"What in the world were you thinking of, coming into my room...?"

Pearl asked in surprise.

The need to feel her was so great, Cal reached out a hand to her, cutting off her words. For the space of a heartbeat he thought about dragging her into his arms and kissing her lips until she was breathless. Then, suddenly coming to his senses, he snatched his hand away as if burned. His eyes hardened. His voice deepened with anger. "Go back to bed."

"Not until—"

"I said go back to bed, Pearl."

"You're drunk," she said accusingly.

He swore. "Not nearly drunk enough."

"Then you should have stayed in town until you did a proper job of it."

"My thoughts exactly," Cal retorted, stepping through the doorway and pulling the door shut behind him.

Dear Reader,

Pearl is the second book in *Romantic Times* Lifetime Achievement Award winner Ruth Langan's new THE JEWELS OF TEXAS series featuring four sisters, brought together by the death of their father. *Pearl* is the story of an Eastern-bred schoolteacher and the rough-and-tumble ranch foreman who wants her sent back home where she belongs. Don't miss any of this terrific new series.

In Liz Ireland's delightful new Western, *Millie and the Fugitive*, an innocent man running from the law is forced to take along a spoiled rich girl who turns out to be the best thing that's ever happened to him.

Margaret Moore's new medieval novel, *The Baron's Quest*, is the story of a rough-edged Saxon who falls in love with the refined gentlewoman whom he has inherited along with his new holdings. *Badlands Bride*, by Cheryl St.John, is about a newspaper reporter who goes west pretending to be a mail-order bride, only to find herself stranded in the Dakotas for one long cold winter.

We hope you'll keep a lookout for all four titles wherever Harlequin Historicals are sold.

Sincerely,

Tracy Farrell
Senior Editor

Please address questions and book requests to:
Harlequin Reader Service
U.S.: 3010 Walden Ave., P.O. Box 1325, Buffalo, NY 14269
Canadian: P.O. Box 609, Fort Erie, Ont. L2A 5X3

Ruth Langan
Pearl

Harlequin Books

TORONTO • NEW YORK • LONDON
AMSTERDAM • PARIS • SYDNEY • HAMBURG
STOCKHOLM • ATHENS • TOKYO • MILAN
MADRID • WARSAW • BUDAPEST • AUCKLAND

ISBN 0-373-28929-4

PEARL

Copyright © 1996 by Ruth Ryan Langan.

This edition published by arrangement with Harlequin Books S.A.

® and TM are trademarks of the publisher. Trademarks indicated with ® are registered in the United States Patent and Trademark Office, the Canadian Trade Marks Office and in other countries.

Printed in U.S.A.

Books by Ruth Langan

Harlequin Historicals

Mistress of the Seas #10
†*Texas Heart* #31
**Highland Barbarian* #41
*Highland Heather #65
*Highland Fire #91
*Highland Heart #111
†*Texas Healer* #131
Christmas Miracle #147
†*Texas Hero* #180
Deception #196
*The Highlander #228
Angel #245
*Highland Heaven #269
‡*Diamond* #305
Dulcie's Gift #324
‡*Pearl* #329

Harlequin Books

Harlequin Historicals Christmas Stories 1990
"Christmas at Bitter Creek"

†Texas Series
*The Highland Series
‡The Jewels of Texas

RUTH LANGAN

traces her ancestry to Scotland and Ireland. It is no surprise, then, that she feels a kinship with the characters in her historical novels.

Married to her childhood sweetheart, she has raised five children and lives in Michigan, the state where she was born and raised.

To Taylor Langan Shrader
The newest jewel in our family crown.

To her proud parents, Mary and Dennis,
And Caitlin Bea, Bret and Ally.

And, of course, to Tom.
Always.

Prologue

"Oh, Daddy. What have I done?"

The lone figure stood on a windswept hill, her gaze fastened on a mound of earth covered with rocks. Pearl Jewel looked exactly as she had two months previously, when she stepped off a stage from Boston. Her gown was painstakingly starched and pressed; her hair was neatly beribboned; her ever-present parasol shielded her skin from the sun's scorching rays.

Even now, she could hardly believe her bold reaction to news of her father's murder in this faraway place called Texas. The first thought that occurred to this prim, proper young woman had been to lock herself away with her grief. Instead, acting completely out of character, she had booked passage on the next stage out of town, determined to visit her father's burial site. And here, in this strange land, she had discovered so much more than she'd bargained for. Three half sisters, as different as possible from each other. Diamond, Texas-born and -bred, was tough, strong, defiant. Jade was a fragile Oriental beauty with a mind as sharp as the jewel-encrusted dagger she carried at her waist. Ruby was a sultry bayou beauty whose voluptuous body turned men's heads wherever she went.

Best of all, Pearl had discovered a home, the Jewel ranch. Her father's will accorded each of his daughters an equal share of his Texas empire, along with a share for his devoted ranch foreman, Cal McCabe.

Why, then, was she feeling so distressed?

"I feel so useless here," she cried, dropping to her knees. "So helpless. Everything is so foreign to me here in your home." She thought of the dusty, sleepy little town, so different from the streets of Boston. "I don't know if I'll ever get used to this primitive place," she said with a sigh. "There's the weather. Everyone says this is a typical Texas spring. Rain. Drought. Heat. Cold. From one day to the next, I don't know what to expect. Then there are the wild animals. Some of them coming right up to the house and barns. And the people. So rough. So...uncivilized. Fear has become my constant companion." A shudder trembled through her. "Perhaps I've made a terrible mistake."

She touched a hand to the stone marker over her mother's remains, which she'd had shipped from Boston, so that her two parents could be joined in death. "Was I wrong to come here, Mama?"

She could still hear her mother's words, fearful, cautious, whenever she'd mentioned following her father to Texas. "It's a wild, fearsome place, Pearl. Women like us would wither and die in such a wilderness."

Women like us.

She shivered again. Tears stung her eyes, and she blinked them away.

Touching the great mound of stones over her father's grave, she whispered, "Oh, Daddy, if only you were here to tell me what I should do."

In the silence that followed, the wind picked up, catching a strand of her hair, blowing it across her cheek. With her eyes closed, it felt exactly like the caress of her father's hand. Strong. Sure. Gentle.

She was jolted by a sudden memory.

She was eight years old. Her father had come to Boston for one of his rare visits. As always, her mother had dressed her little daughter in her finest dress, arranging her long blond hair into fat sausage curls, and commanding her to greet her long-absent father with a recitation. In a clear voice, Pearl spoke the first lines of William Blake's "Auguries of Innocence."

"To see a world in a grain of sand and heaven in a wildflower, hold infinity in the palm of your hand and eternity in an hour..."

Her father's jaw dropped, and he sat, enthralled, as his little daughter recited the entire lengthy poem flawlessly.

"Why, that was amazing, Pearl," he said. "What a delightful, serious little creature you are. What will you do with that facile mind of yours, my child?"

She stared at the floor, fighting tears. "Mama says I have no talents worth developing. I have no ear for music. No patience for sewing a fine seam. Mama says I am useless."

"Useless?" He drew her into his arms and pressed kisses over her upturned face. *"Do you know how proud you make me?"*

The sad, solemn little girl shook her head.

"Oh, my dear little one. A fine mind is a precious gift. If I give you a promise," he whispered against her temple, *"will you give me one in return?"*

She nodded, bewildered by the excitement trembling in his voice.

"This I promise you. You shall have the education I never had. And I ask that someday you will use it to teach others. Ah, Pearl. There is no nobler calling than to shape and mold children's minds, to lift them out of their dreary lives and take them to places they might never see, except in books. Will you do it? Will you use this fine mind to teach others?"

Pearl's eyes snapped open. She was alone. Except for the wind, there was no sound. But she had heard her father's voice, as clearly as if he'd been standing here, speaking to her aloud, instead of in her memory.

A tear slipped from the corner of her eye. She paid it no heed as she bent and reverently kissed the boulder.

Maybe it was her imagination. Or maybe it was a sign. She knew only that she felt a rare sense of peace. In the blink of an eye, she'd been given her answer.

"Thank you, Daddy. I'll do it. I'll do my best to make you proud."

Chapter One

⁓⌇⌇⌇⌇⌇⌇⌇⁓

"If you good folks don't mind, we've been asked to stick around after the prayer service for a town meeting."

Lavinia Thurlong stopped fanning herself and glanced about in surprise. Several other women did the same, as the congregation came to attention.

Not that they hadn't been attentive throughout the hour-long service. Reverend Wade Weston, a charismatic young preacher with flowing blond hair and resonant voice, had begun to attract quite a following. Townspeople and ranchers alike came together every Sunday to have their consciences poked and prodded.

The service was being held in the back of Durfee's Mercantile. It was the only room in the town of Hanging Tree big enough to hold the growing crowd. Besides, Rufus Durfee had agreed to act as mayor for the next year, since no one else wanted the job.

He'd scoured the town, bringing in all those who didn't bother coming to Sunday services. Among them were the marshal and a couple of ranchers in town for supplies.

"Is something wrong, Quent?" Gladys Witherspoon turned to Quent Regan, the federal marshal, who straddled a chair in the back row. He was assigned to cover most of Texas, and made his home in Hanging Tree.

"Not that I know of." He shook his head for emphasis.

"Rufus Durfee doesn't call a town meeting unless there's bad news," Millie Potter remarked aloud. Millie ran a tidy boardinghouse at the end of the dirt track that formed the main street of Hanging Tree. "There's got to be trouble afoot."

A murmur ran through the crowd as heads began to nod in agreement.

"Now, now. This isn't bad news," Reverend Weston hastened to assure them. "In fact, I'd say it's downright good news for all of us." He glanced at the mayor. "Rufus, would you like me to do the honors?"

When Durfee nodded, Reverend Weston cleared his throat. "Miss Jewel, if you'd come up here, please..."

All heads swiveled to study the young woman who made her way to the front of the room. As always, Pearl Jewel was spotlessly gowned and coiffed. This day she wore a pale pink confection with a high neck, tiny sashed waist and flounced skirt. Matching pink ribbons held her long blond hair away from her face. In her hands was an elegant pink parasol, carefully closed, which she held pointing downward, like a walking stick. Despite the fact that she'd been here for two months, her skin seemed untouched by the harsh Texas sun. It was as cool and pale as when she'd first arrived, fresh off the stage from Boston. She would have looked fashionable in her hometown, but here in Hanging Tree, she looked just plain frivolous. Everybody knew the Texas dust didn't discriminate between silk and calico.

"Miss Pearl Jewel has offered to teach our children." Reverend Weston's voice rang with pride.

"What could she possibly teach our kids?" someone called out.

"Miss Pearl attended..." Reverend Weston glanced at Pearl for guidance.

"Miss Thackery's School for Young Ladies," she finished for him.

"Yes, indeed. A fine school in Boston," he added. "Where she earned a certificate for teaching reading, writing, 'rithmetic and such."

"What do children need with that stuff?" Rollie Ingram, a burly rancher who had already buried a wife and three children, got to his feet and started for the door, signaling for his two sons to follow.

Rollie never bothered with Sunday services. As a matter of fact, Rollie didn't bother much with anything or anybody in town. The only times he was seen were when he needed supplies, or those rare occasions when he scraped enough money together to visit Buck's saloon.

His older son, a head shorter than his father but almost as muscular, dropped an arm around his younger brother, who appeared to be no more than six or seven. The two hung their heads, avoiding eye contact with the people around them.

"Wait." The young preacher held up a hand. "I don't think you understand the gift being offered." He looked out over the faces of the congregation. "A town like ours could never afford to pay a teacher. Or build a schoolhouse. Why, we can't even afford a house of worship. But Miss Jewel is asking no pay. She's willing to teach our children just for the pleasure of it."

"What about a schoolhouse?" one of the women shouted.

The preacher turned to Pearl.

"I—" she thought quickly "—hoped we might convert a building on our ranch for that purpose."

"On sacred Jewel land?" Rollie Ingram's tone was filled with sarcasm. "What does the almighty Cal McCabe think about that?"

At the mention of the foreman of the Jewel ranch, Pearl bit her lip. Cal would be furious when he heard the news. But that was nothing new. He seemed always to be angry in her presence. She sensed his disapproval over her simplest attempts to bring order and civility to this rough land. At the dinner table, when she sipped her tea, he frowned. In the parlor, when she opened a book, she would look up to see him watching her, scowling. Always scowling.

What did he see when he looked at her? She had no idea. But whatever image she evoked, it must be thoroughly unpleasant. She thought back to the first days after she'd arrived, after her father's brutal murder. In all this time, she couldn't recall ever seeing Cal McCabe smile at her. Oh, he was civil. But just barely.

"Cal is...up at one of the line camps," Pearl replied. "He doesn't know about my offer of a school." She saw the way several of the men smirked, and quickly added, "But as soon as he returns, I know he'll give his approval."

"Yeah, well, I'll believe it when I hear it from McCabe." Rollie's words had the others nodding.

"It doesn't matter." Pearl lifted her head a fraction. "Diamond, Jade and Ruby have already given their approval."

Lavinia Thurlong wrinkled her nose and whispered to her friend Gladys, "That pack of misfits."

Overhearing, several women nearby snickered.

Pearl tried to ignore the little knot of tension that had begun creeping into her neck and shoulder. Though she and her half sisters had met as strangers, they had developed a strong, loving bond that grew stronger with each passing day. A bond that had begun in sorrow, and had now become joy. Though the initial shock of discovery had been prickly, they were slowly becoming a family.

Still, in the eyes of these small-town citizens, the Jewel sisters would always be the object of ridicule.

"So, Miss Pearl. It appears you and your sisters are planning to stay in Hanging Tree." Arlo Spitz, deputy to the marshal, nudged his wife in the ribs, and the two shared a look.

"I can't speak for my sisters. But as for me, I've decided to put down roots here." Pearl glanced around, seeing the doubt and suspicion on their faces. "I would like to be of some use. And I think the best way to do that is to share my knowledge with your children.''

"Schooling's for rich kids." Rollie spat. "We're simple ranchers, scratching a living out of the land. We need all the help we can find. In case you didn't notice, city woman, it's springtime. Time for planting crops."

He heard the ripple of laughter in the crowd, and saw the flush that crept over Pearl's cheeks. That made him even bolder. "Our kids work right along with us, from sunup to sundown. There's no time left over for schoolin'. Besides, the things you can teach our children aren't things they'll use out here in Texas. If you want to teach, Miss High-and-Mighty Jewel, go back to Boston."

He turned and stalked from the room, shoving his two sons out the door ahead of him.

Pearl watched as several other ranchers scrambled to their feet. She began speaking quickly, hoping to soften their hearts.

"I realize this isn't the best time. But I intend to go ahead with my plan to open a school on the Jewel ranch. I hope some of you will consider sending your children."

"Thank you, Miss Pearl." Reverend Weston left her at the front of the room and hurried to the door, to shake the hands of his flock before they scattered.

As Pearl trailed the others from the mercantile, she offered her hand to the minister.

"I hope you understand," he said gently, "that these folks aren't rejecting your fine offer. And they aren't being selfish. It's just that they need the cooperation of every member of the family if they're to survive. Schooling is a luxury many of them can't afford."

"I do understand," Pearl said softly. "But these children deserve a chance for something better. What I'm offering them is a glimpse of all that's out there beyond the borders of Texas."

Reverend Weston squeezed her hand. "Then I wish you well, Miss Pearl. And I'll pray for your success."

"Thank you." As she walked away, she wondered if there were enough prayers in all of Texas to soften the hearts of these tough, independent people.

Outside, ranchers' wives lifted baskets of food from the backs of wagons and carried them to a grassy spot, where they joined other families. This brief, festive hour was the only relief from a life of never-ending chores.

Pearl lingered a few moments, hoping someone would offer to speak with her, or share their lunch. But, though a few of the women gave her smiles before turning away, most of them refused to even look at her.

What had she expected? Her father had been the richest man in the territory. Perhaps in all of Texas. That was a barrier between her and these good people, who barely managed to eke out a living. Add to that the fact that she was an outsider. An Easterner, they would say, in a tone reserved for an outlaw or villain.

With a sigh, Pearl climbed into her rig and flicked the reins. Within minutes, the town of Hanging Tree was left in her dust.

When she arrived at the ranch house, she was pleased to see Diamond's horse. This generous young woman, who had opened her home and heart to a sister she hadn't even known existed, always made Pearl's day brighter. She turned over the reins to a wrangler and hurried inside.

Diamond, Jade and Ruby looked up as Pearl entered the kitchen. At once, Carmelita Alvarez, cook and housekeeper for the Jewel ranch, placed a pan of milk on the stove for Pearl's midday chocolate, preparing it just the way the young woman had always had it in Boston. Jade preferred tea. Diamond drank only strong, bitter coffee. And Ruby preferred an occasional lemonade to quench her thirst.

Seeing the look on Pearl's face, Diamond said, "I'd say the town didn't take kindly to your offer to teach."

"That's putting it mildly. I was told, in no uncertain terms, that the people of Hanging Tree don't want a teacher." Pearl slumped down at the table. "Do you know a man named Rollie Ingram?"

Diamond nodded. Dressed in her usual rough wrangler garb of chaps and leather, she sipped strong black coffee. "A mean man. With a mean mouth. Pa used to say the only peace his wife ever found was when she was put in the ground."

Pearl shuddered. After a moment of silence, she said, "On the way home from town, I started thinking..."

"Oh! Oh! Not again!" came a chorus of laughing voices.

Ignoring her sisters' teasing giggles, Pearl continued. "I've been thinking that the best way to deal with this problem is to prepare a schoolhouse somewhere here on Jewel land, and then invite the townspeople to see what I have to offer their children.''

"You might go to a lot of work for nothing," Diamond said softly. "You ought to be prepared for the fact that no one will come.''

"Why waste your time?" Jade asked. The Oriental beauty sipped her tea and smiled at the thought of the thriving business her mother had once operated in San Francisco. A business she fully intended to duplicate in Hanging Tree. "Why not build a pleasure palace instead?"

"Or hire a seamstress and milliner who can create elegant satin gowns and feathered bonnets, *chérie*,'' Ruby interjected. It was the thing she most missed from her former life on the bayou. Here in Texas, she'd actually been forced to take up needle and thread and create her own gowns to keep her wardrobe from becoming dowdy.

She lowered the red-satin-fringed shawl to reveal a matching gown that molded her lush figure like a second skin. "Every woman in Hanging Tree would bless you.''

Pearl fell silent, gritting her teeth.

Diamond couldn't help laughing at the differences between these young women. Now that she and Adam Winter were husband and wife, she didn't see them as often as she would have liked. She missed this friendly banter that went on constantly.

"Have you found a place that suits you?" she asked.

"I've been exploring the ranch. There's an empty shed just over the creek. Do you know what it's used for?"

Diamond nodded. "It was Pa's first cabin, before he made enough money to build this house. I don't think it's used for anything now."

"It would be far enough away from the ranch so that my students and I wouldn't disturb the wranglers. And close enough so I could easily ride out there every morning and prepare for my classes."

"Your classes." Diamond studied this prim, proper woman who still seemed so out of place in her new home. "You understand that the children of Hanging Tree are needed to help out on their parents' ranches? There's little time or energy left for such things as reading and writing."

"But there's more to life than mucking stalls and feeding cattle." Pearl glanced toward Jade and Ruby, seeking their support. "Don't you agree?"

"I do indeed," Ruby said emphatically. "There are fine clothes to be worn, and..."

"Pleasures to be sought," Jade added.

"I can't believe the two of you," Pearl cried with dismay. "How can you only think about fancy clothes and personal pleasure?"

"Can't you see they're just having fun with you?" Diamond shot a warning glance from one of them to the other, then gave in to the laughter that was bubbling up. She circled the table to press a kiss to Pearl's smooth cheek. "If you want to turn Pa's old cabin into a schoolroom, and fill the children's heads with sums and letters, I'll go along with it. It would be nice to see

the old place used for something good.'' She glanced
at Jade and Ruby. ''How about the two of you?''

The two young women nodded enthusiastically.

''Do whatever you wish, chérie.'' Ruby sipped her
lemonade. ''Just so you do not ask me to assist you. I
was never much of a scholar.''

''Nor was I,'' Jade said with a shake of her head.
''But I think it is a noble task to tutor the young.''

''That just leaves Cal's vote.'' Pearl glanced anx-
iously at Diamond. ''You've known him all your life.
What do you think he'll say?''

Diamond had to swallow back her smile. She could
already imagine their tough ranch foreman's reaction
when he learned that his ranch might be invaded by the
town's children. Cal McCabe had a reputation among
the wranglers as a tough boss with a quick temper. A
man good with both guns and fists. And a man who,
once his mind was made up, was as immovable as a
mountain.

''He'll object. Violently,'' she added with a chuckle.
''I think we had better meet with him as soon as he
returns from the line camp. He can listen to your arguments, and weigh the issue from all sides.''

Seeing Pearl's look of dismay, she said, ''Don't
worry. We'll all be there to support you. And in time
Cal will come around.'' She crossed her fingers behind her back. ''Now I'd better run.'' She hugged the
three young women, then kissed Carmelita's cheek. ''I
promised Adam I'd ride with him to the south range.''

Everyone was aware of the tenderness that came
into her voice when she spoke of her husband. Married less than two months, they'd become insepar-

able. It was plain that their love had enriched both their lives. Their ranch, which adjoined the Jewel ranch, had already begun to prosper.

As Diamond headed out the door, Pearl followed her. Diamond pulled herself into the saddle. Pearl snapped open her dainty pink parasol and lifted it over her head to shield her pale skin from the sun.

"I hope you're right about Cal. I really want to do this. I'm afraid he'll dismiss it as a foolish dream."

"Don't ever think your dreams are foolish, Pearl." Diamond's voice took on a wistful note. "Pa used to say that Texans were a different breed. And maybe we are. But I think what makes us so special is all the people who come here with heads full of dreams. Like Adam's dream of a piece of land even better than the one he left in Maryland after the war. And your dream of opening up the world to children. You just keep on chasing your dreams. And make them all come true."

With Diamond's words ringing in her mind, Pearl set off on foot to examine the old cabin. Now, more than ever, she was determined to turn it into a school-house. And to share her knowledge with the children of Hanging Tree.

Chapter Two

Cal McCabe rubbed his knuckles over eyes gritty with trail dust. The lower half of his face was covered with a scraggly growth of beard. He'd spent the past weeks hauling supplies to Will Culver at the isolated line camp on the northern boundary of the vast Jewel ranch. Once there, he'd mended fence and cut logs for a new storage shed. On the return trip, he'd rounded up a herd of stray cattle that had grown from a few dozen until they now reached over a hundred. They fanned out in front of him, moving in an undulating black wave.

As his horse crested a hill, he drank in the sight of the big, sprawling ranch house, surrounded by outbuildings. This place had been his home since he was twelve years old. Onyx Jewel had taken a chance on a scrawny, half-starved misfit, and had turned him into the roughest, toughest wrangler in Texas. What was more, he'd trusted him with his most precious treasure, his ranch. Just thinking about the fact that he was now part owner brought a smile to Cal's face.

He was itching to get home. All he could think of was a hot bath, a change of clothes and a bottle of whiskey.

The herd, sensing food at the end of a tedious journey, broke into a run. Cal's mount did the same.

Suddenly, up ahead, Cal spotted the flutter of a pink gown. An unsuspecting female had stepped directly in the path of the thundering herd. Now she stood, frozen to the spot, her hands gripping a ridiculous pink parasol.

"Pearl!" Her name was torn from his lips, though he knew she couldn't hear over the roar of the stampeding cattle.

He swore, loudly, fiercely, as he dug in his heels and urged his horse into a full gallop. Cutting a path through the wild-eyed cows, horse and rider raced at breakneck speed. And all the while, Cal's line of vision was filled with a flutter of pink.

The faster his horse moved, the more desperately the herd attempted to outrun him. The lead steer was bearing down directly toward Pearl, with the rest of the herd following close on its heels.

Sensing that his horse was tiring, Cal whipped him into a frenzy, leaning low over his neck and shouting a string of curses. The horse responded, reaching for even greater speed, until he began to pull ahead. Passing the lead steer, they kept up their terrible pace until they reached their goal.

In one swift movement, Cal leaned over and snatched up the slender figure, holding her in one arm like a rag doll. The horse veered off the path and came to an abrupt halt, just as the herd thundered past.

Without a word, Cal set her down, none too gently, and slid from the saddle. His face was a mask of fury, hiding the razor's edge of terror that still sliced through him.

"Damn it, woman, do you know how close you came to being trampled?"

"I..." She brought her hand to her throat, struggling for breath. All the color had drained from her face. It was plain that she was still paralyzed with fear. She was holding herself together by a thread.

She wanted to throw herself into his arms and thank him for saving her life. She wanted to weep with relief. But pride and propriety wouldn't permit it. Instead, she stood stiffly, head high, chin lifted in a pose that could be misinterpreted as haughty. "I...couldn't move. I've never felt so helpless in my life."

"Helpless." He couldn't hide his disgust. "There's no room in Texas for helpless females." He glanced around, missing the wounded look that came into her eyes. "What in the hell were you doing way out here, so far from the house?"

"I was...examining my new schoolhouse."

His head swung around. Eyes narrowed, he speared her with a look. "Your what?"

She swallowed. "The children of Hanging Tree need to be taught. And I'm a teacher. So I thought..."

"You thought?" His hands were still shaking. To cover up, he clenched them into fists. "Think about this. What we have here is a ranch." His tone, his manner, had become so menacing, she actually cringed. "I won't have my wranglers playing nursemaid to a useless female and a handful of dirty raga-muffins.''

''Useless fe—?'' Her mouth snapped shut. Her lips thinned. Wasn't this exactly what she would have expected from a clod like Cal McCabe? Of all the insults he could hurl, this was the worst. Two bright spots of color touched her cheeks as she brought her hands to her hips. ''The children of Hanging Tree deserve an education.''

The cumulative effects of the trail and the last dregs of fear combined to add a sharper edge than usual to Cal's temper. ''This discussion is over. I'll take it up with Diamond. At least she understands how a ranch operates.''

It was another blow to Pearl's already wounded pride. ''Diamond agrees with me. She suggested a meeting.''

His eyes narrowed. ''A meeting? What for?''

''To...persuade you that we should locate a schoolhouse here on Jewel land.'' Oh, this wasn't going at all the way she'd hoped. This was the wrong place, the wrong time, to bring up such an important topic. With each word, she was creating a wider chasm. But now that she had begun, there seemed no way to stop.

Cal swore. ''Onyx Jewel would turn over in his grave if he thought his ranch was going to become nothing more than a glorified playground. Diamond ought to honor her father's wishes.''

''I'll remind you that Onyx was my father, too. And I won't be treated like a—'' in her frustration, her prim and proper Boston accent sharpened "—like an outsider."

He was about to remind her that was exactly what she was. But his gaze was arrested by the dirty smudges on her pink gown. Smudges caused by his big hands when he'd caught and lifted her. They looked so out of place on this woman who always seemed so perfect. He found himself wondering what she'd do if he tugged on those damned silly ribbons and mussed her hair, as well. Or how she'd react if he unbuttoned that row of tiny buttons that ran from neckline to hem. He wondered if the body she kept hidden beneath was as perfect as the wrappings.

The thought brought a trickle of sweat down his back. And caused his lips to curve in the slightest of smiles.

At once, her frown deepened. "Are you laughing at me?"

He wiped the smile from his mouth, annoyed by the direction his thoughts had taken. "Now why would I do a thing like that? What nearly happened is no laughing matter." He bent and retrieved what was left of her parasol. The frame had been shattered beyond repair. The fabric hung in tatters. As he looked at it, his anger grew. It could have been her. God, it could have been her pink gown that was trampled, her slender body that was shattered beyond repair. The knowledge staggered him. He was filled with a sudden blinding rage.

"This is what happens to anything—or anyone—who gets careless around stampeding cattle." He shook the hated parasol under her nose.

"I'll keep that in mind." She held out her hand for it.

His anger grew. She was so damnably cool. And completely unaware of how close she'd come to . . .

Instead of giving her the parasol, he clamped his fingers over her upper arm, dragging her close.

He saw her eyes widen in sudden fear, and cursed himself for his clumsiness. But he couldn't seem to stop. The thought of what had almost happened sent him hurtling out of control.

"Woman, if you've got any sense at all, you'll take the first stage back to Boston."

She started to push against his chest. "I'll have you know I'm not so easily frightened."

He dragged her close, trapping her hand between their bodies. She felt his breath hot against her temple. His voice was a low growl of anger. "Damn you. You ought to be."

He should have released her then. Turned away and never looked back. But he couldn't. His temper had taken over. Besides, the touch of her, the press of that slender body against his, had his blood hot and his breath backing up in his lungs.

"You ought to be scared to death." His big, callused fingers tangled in hair softer than any silk. He drew her head back and saw the way her eyes widened in shock. Without giving a thought to what he was doing, he covered her mouth with his. And then he was lost. Lost in lips that were as cool as a spring-fed lake on a hot summer day.

She made a sound, and tried to pull back, but he was quicker, stronger.

He could taste her fear. Her outrage. And something more. Just beneath that cool veneer was passion. Oh, she kept it buried deep, locked up tight, but it was there. And as the kiss deepened, he could feel it stirring. It was the most purely sensual thing he'd ever experienced.

Her fingers, splayed across his chest, slowly curled into his shirt. Her sound of protest became a sigh, before she caught herself and swallowed back the sound. And though her kiss was awkward, and her lips trembled slightly, they moved under his, causing his pulse to race at full speed.

He knew he had to end this. But he wanted one more taste, one more moment of pleasure. He absorbed her heat, her taste, her woman's scent. At last he lifted his head and took a step back, breaking contact. He saw the look of confusion in her eyes. She blinked, and the soft look was gone, replaced by the stern demeanor of a teacher whose pupil has just committed an unpardonable act.

"There are all kinds of deadly things you ought to look out for here in Texas." He was surprised at how difficult it was to speak. Especially with the taste of her still on his lips.

"I'll remember that." Her throat was as dry as dust, but she wouldn't give him the satisfaction of knowing that. "It isn't just scorpions and rattlesnakes that slither out from under rocks, is it?"

He arched a brow. He'd give her credit. The teacher was tougher than she'd let on.

He thrust the remains of her parasol into her hand. As their fingers brushed, he absorbed the sexual jolt and turned away quickly.

To his retreating back, she called, "I'll ask Diamond to come to a meeting tonight."

"I'll be busy tonight." He didn't turn.

"Then we'll make it earlier. Before supper. This has to be resolved."

"Believe me, it will be."

She watched as, in one smooth motion, he swung into the saddle. His body was all sinew and muscle, taut and lean and sun-bronzed.

A magnificent animal.

A dangerous opponent.

He tipped his hat. In a swirl of dust, he was gone.

Cal pushed his horse to catch up with the strays. As he rode, he called himself every kind of fool for that little scene back there. What in hell had he been thinking of, letting his temper get the better of him? Besides, a lady like Pearl was off-limits. She would never have anything to do with a trail bum like him. Not that he minded. She wasn't his kind. Too prissy. Too perfect. He preferred the girls at Buck's saloon. They knew the rules. No promises. No complications. Just a quick tumble and an even quicker goodbye.

He struggled to wipe Pearl from his mind. But it wasn't easy. The taste of her, like a spring rain, lingered on his lips. The smell of her, clean and fresh and sweet as lilacs, filled his lungs. He glanced down at his rough, callused hands. Hands that had soiled her gown. Though they were loosely holding the reins, he could imagine them holding her, stroking her. His heartbeat accelerated.

Annoyed, he urged his horse into a run and busied himself with the job of herding the strays toward a holding pen. A group of wranglers had already managed to subdue the herd.

"Hey, Cal!" a cowboy shouted.

Cal lifted his hat and waved, then watched with satisfaction as a crew of cowboys swarmed about, opening the gates of a corral, prodding the cattle inside.

"I counted a hundred and twenty-one," a wrangler called as he leaped from the top rail of the corral a short time later. "Whooo-ee! Looks like you've been busy."

Cal nodded and slid from the saddle. "Strays I picked up along the way. See that they're branded by morning. We'll add them to the herd on the north ridge."

"Sure thing. How's Culver doing at the line camp?" the cowboy asked.

Cal's grin was slow, easy. "Glad his time's almost up. Looking forward to seeing all his old friends, and spending a couple of nights in Hanging Tree." His grin widened. "Fact is, so am I."

The cowboy slapped him on the back. "I figured now that you'd moved up to the big house, you'd rather spend your nights eating Carmelita's good cooking and sleeping in Onyx's big feather bed. With that stash of fine liquor, why bother drinking Buck's cheap whiskey in town?"

Cal led his horse toward the barn. Over his shoulder, he called, "There's more to Buck's place than whiskey."

The wranglers winked and nodded and hurried to finish their chores. If the boss was heading to town later, they wanted to be in on the fun.

In the barn, Cal took his time rubbing down his horse and forking hay and hauling water into the stall. Then, slapping his hat against his thigh, he sent up a cloud of dust as he made his way across the yard.

Just outside the bunkhouse, Cookie had a side of beef roasting over a fire.

"Your cooking's all that Culver talked about at the line camp," Cal called.

The leather-skinned old man took a pipe from his mouth and grinned, revealing a gap where several teeth used to be. "Reminds him of his mama's cooking, does it?"

Cal nodded his head. "As a matter of fact, he says his mama was the worst cook he'd ever known. That's why he's so crazy about you. You run a close second."

Cookie slapped Cal on the back, enjoying the joke. "Are we going into town later?"

"You bet. Wouldn't miss it," Cal called as he started toward the ranch house.

It was hard to believe he'd gone from bunkhouse to ranch house in the space of fifteen years. He still found it a source of amazement that he was part owner of this magnificent spread, thanks to Onyx Jewel's generous will. But the truth was, he'd have gladly given it all up to have Onyx back. No man had ever been as important in his life, or treated him better. Like a brother or son. Because of Onyx, his past had been put to rest. And his future was secure.

"Señor Cal," the housekeeper called as he stepped through the back door.

"Hello, Carmelita." He breathed deeply. "Something smells great. Even better'n Cookie's."

She beamed at the compliment. Though she and Cookie shared recipes and supplies, she thought the old man's cooking plain, and tolerable only for cowboys who had no choice but to eat whatever was given them. "Tortillas. And for Señorita Pearl, roast beef."

"She still hasn't learned to like our Texas spices?"

The housekeeper shook her head. "She resists. But one day she will give in. You will see." She nodded over her shoulder. "I have a tub of water already waiting in your room."

He kissed her cheek. "You're an angel of mercy. How much time do I have?"

She lifted a lid to stir something on the stove, sending a cloud of spicy fragrance wafting across the big kitchen. "An hour. No. Make it two."

He snatched a steaming biscuit from a plate on the table and headed for the doorway. "I don't know if I can wait that long."

But when he climbed the stairs and stepped into the suite of rooms that had once been occupied by Onyx Jewel, he forgot about the time. It was enough to know he was home. Home. He stared around the bedroom, with its massive bed hewn from rough timbers and its stone fireplace. In the adjoining room was a desk and several comfortable, overstuffed chairs.

Wide windows offered a sweeping view of mountains glimmering with snow atop Widow's Peak, and below them the mirrored surface of Poison Creek.

He stripped off his clothes and sank into the tub of warm water. Holding a match to the tip of a fine cigar, he blew out a ring of smoke and closed his eyes. This was as close to heaven as he'd get in this life.

He heard the trill of feminine laughter, and the pad of footsteps as Pearl and her half sisters passed his door, clucking like hens.

Even heaven, he reminded himself, had its little imperfections.

Chapter Three

"**S**orry to spoil your first night home with unpleasant business," Diamond murmured as she kissed Cal's cheek. "But this meeting gave us an excuse to stay for supper."

Her husband, Adam Winter, shook Cal's hand and muttered, "Thought I'd come along so you wouldn't feel outnumbered."

"I'm not worried." Cal stared pointedly at Pearl, who had taken a seat between Jade and Ruby for support. "I've faced down loaded guns before."

"We're not here to do battle." Diamond paused as Carmelita moved around the room, offering glasses of wine to the women, and whiskey to the men. When she left the room, Diamond continued, "But since the five of us are equal partners in the ranch, it's only right that all of us should approve or disapprove any changes."

"I agree." Cal's tone was surprisingly cordial as he sipped his whiskey.

"I think we should allow Pearl to give her reasons for wanting to open a school." Diamond turned to the

young woman, who had her hands clasped tightly in
her lap.

"A fine idea." Cal shot Pearl a challenging look.

With an effort, Pearl glanced at him, then away as
she got to her feet. She shivered, struck by how handsome he looked. And how dangerous. Beads of mois-
ture still glistened in his dark hair. With his face clean-
shaven, all the sharp hollows and planes of his cheeks
seemed more defined, and revealed a proud, square
jaw. Not really handsome, she corrected. But rugged.
Powerful. His dark eyes were his most compelling
feature, daring any man, or woman, to look away. His
starched white shirt was a contrast to his sun-darkened
skin. Each time he lifted his tumbler to his lips, his
sleeves stretched tautly over the muscles of his arms.

It galled Pearl that he could be so completely at ease
when she was so tense and edgy. She found herself
blushing every time she looked his way, remembering
the kiss they'd shared. She'd expected him to be apol-
ogetic in her presence. Or at least cool and evasive.
Instead, he seemed pleased with himself.

"Like my mother, I studied at Miss Thackery's
School for Young Ladies in Boston, and am a certi-
fied teacher." Even as she said it, Pearl realized how
pompous she must sound. "And, like my mother, I
yearn to mold the hearts and minds of young people.
To fill their heads with knowledge. To broaden their
horizons, and open up their small world to the larger
world beyond these borders."

A half-dozen arguments filled Cal's mind. But the
point she'd made about enlarging a child's horizon
touched him more deeply than he cared to admit. Be-

sides, just looking at her had him at a disadvantage. Tonight she wore a gown of pale lavender, with mother-of-pearl buttons that ran from her throat to her waist. Her long blond hair had been swept off her face with jeweled combs that caught and reflected the candlelight. She looked every inch a lady. And completely untouchable. His hand clenched around his tumbler, and he turned away.

"That's very noble. But why here, on our ranch?" he demanded disapprovingly. "Why can't you set up a schoolhouse in town?"

The others watched and listened without interruption. It was obvious to them that this duel was between Cal and Pearl. And neither seemed willing to concede a single point to the other.

"Since most of the ranches are scattered in all directions, this is a more central location than the town. Besides, there are no buildings available in town." Pearl had stepped closer now, hands clasped in front of her. "By my calculations, most of my students should have no more than an hour's ride."

"An hour here. An hour back." Cal shook his head. "That's a lot of time taken away from their chores."

Again that note of disapproval.

"I realize that. But it's a small price to pay for knowledge."

"Not a small price for their families. A lot of these ranchers barely eke out a living. Every waking minute is spent tending herds and working the soil. They can't afford to lose even one worker."

"But they're only children, Cal."

"On a ranch, children do the work of grown-ups. The more children a man has, the more land he can work. An eight-year-old girl can rock a baby and make supper, so her ma can plow another field, plant another crop. And a ten-year-old boy can do the work of a man, especially if his pa is off wrangling on a bigger spread for a week's pay."

"I . . . hadn't thought of that." Pearl had a quick vision of some of the ranches in the area, the houses barely more than shacks, the herds spread out over huge sections of land that would take days to cover by horseback.

"I realize now that it might be a hardship for parents to send their children to school, even for a couple of hours," she said softly. "But what about those families who can spare the time? Are you saying I shouldn't make school available to them?"

"Not at all." Cal's eyes narrowed. "My biggest objection is having so many strangers on the Jewel ranch. For the sake of security, I'd like to keep our property off-limits."

"Security?" Pearl glanced helplessly from Diamond to Jade to Ruby.

"Pa's orders were to stop anyone who crossed onto Jewel land," Diamond explained.

"But why?" Pearl was confused.

"Greed," Cal said simply. "When a man becomes as successful as Onyx Jewel, other men start thinking they have the right to some of his wealth."

Pearl clasped a hand to her mouth to stifle her little gasp of alarm.

"Greed is what caused a man to murder your pa," Cal said evenly. "And don't fool yourself that greed died with his killer. There are plenty of other men out there who resent the success of the Jewel ranch."

"But what has that to do with my opening a school?"

Cal's tone grew impatient. "It's obvious that your father knew better than you how to protect what was his." He drained his glass in one swallow and turned away.

She felt the snub as surely as if he'd slapped her.

"Supper is ready," Carmelita said, interrupting.

"Good. I'm starving." Cal pinned Pearl with a challenging look. "Do you have anything more you'd care to say about this?"

"I'm sorry about the distance the children will have to travel. And I'm sorry to open our ranch to strangers. But I am determined to use my skills to teach the children of Hanging Tree. With or without your approval."

"Then I guess you'll do it. Without my approval," he said as he headed for the door.

"Are you saying you will never approve?" Pearl demanded to his retreating back.

"That's what I'm saying." He never even bothered to pause.

The others glanced at one another, unsure what to do.

"Come on," Diamond said, linking arms with her husband. "Maybe after a good meal we'll all feel more civilized."

She left the room, followed by Jade and Ruby.

Pearl stood very still, experiencing a sudden flash of anger. She had managed to scrub Cal's dirty smudges from her pink gown, which was left to dry on a hook in her room. But the fingerprints he'd left on her, and the imprint of his mouth on hers, were another matter. They couldn't be so easily wiped away. And now, as if to prove his male superiority, he had dealt the ultimate blow. He had dismissed her. As easily as if she were one of his wranglers.

As she carried the goblet of wine to the table, her fingers tightened until her knuckles were white from the effort. She didn't need Cal McCabe's approval to live her life. And she would prove it to him.

"What can a man possibly find to do at the line camp for months at a time?" Ruby sprinkled cinnamon sugar over her cup of strong coffee laced with scalded cream. It was the only way she would drink coffee, since it reminded her of the cafe au lait of her beloved bayou.

They ate at the big, scarred wooden table in the kitchen, preferring that to the formal dining room, which was used only for company.

While Pearl brooded, Cal seemed almost jolly.

He chuckled. "You'll have to ask Culver. He chewed my ear off about all the things that needed doing. I barely had time to eat or sleep, with all the chores he had lined up."

"How can you persuade anyone to take such a lonely job?" Jade asked in her melodic voice. She wore a gown of green silk, with mandarin collar and black frog fasteners. Her sleek black hair fell straight to her waist. Her lovely almond eyes were alight with questions.

"Money." Cal took a bite of the spicy tortillas and added a pinch more of chopped chili peppers. "The man who volunteers for six months in the line camp gets a bonus, to compensate for the hard work and the long, lonely hours."

Ruby shivered, drawing a fringed satin shawl around her shoulders. "I could not bear to be alone for that long. I need people around me."

Jade nodded.

"What about you, *chérie?*" Ruby turned to include Pearl, who hadn't said a word since joining them for supper.

"I don't think I would handle the isolation very well," she said softly. "Especially in such a primitive place."

Primitive. The term annoyed Cal. Did this Boston belle really think Texas was the end of the earth? "You get used to it. I've been alone for most of my life," he remarked.

"Have you ever worked the line camp?" Jade asked him.

He nodded. "On and off through the years, I guess I've pulled line-camp duty a dozen times or more."

There was a collective gasp.

"It didn't bother you?" Jade asked.

He shrugged. "I managed to stay busy. And when I felt a need to talk, there was always my horse. Or the cattle." He polished off another of Carmelita's biscuits and added, "There's something satisfying about being alone. Gives a man time to sort through a lot of things. There's time to think, to read."

"You read?" Pearl asked.

He arched a brow, and once again she felt the ice in his steely gaze. "Did you think you were the only one here who's ever opened a book?"

Shamed, she bit her lip.

"I would go mad," Ruby said with a little shudder. "If I thought I had to live like that."

"You'd be surprised what you can do when you have to," Cal answered, his voice low with feeling.

Pearl glanced at him, wondering what had brought that sudden note of passion to his voice.

"Señor Cal," Carmelita said, interrupting, "in honor of your return, I made your favorite dessert." She placed a slice of apple pie, still warm from the oven, in front of him.

As soon as the others were served, he dug in. "Ah, Carmelita," he murmured. "Will you marry me?"

The housekeeper giggled like a schoolgirl. "I think Rosario would have your head if he heard you ask such a thing."

"He's lucky he found you first." Cal polished off the pie and drained his coffee. "If you ever grow tired of your husband, keep me in mind. You're every cowboy's dream."

"You'll never marry, Cal," Diamond said as she finished her meal.

He arched a brow. "And why is that, Di?"

"Because you're already married to this ranch. Pa used to say you love this place the way a man loves a woman."

"He was right." Cal's voice softened, as did his eyes.

"That is true," Carmelita said with a laugh as she lowered the dishes into a pan of warm water that had been heating on the stove. "Besides, according to Cookie, you would break the heart of every woman at Buck's saloon if you ever decided to settle down with a wife."

Pearl set down her cup with a clatter, causing some of the tea to slosh over the rim. She glanced around to see if anyone had noted her reaction.

"Speaking of Buck's..." Cal pushed away from the table and reached for the black jacket draped over the back of his chair. Slipping it on, he buttoned it. "I figure by now the wranglers are itching to ride to town." He nodded his head slightly, acknowledging the others.

When his gaze lingered a moment longer than necessary on Pearl, he pulled himself together. He had an itch of his own to scratch. "I'll say good-night."

"Wait," Diamond called.

He paused at the door.

"We haven't decided about Pearl's schoolhouse."

"We'll talk about it in the morning."

"Adam and I are going to Abilene tomorrow." Diamond closed her hand over Adam's, and the two of them stared at each other with a look of love that was nearly blinding in its intensity. "From there we're taking a train to Maryland."

"Maryland?" Cal's eyes narrowed. "I thought you said you'd never go back to your home, Adam."

Adam Winter nodded. "I never expected to go. But there's a bull I'm interested in. Bred in Scotland. And I thought it would give Diamond a chance to see where I was born."

"And since we'll be gone for several weeks," Diamond put in, "I think we'd better resolve this issue about the schoolhouse before we go."

"For what it is worth, *chérie*," Ruby said with a throaty chuckle, "I vote in the affirmative."

"As do I," Jade said softly.

"Me too," Diamond said with a vigorous nod of her head. "Though I agree with Cal that there could be some risk to our ranch security, I see the need for a school."

They turned to the man in the doorway, hoping their unanimous defense of Pearl would sway him.

"I vote no," Cal said quickly, avoiding Pearl's eyes.

They watched as he strode out into the gathering darkness. A few minutes later, they heard the sound of horses' hooves, as Cal and the wranglers headed out.

In his absence, silence, like the darkness, settled over the Jewel ranch.

Pearl was awakened from sleep by the pounding of hooves, signaling the return of Cal and the wranglers. She squeezed her eyes tightly shut and snuggled deeper under the blankets, determined not to think about Cal McCabe. But her mind could not be closed as easily as her eyes. Heat curled deep inside her at the thought of the way he'd dragged her against him and kissed her. A kiss that had left her breathless. And continued to rob her of breath each time she thought of it. His body had been lean and hard and muscled. As different as possible from her own.

Maybe that was what had excited her. He was unlike anyone she'd ever encountered. But, she warned herself, that was no excuse for the way she'd responded. Shame burned through her each time she remembered it.

She heard the footfall on the stairs and knew that Cal was making his way to his room. Suddenly, without warning, the footsteps paused outside her door.

She sat up, shoving tangled curls from her eyes. The door was thrust inward with such force it reverberated around the room. She strained in the darkness to make out the shadowy figure who paused in the doorway.

"Cal?" Her voice was soft, muffled. "What...is it? What's wrong?"

He strode in an uneven gait across the room, not stopping until he reached the side of her bed.

Moonlight spilled through a crack in the draperies, bathing her in a pool of silvery light. Her lacy ivory night shift had slipped, baring one shoulder. In her agitated state, she took no notice.

But Cal did.

He felt a rush of heat that had nothing to do with the long, hard ride from town or the warmth from the fireplace across the room. This fire started in his belly and moved upward until even the hair at the back of his neck was damp with sweat.

His gaze slid from the swell of breasts visible beneath the gown to the gentle slope of her naked shoulder. He wondered idly what the prim and proper Pearl would do if he dragged her into his arms and pressed his lips to that pale column of flesh.

Hadn't he wondered what it would be like to muss her hair? Now his gaze strayed to the spill of tangled blond curls. He could almost feel his fingers combing through the silken strands. He had to clench his hands into fists to keep from reaching out to her.

Her eyes were wide with surprise, and her lips rounded in an unspoken question. He had spoken not a word. And the longer he stood there, watching her, the more nervous she became.

"What is it, Cal?" Her chest heaved, and the blanket slipped lower, causing his gaze to follow. "What's wrong?"

With an effort, he seemed to pull himself back from his dark thoughts. He turned away. And bumped squarely into the door. He swore, softly but fiercely, under his breath.

Though Pearl had little firsthand knowledge of men, she was reminded of her father. During Onyx Jewel's infrequent visits to her Boston home, she had heard her mother's soft, urgent whispers as she helped him to his bed after a visit to the local inn.

Without thought to her lack of modesty, she swung her legs free of the covers and hurried to the door.

"What in the world were you thinking of, coming into my room—"

The need to feel her was so great, he actually reached out a hand to her, cutting off her words. For the space of a heartbeat, he thought about dragging her into his arms and kissing her lips until she was breathless. Then, suddenly coming to his senses, he snatched his hand away as if he'd been burned. His eyes hardened. His voice deepened with anger. "Go back to bed."

"Not until—"

"I said go back to bed, Pearl."

"You're drunk," she said accusingly.

He swore. "Not nearly drunk enough."

Stung by his abrupt tone, she whispered, "Then you should have stayed in town until you did a proper job of it."

"My thoughts exactly." He stepped through the doorway, firmly pulling the door shut behind him.

As he crossed the hall to his own room, he cursed and called himself every kind of fool.

Balancing on the edge of the bed, he struggled to remove his boots. As each one hit the floor, he added another oath of disgust.

After a lonely month at the line camp, he'd found himself resisting the pleasures offered by Buck's women tonight. And all because of one damnably independent little prude who'd kept slipping into his mind, ruining his poker game, spoiling any fun he might have had. A female who probably didn't care if he lived or died. A female who didn't know the first thing about men. Who wouldn't know what to do with a man if she found one in her bed.

He tossed aside his gunbelt, then his shirt and pants, and sprawled naked across the big bed. The mattress shifted beneath his weight. He pressed an arm across his eyes, hoping to blot out all thought. But it was impossible. She was there in his mind, all shimmery in the moonlight. Taunting him. Tormenting him. Causing an ache unlike anything he'd ever known.

Across the hall, Pearl lay in her bed, wondering what she had done to make Cal hate her so. Was it merely the fact that she wanted to open a schoolhouse for the town's children? Was that what had brought out this anger? Or was there something more?

She'd never before provoked such intense feelings in another human being. She didn't know how to react. Should she ignore him? Try to make him see her point of view?

The man confused her. He'd kissed her. Kissed her as she'd never been kissed before. She touched a finger to her lips. In fact, she could still taste that kiss. It had been shocking, unexpected, jolting.

But it had also hinted of darker, more intense feelings. Violence? Was there a violent side to Cal that she ought to fear? She knew nothing about him. His past. Even his present life. All she knew was that her father had loved him, and trusted him enough to give him a piece of this ranch. But who was he, really? What was he?

Oh, if only she knew about men. But the only man she had ever known was her father. And Onyx's visits had been so sporadic, she'd had little time to uncover any depth to him. The only thing she knew for certain was that Onyx Jewel had lifted her mother to the heights of ecstasy. And had broken her heart.

Pearl's confusion slowly gave way to anger. Damn Cal McCabe. He had no right to intrude himself into her life. She had a right to use her education, her talents, to help others. And if he didn't like it, that was his problem. After all, she owned a piece of this ranch, too. That gave her some rights.

Closing her eyes tightly against the light of the moon, she rolled onto her side, determined to put all thought of the rough, tough ranch foreman out of her mind.

Chapter Four

The sun was already high in the sky. A sky so clear, so cloudless, it hurt to look at it. Especially since Cal's eyes burned as though they'd been through a sandstorm. His mouth felt as if it was stuffed with a wool sock. And instead of the pleasant satisfaction he usually enjoyed after a night at Buck's, he was as cranky as a bobcat with his tail in a trap.

And all because of a female who'd gotten under his hide. A female who didn't have a lick of sense. A female who was as out of place in Texas as a cowboy in Boston.

Not that he cared about her, he reminded himself. It was just that she irritated him. Like a burr that couldn't be dislodged.

He stalked to the barn and saddled his mount. Seeing the murderous look in his eyes, the wranglers gave him a wide berth.

"Let's get this herd moving," he called as he headed toward the corral. It was already high noon. The branding had begun at sunup, and the strays were ready to join the larger herd.

"Right." One of the cowboys opened the gate to the holding pen, and the cattle were prodded until they began to follow the lead steer.

"I'll take point!" Cal shouted. He had no intention of eating their dust.

The procession moved out, with Cal and two other wranglers riding in front.

The eggs and corn bread he'd washed down with strong black coffee sloshed in his stomach. He should have skipped the breakfast Carmelita had pressed on him. But he'd accepted, hoping the food would steady his jumping nerves.

"We'll take them over Poison Creek and up toward the north range," Cal called to the others.

They nodded, and he gave his horse its head, lifting his face to the sun. Maybe, if he was lucky, he'd feel human by suppertime.

His mount splashed through the waters of the creek and scrambled up the other side. There Cal was joined by two other cowboys.

As they rounded a corner of a small vacant shed, they were forced to come to an abrupt halt, sending dust spewing and chickens squawking.

"What in hell is going on here?" Cal demanded.

Half a dozen ranch hands were busily unloading boxes and parcels from a wagon. One of them looked up and said sheepishly, "Just doing what we're told, Cal."

"Who's giving the orders?" he demanded.

The cowboy nodded toward the open door of the shed.

Cal slid from the saddle and pushed his way through the crowd. Standing in the midst of the wranglers was Pearl, calling out directions in her proper Boston accent.

"That box can go over there, by the shelf. And you can set that smaller one over here beside my desk . . ."

The words died in her throat. The man in her line of vision had cost her a night's sleep. The look in his eyes had her hand going to her throat. Composing herself, she lifted her head in that familiar haughty gesture that never failed to annoy him. "Good morning. I hope you had no trouble finding your bed."

She looked as pretty as a Texas bluebell. Her gown was the same color as her eyes, and, as usual, buttoned clear to her throat. The skirt was full, gathered here and there with darker blue ribbons. Her only concession to the job at hand had been to roll her sleeves to the elbows, and to add a spotless white apron that emphasized her tiny waist.

He had to swallow twice before he managed to speak. "No trouble at all."

"I trust you slept well."

"Slept like a bear in hibernation." Liar, he thought. He'd spent the worst night of his life.

"And today? It looks like you and your men are headed—"

He held up his hand to silence her. He was no good at small talk. Instead, he got directly to the point. "What in hell do you think you're doing?"

She turned away, to escape his burning gaze. "What does it look like? I'm preparing my schoolhouse."

"Just like that? With no further discussion?"

She nodded and began to unload books from a tapestry valise that she'd brought all the way from Boston. "There was nothing more to discuss. Diamond, Jade and Ruby agreed with my decision to teach. Yours was the only objection." She glanced over her shoulder. "The vote is cast. The ayes have it. Discussion closed."

He turned a furious scowl on the wranglers. "Get out," he snapped, causing them to deposit their burdens and scurry from the cabin. "Miss Jewel and I need a few minutes to discuss some things."

"But I . . ." she began.

It was too late. He slammed the door behind the last wrangler, then leaned against it, crossing his arms over his chest.

She was feeling very much alone. And determined not to show it. She would not be intimidated by this tough-talking Texan.

"Do you know what you're doing?" he demanded.

Unnerved, she turned her back on him. "Unpacking books."

"You know what I mean." He stepped closer and caught her arm, forcing her to stop. But she refused to meet his eyes, knowing what she would see there.

"I'm preparing a classroom so the children of Hanging Tree will learn something about the world beyond Texas."

His fingers tightened on her arm. At some other time, in some other place, he might have acknowledged the sexual jolt. Right now, anger was the only emotion he would admit to. "You're inviting everyone in town to trespass on our property."

She was determined to ignore the heat generated by his touch.

"Is that so terrible?"

"You don't understand, do you?" There was a note of disdain in his voice that wounded her more deeply than a blow could have. His voice was low and angry, his breath hot against her cheek. "Onyx Jewel built an empire in the middle of nowhere. That makes a lot of people more than just curious. It makes them jealous."

"What has that to do with...?"

"I wouldn't expect you to understand. Onyx may have been your father, but he was practically a stranger to you. And the ways of Texas aren't always the ways of the rest of the country." His tone sharpened, as though he were addressing a witless child. "Always before, we've had control over the land. No one crossed onto Jewel property without being challenged for trespassing. Now, if someone should decide to spoil our water supply, steal our cattle or damage our buildings, how will we stop him if the place is crawling with strangers?"

"I...don't know. I never gave it any thought," she admitted grudgingly.

He grasped her other arm and turned her fully to face him. As before, the touch of her had his nerves jangling, his heart racing. His voice warmed, turning persuasive. "It isn't too late to put a halt to this foolishness. You need time," he said urgently, "to really think this through."

Foolishness? He thought her dream a folly? Oh, how she intended to prove him wrong. "It's already too late. I sent a wrangler into town this morning with a letter to Reverend Weston.''

''A letter?''

She nodded. ''Asking him to announce to all the families with children that I would begin teaching school on Monday.''

Cal dropped his hands to his sides, clenching them into fists. He made a sound of disgust before turning away. At the door he said, ''You couldn't wait, could you? You've just knocked down a very well-constructed dam. A dam that's managed to hold back dozens of adversaries in the past years. I hope you're ready for the flood that's bound to follow.''

''I'm sorry you feel so strongly about this.''

''Sorry doesn't stop the rain.'' Without a backward glance, he hauled open the door and strode out, slamming it behind him with such force the windows rattled.

A minute later, the sound of galloping hoofbeats signalled that he'd ridden off to rejoin the herd.

The sun dropped behind Widow's Peak, trailing ribbons of blood in its wake. The foothills were bathed in lavender shadows.

As always, the effects of Cal's night in town had been purged by a couple of days filled with hard, satisfying work. Long after the wranglers had finished their jobs, he'd remained with the herd, seeing to all the details, not only because he was needed, but because he wanted to put some distance between himself and the object of so much of his anger. Pearl Jewel. He was still shocked by the way she'd affected him the other night. After only a couple of drinks, he'd behaved like an absolute fool, tearing into her room, scaring her half to death. And tempting himself with thoughts of...

Now, at last, his head was clear, his mind focused and his body energized.

This was Cal's favorite time of the day. The chores were behind him. The evening stretched out before him like a gift to be savored. Oh, there were still chores to see to. Frayed harnesses to be mended. Guns to be cleaned and oiled. But they were armchair chores that kept the hands busy and left the mind free to soar, to explore.

There had been a time when he spent his nights huddled in darkness, eyes wide, senses alert, too afraid to even light a fire for warmth. A man in a boy's body. His childhood swept away by a single mindless act. But Onyx Jewel had changed all that. He'd taken a chance when all others had turned their backs. And, with patience, had given Cal back his self-respect. And his soul.

Deep in thought, Cal reined in his mount. Rolling a cigarette, he held a match to the tip. The light flared briefly before being extinguished. He drew smoke into his lungs, then watched it dissipate into the night air.

He found himself in a thoughtful, contemplative mood. He'd never dreamed his life could be so rewarding. He directed an empire. He had the respect of his men. The hard work, the demands of the land, satisfied him. And yet... He struggled with vaguely unsettling feelings.

Onyx would say it was just man's nature. There was always one more mountain to climb. One more challenge to meet.

On a sigh of impatience, Cal exhaled a cloud of smoke and tossed the butt aside. He'd had enough challenges to last him a lifetime. All he wanted now was some peace. And time to enjoy the fruits of his labors.

Still, he'd found his long evening talks with Onyx Jewel stimulating. No one had ever taken the time to open up to him before. Or to listen. The exchange of ideas, the flow of good conversation, had been food for a starving soul. He missed Onyx. Every day. Felt empty sometimes, when he realized there was no one else with whom he could ever converse so freely. No one else who knew him so well. Who understood where he'd come from. No one else who cared about the boy he'd been and the man he'd become.

He urged his horse into a slow, easy gait. No need to rush back. He'd already missed supper. But Cookie could be counted on to have a few biscuits left in his chuck wagon. Not to mention a couple of slices of dried beef.

As he crested a ridge, he was surprised to see a flicker of light in the deserted cabin. At that moment, Pearl emerged, carrying a parcel. She placed it in the back of the rig. As he urged his mount closer, she made several more trips from the cabin to the cart.

"Putting in long days, aren't you?"

"Oh." When she spotted Cal, astride his horse in the shadows, her hand went to her throat in a gesture of surprise. "I didn't hear you approach. How long have you been out here?"

"Long enough that if I intended you harm, it would already be an accomplished deed." He could see that his words caused her alarm. He hadn't intended to frighten her. But he couldn't seem to stop himself. There was something about this woman that always brought out the worst in him.

Her chin lifted in that infuriating manner. "I doubt there are many madmen loose on the Jewel ranch."

"Not now, maybe. But who's to say what tomorrow will bring?"

"Instead of dwelling on the worst that might happen, I prefer to think about the best." She latched the door and climbed into the rig.

He surprised her by tying his horse behind the wagon and climbing up beside her. In answer to her unspoken question, he muttered, "Since we're both heading in the same direction, it's best if we ride together."

With a flick of the reins, they started off.

The cart danced over the ruts, causing little tendrils of her hair to flutter at the temples.

"Have you given any more thought to what I said the other morning?"

She nodded. "I've thought of little else. And I'm sorry if I've exposed our land to any danger. But I won't be swayed from my course. I intend to teach the children. And for now, this is the best place to hold classes."

"Then I won't put any more barriers in your path," he said simply.

She was stunned. "Cal, do you mean it?"

He nodded, unsure of just how or when he'd come to this decision. Though he'd been mulling it over the past few days, he hadn't really known until that moment what he'd say. "But be warned. If I find the townspeople taking advantage of this opportunity and encroaching on our land, I'll convince Diamond and the others to shut down your schoolhouse. Agreed?"

Her voice softened in the darkness. "That's more than fair, Cal. I agree."

She felt as if the weight of the world had just been lifted from her shoulders. For the moment, it would seem, she and Cal McCabe had reached some sort of tentative truce.

Of course, things were far from comfortable between them. In fact, if anything, they seemed to be tiptoeing around each other, like two prickly rivals. But she wouldn't dwell on that. For now, for the moment, Cal had called a halt to their battle.

With a light heart, Pearl watched as darkness settled over the land. A full moon sent ribbons of gold trailing across the hills.

"What do you do for days on end when you stay with the herd?" She'd been harboring the nagging little fear that it was the cross words spoken between them that had kept him away so long.

"There are so many chores, I usually don't know where to begin. The cattle keep me busy, of course. And when I'm left on my own, I have to hunt or go without supper. My sleep is always disturbed. Most nights I'm up a couple of times, fending off scavengers. Wolves,'' he added, ''or maybe a wildcat that wants a quick meal of tender, helpless calf.''

Pearl found herself studying Cal's big, callused hands as they guided the reins. In everything he did, he seemed so sure and confident. He made it all look so easy. The operation of this vast empire. The million and one chores needed to keep everything going.

She had seen the way the cowboys looked to him for guidance, for advice. And the way they avoided facing him when they knew they'd made an error in judgment. He could be as tough as he was fair. And as unforgiving as an avenging angel when he'd been wronged.

''I hope I'm not keeping you from something important right now,'' she said.

He shook his head. ''The chores will be there tomorrow.''

They rode some distance in silence.

A mournful howl pierced the night air, and Pearl shivered.

''No need to be afraid,'' Cal said softly. ''It's just a lonesome coyote singing to his mate.''

''How do you know?'' she asked.

''If you live here long enough, you'll learn to sort through the different sounds. The hiss of a rattler, the growl of a wolf, the cry of a mountain cat.''

She drew her shawl tighter around her shoulders. ''Are you trying to frighten me more?''

''Not at all.'' He turned his head. ''Are you afraid?''

She shrugged. "Texas is wild and strange. There are so many things out here that I don't know about. Wild animals. Inhospitable weather."

His shoulder brushed hers as he guided the team over the rough terrain. "It's natural to be afraid of what you don't understand. But whether you're in a civilized city like Boston, or the hills of Texas, the biggest danger is always the same."

"What?" she asked.

"It isn't the animals or the weather. It's always people. People who've been through a bloody war and haven't learned to put the hatred and fear behind them. People who shoot first and ask questions later. People who just hate."

She thought about some she'd known in her childhood. Though they hadn't carried guns, they'd used their words like weapons, to wound, to destroy confidence.

"What causes people to be cruel?" she wondered aloud.

"Jealousy." He spoke the word like a curse. "They're jealous of those who've prospered while they're going hungry. Jealous of those who've succeeded while they've failed. Some are just jealous for the sake of jealousy. And there's no reasoning with them. That jealousy and hatred festers until they go mad with it." His tone changed, lowered, until his voice throbbed with passion. "It's always the innocent who are made to suffer at the hands of such people."

She glanced at his hard, chiseled profile and sensed that he'd had more than a passing acquaintance with the subject.

Without warning, he said, "I'd like you to learn how to handle a rifle."

"A rifle?" She turned to him, shocked at his suggestion. "I... couldn't."

"Sure you could. It isn't that hard. I could teach you."

"No." She spoke the word quickly. "I won't. You can't make me."

"Listen to me, Pearl," he said calmly, reasonably. "You're going to be isolated. Too far from the ranch house to call for help. And too far from the nearest rancher. You'll have to depend on yourself."

She continued shaking her head. "Absolutely not. I won't even consider the idea."

He sucked in an angry breath. Obstinate little fool.

Defeated, he centered all his attention on the task of guiding the horse and rig across the rushing waters of Poison Creek.

"Creek's high," he muttered as water sloshed over their boots. He was determined to find some common ground where they might talk without fighting. "Snow's melting up on Widow's Peak. That's good for the ranchers."

She seemed equally determined to avoid another battle. "Why?" she asked.

"Water's the lifeblood of the cattle rancher. Without it, we could lose an entire herd in one season."

"Has that ever happened?"

He nodded. "We suffered through a drought in '63. Onyx wasn't sure he'd be able to hold on to the ranch. By the time the rains finally came, Poison Creek had been reduced to a dry gulch and we'd lost all but remnants of the herds up in the foothills."

"What did Daddy do?" Pearl asked in alarm.

"He had to let the wranglers go. Couldn't pay them," Cal added when she glanced at him in surprise.

Pearl watched as he urged the horse up the steep banks of the creek. But it wasn't the progress of the horse and rig that held her attention; it was the muscles of Cal's arms, rippling with each movement. He had such incredible strength. Such power. And yet, for all his toughness, there was an aura of calm capability, of quiet authority, about him. She knew, from things she'd heard, that the wranglers respected him. She knew, too, that he could be quick with fist or gun. But she suspected that such things would be a last resort with Cal McCabe. He was a man of few words. But when he spoke, others listened respectfully.

"How did the Jewel ranch survive?" she asked.

"Your father sent me to sweep the north and east ranges, while he rode the south and west. When we brought back the few stragglers who'd survived the drought, we had a herd of less than a hundred."

"You stayed? I thought you said my father couldn't pay his wranglers. How could he pay you?" Pearl asked.

Cal gave a short laugh. "I didn't stay with Onyx Jewel for money." His tone roughened. "I'd have walked through fire for that man."

They fell silent for a few minutes, as the horse and rig neared the ranch. But now it was a comfortable silence. Onyx Jewel was someone they had both loved. And both had suffered his loss.

Lanternlight filtered through the curtained windows of the big house. The haunting notes of a mouth organ could be heard drifting faintly from the bunkhouse.

"It's hard to believe my father almost lost all of this," she said softly.

Cal nodded, enjoying, as he always did, the beauty, the serenity of the scene. "Onyx mortgaged everything, then went to St. Louis and brought back the finest bull money could buy. We built breeding pens, and even Diamond and Carmelita were pressed into service when the calves were born. Onyx was determined that his cattle would be the sturdiest, the healthiest, in all of Texas. And they were, because they'd come from sturdy survivors. Within five years, the herd numbered more than a thousand. And Onyx lived to see his dream fulfilled."

"I'm glad," she whispered. "But he couldn't have done it without you."

"Oh, Onyx would have managed, even if he was the last man on earth." Cal drew on the reins, bringing the horse and rig to a stop at the back door. He stepped down, then offered a hand to her. "Your father was an extraordinary man, Pearl. I wish you could have known him the way I did."

"So do I. You don't know how it grieves me that I was denied the chance to really know my own father." She held out her hand and caught up the hem of her skirt, preparing to climb down.

She was startled when she felt herself lifted in Cal's powerful arms. He scooped her from the rig and held her as easily as if she weighed nothing at all. For the space of a heartbeat, he held her slightly above him, so that she was forced to look down at him. Then he lowered her slowly, so slowly that time seemed to stand still. Their gazes locked, and she felt a sizzling current go through her at the intensity of his look. Fear? she wondered. Or anticipation? She sensed that he was going to kiss her again. And though in her heart she wanted desperately to feel his lips on hers, her common sense told her she had to resist.

Cal, too, seemed torn. It would be an easy matter to steal a kiss. Held helplessly in his arms, Pearl was in no position to refuse. And if she was any other female, he wouldn't have given it a second thought. He was, after all, a man with a healthy appetite. But this was Pearl Jewel. The daughter of the man to whom he owed more than life itself. Besides, she wasn't like other women. After just one taste, he'd come to realize that she was more potent than Buck's whiskey. He could never dally with this woman. Or walk away, once he'd begun.

But, oh, the temptation was great.

He continued to lower her, and she absorbed a tingle along her spine as her breasts brushed his chest. And then he set her on her feet, and she had the strangest sensation that the ground was shifting and tilting beneath her.

"I'll see to your horse and rig."

Even after he released her, she could feel the warmth of his touch against her flesh.

"Thank you. Good night, Cal."

She stood at the door a moment, watching as he climbed to the seat and caught the reins. He gave a tip of his hat before blending into the shadows.

It occurred to her that he had offered her much more tonight than just his approval for the schoolhouse. By sharing his memories of her father, he had reached out a tentative hand of friendship.

Still, there was something there, just below the surface, that disturbed her. Something raw and primitive. Something dark and dangerous. And, though he kept it carefully controlled, she could sense it.

Unleashed, it could consume them both.

Chapter Five

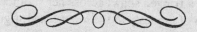

The sky was a dark, churning blue. A mild spring morning, though the air hinted of cool winds and distant storms.

Pearl took pains with her appearance this morning, knowing she would be the object of much speculation at Sunday services. She fumbled with the buttons of her buttercup-yellow gown. Where had the week gone? She wasn't nearly ready for school to begin. Oh, why had she sent that letter to Reverend Weston, promising to start tomorrow?

Because she had wanted to get even with Cal for taking up a position against her. And now she would have to pay the price for her act of defiance.

Cal. The very thought of him had her insides turning to mush. Though she was intimidated by him, she was determined not to let him know it.

As she descended the stairs, she was surprised to see Jade and Ruby, dressed in their Sunday best.

"Wherever are you going?" she asked.

"To town with you." Jade smoothed down the sheath of pale green silk and added a matching coat lined in deep green. Like the gown, it had a mandarin collar and a frog closing, and was slit on either side to the knee to allow for easier walking.

"But why? You've never gone before."

"We talked it over, *chérie*." Ruby gave a deep, throaty laugh. "And decided that you should not have to face the townspeople alone. Are we not family?" She tossed a fringed shawl across her shoulders, adding a touch of modesty to the low-necked, figure-hugging gown of crimson satin. "Let them see that the Jewel sisters stand together."

"And if anyone should malign our good name," Jade said in her soft, melodious voice, "they will find themselves against three dangerous opponents."

With a lighthearted laugh, Pearl linked her arms with theirs. This was her father's greatest gift to her. Sisters.

When a clatter marked the arrival of their horse and carriage, they walked outside, and were surprised to see Cal.

"What are you doing in the carriage?" Pearl asked. "Why didn't you leave that for one of the wranglers?" Again that flutter in the pit of her stomach. And again she had to struggle to calm herself.

"I'm driving you ladies to Sunday services." He stepped down and helped them get settled.

At the touch of his hand at her elbow, she felt her skin soften and heat. She glanced at his hard, chiseled profile. If he felt it, he gave no indication.

He climbed aboard and flicked the reins. "Before she left, Diamond reminded me that now that I'm part owner of the Jewel ranch, I have an obligation to act the part."

"You mean this is to become a weekly ritual, *mon cher?*" Ruby's eyes lit with laughter.

He shook his head. "I wouldn't go that far. Most weeks, I'm up on the range with one of the herds. But I guess whenever I'm around I'll have to sit through an hour of Reverend Weston's famous sermons."

"You won't be sorry," Pearl assured him.

"I'm not sure about that. I think I'm already sorry." To soften his words, he winked, and she felt her heart tumble. "But I can't forget your father's example. As busy as he was, Onyx always managed to find time on Sunday to attend services. The least I can do is follow his lead."

Pearl had no idea why Cal's presence should make her heart feel so light. But suddenly the morning had taken on a festive air. There was nothing the townspeople could say or do that would spoil her day.

The gilt carriage, with its matched white horses, had belonged to Jade's mother. At the news of her father's death, she had driven it all the way from San Francisco. Though it looked as out of place in this dusty landscape as the three women who rode in it, they took no notice. Instead, as they rolled across the countryside, they found themselves laughing and chatting like carefree children.

"What is that?" Jade asked, pointing to a tall column of rocks in the distance.

"Dead Man's Leap," Cal replied.

Ruby shivered. "*Mon Dieu!* Did a man really leap to his death from those rocks?"

"Legend has it that a Comanche chief lost his heart to a woman who had promised her love to another. So the chief spirited her away to the top of that pile of rocks and forced her to remain there until she agreed to be his. In desperation, she leaped, choosing death over a loveless union. But the gods, taking pity on her, turned her into an eagle, and as the chief watched, she spread her wings and flew back to her beloved. The chief followed, expecting the gods to bless him, as well. But instead of sprouting wings, he fell to his death."

"That's so sad," Pearl cried.

"Oh, *chérie*. It is just a story."

"I suppose so. But why must everything in this place reflect such unhappiness?" Pearl shivered. "Poison Creek. Widow's Peak. And now Dead Man's Leap."

"Life has always been hard for the people who forged new trails," Cal said. "And it's the saddest and most dramatic events that get repeated over and over until they become legends."

"But weren't there any happy events in this place?" Pearl folded her arms across her chest. "Must everything be so dreary?"

"You are right, *chérie*," Ruby said, with laughter bubbling in her throat. "We will give them new names. How about Nectar of the Gods Creek?"

"And Cupid's Peak," Jade added, getting into the spirit of things.

"Why not Lovers' Tower?" Pearl mused.

"And Sweetheart's Ridge," Ruby shouted, enjoying the way her voice bounced and echoed off the surrounding buttes.

The air rang with their laughter, as they gave improbable names to every hill and gully in the area.

Though Cal didn't join in the silliness, it was clear from the way he bit back a smile that he was enjoying himself. More, he was enjoying a side of Pearl he rarely saw.

By the time they arrived in town, they had laughed and shouted so much, it was an effort to settle down. They were still smiling as Cal helped them from the carriage and they made their way to the back room of Durfee's Mercantile for Sunday services.

Pearl saw the way heads turned when they entered. The Jewel sisters were still objects of curiosity to the townspeople. And when Cal McCabe trailed after them and took his seat, a murmur went up in the crowd. He took no notice as he removed his wide-brimmed hat and nodded greetings to several of the ranchers.

"Morning, Cal." Marshal Quent Regan took a seat beside him and leaned over to mutter, "Morning, ladies."

"Good morning, Marshal," they said in unison.

"I'm surprised to see you here, Cal."

"I don't know why. You're here, aren't you?"

The two men shared a laugh.

Cal glanced around. "It looks like word of the reverend's rousing sermons is spreading. He's got a full house."

"I haven't decided yet if it's Reverend Weston's sermons that fill this room every week, or the chance to see so many pretty ladies all in one place." The marshal cast an admiring glance at the three Jewel sisters, then quickly looked away when Ruby shot him a sultry smile.

The crowd fell silent when Reverend Wade Weston walked in and strode to the front of the room. Even his dark suit and starched white shirt couldn't conceal the ripple of muscles. Hair the color of a golden halo fell nearly to his shoulders. More than a few young women, as well as several of their mothers, were heard to sigh. After leading them in song, he signaled for them to be seated. And for the next half hour they listened attentively as his rich voice rolled over them, exhorting them to love one another and to forgive one another. At the end of his rousing sermon, the congregation were on their feet, singing with even greater fervor.

When Jade and Ruby shared a songbook, Pearl had no choice but to share hers with Cal. As their hands brushed, she glanced up to find him looking down at her. She looked away quickly. With heat staining her cheeks, she joined in the singing, and was surprised to hear Cal's rich, deep voice blending perfectly with hers.

When the song ended, Reverend Weston announced, "For those who haven't heard, Miss Pearl Jewel will open her schoolhouse tomorrow. Classes will be held in the old cabin, located on the north ridge of the Jewel ranch, just across the banks of Poison Creek. All are welcome."

He walked to the doorway and began greeting the members of his congregation as they took their leave. When Pearl stood before him, her hand was engulfed in a warm, firm handshake.

"Do you think anyone will show up tomorrow, Reverend Weston?" she asked.

"I certainly hope so," he replied. "It would be a shame if the children of Hanging Tree couldn't take advantage of your generous gift."

As she followed her sisters from the mercantile, a little boy who'd been standing to one side tugged on her skirt. His arms were painfully thin, and his clothes were patched and faded. His fine blond hair was in need of a trim. She recognized him at once as Rollie Ingram's son. As usual, the Ingram family had not been at services.

"Are you a princess?" he asked.

Pearl knelt, so that her eyes were level with his. "No. I'm not a princess. I'm a teacher." She solemnly offered her hand. "My name is Miss Pearl Jewel. What is yours?"

"Daniel."

His hands, she noted, hadn't seen soap or water in a very long time. Dirt and grime seemed to have settled deep in his sunburned skin. "Would you like me to teach you to read and write, Daniel?"

He nodded his head, afraid to speak. At last, finding his tongue, he managed to say, "Before she died, my ma showed me a picture of a princess. She looked just like you, only not as pretty."

"Why, thank you, Daniel." Still clutching his hand, Pearl gave him her sweetest smile. "I'll bet your mama was pretty, too."

"Yes'm. Gilbert says she's with the angels now."

They both looked up as a shadow fell over them. For a moment Daniel cringed, then, seeing that it was his older brother, he gave him a wide smile. "Gilbert, this is Miss Pearl Jewel. She's the new teacher. She said she could teach me to read and write."

Pearl got to her feet and brushed down her skirts. With a smile, she held out her hand. "Hello, Gil . . ."

"It's Gilbert." Though the older boy couldn't have been more than twelve or thirteen, he already stood a head taller than her. He resembled his father, with hair that was thick and dark and curly, and shoulders almost as broad as a man's. He avoided looking at her. Instead, he frowned at his little brother. "Pa's mad as a hornet," he said in a furious whisper. "Get in the back of the wagon, and don't say anything to rile him."

"But . . ."

"Come on now." He pushed the little boy ahead of him.

Pearl noticed that he kept his hands on Daniel's shoulders, steering him to the back of a rickety wagon and settling him amid some sacks of flour and sugar.

Without a backward glance, he pulled himself up to the seat beside his father. The horse and wagon took off in a cloud of dust.

"Looks like I just lost my first student," she said.

"Maybe it's just as well," Cal muttered, watching the wagon until it disappeared over a ridge. "That's one man I'd rather not have on Jewel property."

Just then, he heard a feminine voice calling his name. He glanced up to see a dark-haired young woman in a flimsy wrap waving her hand from an upstairs window of Buck's saloon. A slight red flush crept up his neck.

"I believe that young lady is calling you." Jade's eyes twinkled with humor at Cal's discomfort.

"Come on," he added tersely. "It's time we took our leave."

As he turned away, Millie Potter, who owned the boardinghouse at the end of town, stepped directly in front of him. From behind her skirts peeked three little girls, all with their mother's curly red hair and freckled noses.

"Good morning, Cal. I knew you were back. At least I'd heard you'd been to town." She glanced toward Buck's with a look of distaste. "But it's been a long time since you graced my boardinghouse."

"'Morning, Millie." He removed his hat and held it stiffly in one hand before winking at the three girls, who giggled and hid their faces. "Hello April, May and June. Say hello to Miss Pearl, Miss Jade and Miss Ruby."

The three children blushed beet red and ducked behind their mother's skirts.

"Children, mind your manners." At a stern word from their pretty mother, the three children stepped forward and made a slight bow. They appeared to be about five, six and seven.

"How do, Miss Pearl. Miss Jade. Miss Ruby," they called before ducking away again.

Cal cleared his throat, uncomfortable, in the silence that followed. "With Onyx gone, there's a lot needing my attention out at the ranch."

"Yes. I'm sure of that. Still, we miss you." Millie Potter shot a swift, fleeting smile toward the three women, allowing her gaze to linger a moment on

Pearl, who stood to one side of Cal. "I was hoping you'd find time to come by for a while. I have a pot of stew simmering. And fresh biscuits I baked early this morning."

Before Cal could politely refuse, Ruby stepped forward. "Oh, yes. Please, Cal. It is such a long ride back to the ranch. And we have so few opportunities to visit with the people of Hanging Tree."

"Marshal Regan always takes his meal with us on Sunday. So does the Reverend Weston," Millie urged.

Cal glanced at the families seated in grassy areas around the mercantile, enjoying baskets of cold chicken and jugs of buttermilk, while children chased each other in games of tag. He thought of all the chores needing his attention back at the ranch. Then he saw the eager looks of the three Jewel women.

"I suppose, since it's Sunday..." Seeing Millie's wide, expectant smile, he added, "You folks can go ahead."

Millie shot an arched look toward Buck's saloon. Seeing it, he added quickly, "I have a few supplies to pick up at Durfee's, and I'll be along in a little while."

Satisfied, she nodded. "Fine. We'll see you at my place." With her daughters in tow, Millie hitched up her skirts and headed briskly along the wooden walkway, greeting friends as she went. The three Jewel sisters followed in her wake, aware that they were being watched with every step they took.

Potter's Boardinghouse was a large, cheery place, with a formal front parlor boasting a horsehair sofa and several overstuffed chairs set around a stone fireplace. Millie led them past the parlor, toward the rear of the house, where the air was sweet with the aroma of cooking. In the dining room, a long table had already been set for company, with starched white linens and an assortment of mismatched dishes and cutlery. On a sideboard was a jug holding a bouquet of wildflowers, set amid several towel-draped mounds. Millie removed the towels to reveal loaves of freshly baked breads and cakes.

"You must have been working since dawn," Pearl remarked.

"I actually started last night," the young woman admitted. "Sunday is a big day here at my place. Many of the ranchers bring their own baskets of food. But those who have no wives to cook for them usually eat here after Sunday services."

A girl of twelve or thirteen poked her head out of the kitchen. "Stew's ready," she called. "And your chicken and biscuits are done to perfection, Mrs. Potter."

"Thanks, Birdie." Millie nodded toward her three guests. "Birdie Bidwell, meet Miss Pearl Jewel, Miss Jade Jewel and Miss Ruby Jewel."

The girl's eyes widened. The Jewel women were the closest thing Hanging Tree had to royalty.

"Hello, Birdie." Pearl stuck out her hand, and the girl self-consciously wiped her hands on her big, stained apron before accepting her handshake.

"You're the teacher lady," Birdie said.

"Yes. That is, if anyone shows up to be taught."

"I wish my girls could attend," Millie said wistfully.

"Why can't they?" Pearl asked.

"It's just too far. They're too young to travel that distance alone. And with my husband dead these past five years, I can't spare the time every day."

"How about you, Birdie?" Pearl turned to Millie's young assistant.

Birdie sadly shook her head. "I surely would like to learn to read and write. But I got to earn my keep." She went back to the kitchen.

When the door closed behind her, Millie said softly, "Birdie's father was thrown from a horse more than a year ago. His broken bones mended, but Doc Prentice can't fix his back. He hasn't been able to work since the accident. Even though I can't afford to pay Birdie very much, it's a help to her ma just to pay her something. And though she's clumsy, the girl has a big heart."

"I see." Once again, Pearl felt the distance between herself and these people created by her father's wealth. "Could we give you a hand before the others get here?"

"Oh, no. You're paying guests." Millie reached for their shawls. When they relinquished them, she carried them to the front hall and draped them over wooden pegs. "Make yourselves comfortable in the dining room, and I'll have Birdie serve you some tea.

"But we would like to help, *chérie!*" Ruby exclaimed.

"I won't hear of it."

Before they could argue, a knock sounded on the front door. Looking almost relieved, Millie Potter invited them to take their seats at the table while she hurried from the room.

Soon the sounds of men's voices signaled the arrival of the rest of her guests.

"Something smells wonderful," Marshal Regan said as he removed his gunbelt and hat and hung them on a peg. "I think you've made my favorite stew, Millie."

"And cinnamon biscuits," Reverend Weston added. "Nothing perfumes the air like your cinnamon biscuits."

Millie's laughter trilled as she led them along the hallway and into the dining room. It was obvious, from the way she handled the introductions, that she was a woman who was comfortable in the presence of men. When everyone was seated, she made her way to the kitchen. Just as Millie and Birdie began serving the meal, Cal arrived.

"You're just in time," Millie said in an admonishing tone.

"A few minutes longer and I'd have had your share," Marshal Regan said with a laugh.

Cal took a seat beside Pearl. Once again she absorbed the shock of his thigh brushing hers, and the touch of his shoulder against hers. It occurred to her that it was not an altogether unpleasant sensation. It was one that she might learn to enjoy, if she could only relax in his presence.

As he ladled stew onto his plate, Millie paused beside him and set down a plate of chopped chili peppers. With an air of easy familiarity, she dropped a hand on his shoulder and murmured, "I guess I know your taste by now, Cal."

"That's right," Marshal Quent Regan said. His words brought knowing laughter from the others. "Nothing bland for a man like Cal McCabe. He likes his food the way he likes his life. And we all know what that is."

Millie finished for him. "The spicier the better."

Chapter Six

The spicier the better.

Conversation swirled around Pearl, but she was hardly aware of it. She seemed unable to get beyond one inescapable fact. She had been fooling herself. Tempting herself with the idea that a man like Cal McCabe could be interested in someone like her.

She had never had any illusions about herself. She was aware that, in a world filled with dangerous, exciting people, she was easily overlooked. She had always been the good daughter, doing as she was told. The good student, following the rules. The good citizen, living by the law. It never occurred to her to rebel, to be defiant. She couldn't help the way she was. She knew what others thought of her. Prim. Proper. What was the word Millie Potter had used? *Bland.* Certainly not spicy. The only bold thing she'd ever attempted was this trip to Texas. And every day she found herself questioning that decision.

She sat locked in misery as Millie laughed and chatted. And flirted shamelessly with Cal and the other men.

"There's been a good bit of interest in your school, Miss Pearl."

At the sound of Reverend Weston's voice, Pearl roused herself from her thoughts. "Interest, perhaps. But so far, no one has promised to attend."

"It's a long way for children to ride," Millie Potter said. "I can't, in good conscience, let my three girls travel that far alone. And I've heard several other townspeople say the same."

Pearl had a sudden inspiration. "What if the townspeople could transport them all together in one wagon?"

Millie's brows lifted. "What an interesting thought..."

Marshal Regan nodded. "If several of the families took turns hauling the children to school and back, it wouldn't feel like such a burden."

Reverend Weston nodded. "It's a fine idea, Miss Pearl. Before this day is over, I intend to discuss it with as many families as I can."

Beside her, she could feel Cal's probing stare. She lowered her head and took a bite of stew. It was the best she'd ever tasted. Which was one more reason not to like Millie Potter. But the truth was, she couldn't deny the fact that she liked this young woman. Pearl admired the way she held her family together, despite the loss of her husband. Five years alone, Millie had said. A long time for a pretty young woman to survive in this tough town, and to raise three daughters. No wonder she found all the men so charming and interesting. She saw them all as potential husbands. And from the looks of things, she would have her pick of them. She had everything to offer a man. A cozy home. A ready-made family. A respectable standing in the community.

When the meal was finished, Millie poured coffee, lingering beside Cal as she leaned close to remove his empty plate.

"I made apple cobbler," she announced.

When she returned from the kitchen, she placed an oversize slice in front of Cal.

"How did that cowboy get so lucky?" the marshal asked.

"I happen to know it's his favorite." Millie added a dollop of sweet cream before returning to the kitchen for more coffee.

"I thought Carmelita's pie was your favorite," Pearl muttered under her breath.

"It is. When Carmelita's doing the cooking," he said with a grin.

"Why, I didn't realize what a charmer you were, Mr. McCabe," she whispered in sugary tones.

Before he could manage a reply, Millie returned to top off their cups with more coffee.

"Did you get enough to eat?" she asked as she refilled Cal's cup.

"More than enough." His smile faded when he caught the knowing look in Pearl's eye. He nearly burned his tongue as he downed the scalding liquid, then hurriedly pushed away from the table. "It's time we got moving. We have a long ride ahead of us."

He held their chairs as the three Jewel sisters got to their feet and said their goodbyes. In the hallway, Millie retrieved their shawls and escorted them to the front door. As they took their leave, she placed a hand on Cal's sleeve, holding him back.

Jade and Ruby chatted as they made their way to the waiting carriage. But, even over the sound of her sisters' voices, Pearl managed to overhear snatches of Millie's words to Cal.

"I'd forgotten what a good cook you were," he said as he counted out the coins for their meal.

"Now that your memory has been refreshed, I hope you won't stay away so long."

"I'll try not to."

The three little girls ran up behind their mother and peeked out at Cal. He winked and tugged on their curls, causing them to giggle and squeal in laughter.

Pulling on his hat, he strolled to the carriage. As he flicked the reins, he gave a brief wave of his hand. The woman and her daughters remained in the doorway, waving until the carriage and its occupants were out of sight.

Pearl studied Cal's straight back, his broad shoulders, the way his sun-bronzed fingers curled around the leather reins. While Jade and Ruby laughed and chatted, she fell deeper into silence. What was the matter with her? The Reverend Weston's sermon had been rousing. The singing soothing. And Millie Potter's food as satisfying as any she'd tasted since she left Boston. She ought to feel on top of the world. Instead, she had to struggle to chase away a feeling of gloom.

There was only one cure for it. As soon as they returned to the ranch, she would ride out to the cabin. Even though the day was half-over, there would be a couple of hours of daylight left. Enough time to polish the classroom in preparation for the morning.

Hard work. That was what was needed to keep her mind off her troubling thoughts.

Cal's horse ambled up the hill, moving at a slow, leisurely pace. Twilight was settling over the land, casting the hills in bloodred shadows.

As his gaze scanned the land, he noted the flicker of light in Onyx's old deserted cabin. He would have to stop thinking of it as that, he told himself. It was no longer a deserted cabin. Now it was the new schoolhouse.

Tied to a rail out front was a horse and rig, signaling that Pearl was still there.

Drawing near, he could make out her figure, cloth in hand, scrubbing a row of mismatched chairs and overturned barrels that would serve as desks.

Cal dismounted and watched through the open door. Pearl paused, pressing a hand to the small of her back. She straightened and gave a little sigh, then resumed her work until the chair she was scrubbing was as clean as the others.

Satisfied, she gave a look around. In the glow of the lantern, her eyes danced with unconcealed pleasure. The floor and walls sparkled. The clean desks were arranged in a neat, orderly row. A shelf along one wall held a cache of precious books. She dropped the rag into a bucket of water and wrung it out, then began to wash another desk.

He watched her a few minutes, then stepped inside, alerting her to his presence. "Looks like you've been busy."

"Oh, you startled me!" She turned to face him.

There was a smudge of dirt on her cheek, and he thought about brushing it off. Instead, he curled his hand into a fist at his side. A wisp of her hair had pried loose from the ribbons to fall seductively over one eye. It was the closest she'd ever come to looking mussed.

"Why don't you leave that for the men to do?" he asked.

"I wouldn't dream of taking them away from their chores to do something I can manage on my own."

She was surprised when Cal picked up a second rag and began to work alongside her. "Haven't you done enough today?"

He shrugged. "After the day I put in, this seems like child's play."

"This child's play," she said lightly, "has my muscles aching and my back protesting."

He shot her an admiring glance as she continued to work despite her weariness.

They worked together in companionable silence.

When the last desk was clean, she tossed aside the cloth and washed her hands, while he went outside and returned with an armload of wood for the fireplace. He knelt and positioned the logs, then added kindling.

"All you'll have to do in the morning is light this to take the chill off the cabin," he told her.

"Thank you." She watched as he stood and wiped his hands on his pants. "Carmelita sent one of the wranglers out here with a basket of food. Will you join me?"

He was surprised by the offer. And unnerved by it. He didn't think he was ready to share a secluded supper with Pearl Jewel. Not the way she'd been affecting him lately.

"No, thanks. I'll just be on my way."

At that moment, she uncovered the basket, displaying fried chicken and golden biscuits still warm from the oven.

"I'll never eat all this." She laughed, and the warm, lilting sound had his tension evaporating. "It's obvious that Carmelita is accustomed to cooking for men. Men with hearty appetites, I might add."

Cal's mouth watered, and before he could stop himself he said, "I guess I could eat something. It's been a long day. And since it's so late, I figured I'd have to settle for whatever Cookie had left."

Pearl spread the linen covering over her desktop and began setting out the food. Along with assorted pieces of chicken and biscuits were several spring vegetables and a canteen of water.

"Now I know Carmelita thinks she's cooking for wranglers," Pearl said with a chuckle. "I haven't eaten this much since I was twelve, when Charley Springer dared me to enter the pie-eating contest at our church picnic."

Cal shot her a look of disbelief. "You accepted his dare?"

"How could I refuse?" She laughed again. "I was sick for two days. And I haven't been able to look at a blueberry pie since. But I beat Charley. And took home the ribbon."

Cal tried to picture this perfect woman with her face buried in blueberry pies. But it was an impossible task. Even as a child, she'd probably been all pink and spotless. And driving the boys crazy. Still, the fact that she'd accepted a dare had him looking at her with new respect. He was going to have to adjust his perception of Pearl Jewel.

He held her chair, then pulled a wooden stool beside the desk and straddled it. He bit into the chicken, closing his eyes a moment in pure pleasure.

Pearl enjoyed watching him eat. He made the ordinary act of chewing food seem like a rare treat. With each taste of Carmelita's biscuits, each bite of chicken, he seemed to soften, to grow more mellow.

"Why do you want to teach?" he asked as he ate.

His question brought a gentle smile to her lips. "I guess I've always known I would be a teacher. It was what my father wanted for me. My mother was a teacher. A good one. And I watched as the children in our neighborhood learned to read and write under her guidance. There's something wonderful about satisfying the need for knowledge." She glanced at the chicken in his big hand. "It's like filling a hunger. Any hunger."

Now that was a simple, succinct answer that Cal readily understood. And one that caught him by surprise.

"I'd like the future to be brighter for the children of Hanging Tree," she added softly. "And if I can be a small part of that future, I'll be grateful."

"I hope you're right, Pearl. I hope the things you teach the children will improve their lives. I only wish you'd chosen to teach them in town, instead of way out here."

There it was again. That note of censure. And though she tried to ignore the little twinge of pain, it slipped through her defenses, cutting as sharply, as unexpectedly, as the page of one of her precious books had cut her finger earlier.

"I don't mean that as criticism," he said gently. "But this place is awfully secluded. If you discovered yourself in need of help, there would be none to be found."

"It isn't that far to the ranch house. Besides, I'm sure there are a lot of ranchers who find themselves secluded." She shrugged. "They survive, don't they?"

Cal could tell her a lot about survival in this rough country. He thought of the women, old before their time. And the children, forced to do the work of adults, for the sake of survival. Instead, he decided to change the subject. "Tell me about your childhood in Boston," he said unexpectedly.

She was caught by surprise, and was more than a little flattered that he would care. "I suppose to some it seemed lonely. My mother and I kept to ourselves."

"Why?" he asked.

"We...kept to a very small circle of friends." Uncomfortable beneath his gaze, she ducked her head and uncovered a linen-wrapped mound, which turned out to be an enormous slice of apple pie.

Grateful for the interruption, she shoved the pie toward Cal. "I'm afraid you'll have to eat this," she said. "I don't have room for another thing."

"No, thanks." He was determined to be polite. But his mouth was already watering. "I've eaten enough of your supper. Besides, it isn't blueberry. Go ahead and enjoy it."

They laughed at the shared joke. To settle the dispute, she cut off a small portion for herself, then passed the rest to him.

He needed no prodding as he dug into the pie, then washed it down with a long, cool drink from the canteen.

"You still haven't told me much about your childhood," he said.

She sighed, reluctant to pursue the topic further. "By the time I was barely past crawling, my mother saw to it that I could read and write and do sums. A neighbor taught me music...." She blushed slightly, seeing the way he lifted a brow.

"Music?"

"Piano and voice," she explained. "Though I had no aptitude for it. And another neighbor taught me needlework, which I greatly disliked. My mother believed that everyone should be taught to be useful. In exchange for their lessons, my mother taught their children reading and writing. When I grew old enough, I was sent to a women's academy, where I completed my education."

"You actually attended an academy?"

She nodded. "I needed to prepare myself for a profession. And there was never any doubt that I would choose to become a teacher like my mother."

He didn't say anything. Merely stared at her in a strange, guarded way.

She felt her cheeks redden. Though she couldn't think why, she had the distinct impression that she had said something revealing. To a man who had grown up in a harsh, demanding wilderness, her childhood probably sounded foolish. Perhaps he had already dismissed her as a spoiled, pampered female who knew nothing more than how to read, sew a pretty seam and make silly, useless music.

"My mother died just before graduation, and then, before I could put my education to good use, Daddy died." She shrugged expressively. "And here I am. In Hanging Tree, Texas."

Again he said nothing. He helped her gather the remains of their supper into the basket. After replacing the linen wrap on top, she glanced up to find him still studying her.

He swung away, returning the wooden stool to the corner of the room. "Thanks for sharing your supper with me, Pearl."

"I...enjoyed it." And, she realized, that was the truth. She had enjoyed this unexpected interruption in her evening.

But, as usual, she had said or done something to keep it from going smoothly, though she couldn't think what it had been.

"Come on." Cal blew out the lantern, then picked up the basket and placed a hand beneath her elbow. "It's time we got back to the ranch."

Outside, he secured the latch, then helped her into the rig and tied his horse behind it. He climbed up beside her and flicked the reins.

"I have a question."

At the deep timbre of his voice, she turned to him.

The moonlight cast his face in light and shadow, giving him a dangerous, mysterious look. "You said you needed to prepare yourself for a profession. Why?"

"Did I—?" She nearly lost her voice and tried again. "Did I say that?"

He nodded.

She ran a tongue over her lips, cursing her clumsiness. Now that she had let it slip, there was nothing to do but try to muddle through. But, oh, how she wished she'd never allowed herself to reveal something so personal.

"Because," Her voice lowered to almost a whisper. "The students at the academy were divided into two groups. Those who would marry, and needed to learn certain social skills, and those who were preparing for a profession." She took a deep breath. "I fell into the second group."

He kept his gaze on the trail. "And why would a young, pretty female think she would never marry?"

She should have been flattered by his question. Instead, it only made her all the more uncomfortable. "I was... That is, my mother wasn't..." She squared her shoulders and said in a rush of words, "As you well know, my mother and Onyx Jewel were never married. In Boston, no proper gentleman would ever consider marrying a woman who wasn't...respectable."

He opened his mouth to protest, but she went on quickly, "A woman who couldn't be welcomed into a man's family, his church and his community was not marriageable. So I knew I would never marry. I needed to prepare for my future. A future of service."

She ducked her head and missed the look of anger that crossed Cal's face.

His hands tightened perceptibly on the reins. "What went on between your father and mother has nothing to do with you, Pearl."

"Of course it does." She lifted her head to study the canopy of glittering stars in the sky. "All my life, I've had to live with the knowledge that I was being judged, not only on the way I lived my life, but on how my parents chose to live theirs. If I should make one mistake, one misstep, people would say I was just doing what came naturally."

"You make it sound as though you were ashamed of your mother and father."

"Don't ever think that," she said in protest. "I was very proud of my mother. And I want to be like her. I want to fill young minds with knowledge. As for my father, I adored him, though I hardly knew him." She struggled to keep her tone even. "But people can be very cruel. The fact that my parents never married was common knowledge. And for the very proper people of Boston, it was a barrier. Though they tried to be fair, they thought less of me."

"What do you care what others think?"

She shrugged and tried to smile. But her voice wavered slightly. "When you hear it often enough, Cal, you care."

Oh, how well he knew that.

His tone softened. Without thinking, he patted her hands, which were clenched tightly together. At once he felt the familiar rush of heat. "I guess it's time you heard what your father told me many years ago."

Surprised, she lifted her head to glance up at him.

"You're in Texas now, Pearl." His fingers squeezed lightly, as if to emphasize his words. "Out here, you're not judged by the cards you're dealt, but by the way you play them."

For some strange reason, her throat felt clogged. She had to swallow several times before she managed to say, "I'll . . . try to remember."

The silence of the night seemed to close in around them. Even the clatter of the wheels, and the horses' hoofbeats, seemed muffled.

This time, as they pulled up at the door to the ranch house, Cal made no move to climb down.

Surprised, Pearl turned toward him. And found him staring intently at her.

"What's wrong?" she whispered.

"Nothing. It's just that I . . ." He leaned toward her, and she felt the warmth of his breath against her cheek. "I like looking at you."

Sweet heaven, he was going to kiss her. She started to draw back, but his hand was at the back of her head, holding her still. And then his lips moved over hers, in a kiss as soft as a misty raindrop.

She thought about pulling away. Thought about it, but didn't. Couldn't. The fact was, she found it impossible to move. All she could do was sit, rigid with shock, while his mouth nuzzled hers.

He drew back a moment. With his big hands framing her face, he stared down into her eyes. His thumbs traced the outline of her lower lip. ''You taste sweeter than apple cobbler. I'm afraid I'm going to have to ask for seconds.''

She sighed as he lowered his head. This time, caught up in the intensity of the moment, she leaned into him, offering him what he sought.

His mouth covered hers in a hot, hungry kiss. Now there was no tenderness, no gentleness. His arms closed around her, pressing her so tightly to him, she could feel his heartbeat thundering in her own chest.

A little moan escaped her lips as she gave herself up to the pleasure. When his tongue slid between her parted lips, she was shocked at her reaction. Instead of backing away, she touched her tongue tentatively to his and felt a jolt clear to her toes.

And all the while he was kissing her, his hands were moving along her back, igniting little fires over her flesh. Awash in strange new feelings, her blood heated. Needs she'd never even known existed began pulsing and throbbing deep inside.

Cal knew he was treading on dangerous ground. He had no right to the things he was thinking. Or wanting. It was time to step back. But still he lingered over her lips, seeking one more taste. One more touch of her.

His rough hands moved up her sides until they encountered the swell of her breasts. For one brief moment, he allowed his thumbs to brush across the tips. At once they hardened, and he heard her quick intake of breath. He swallowed her protest with a hard, quick kiss before lifting his head.

Pearl dragged air into her lungs. Her fingers were curled into Cal's shirt, though she couldn't recall how they got there. And her body was pressed to his in a most provocative way.

As her head slowly cleared, she lowered her hands and moved away.

Without a word, Cal climbed down from the wagon, then lifted her in his arms. The flare of heat was instantaneous. He set her down, then lowered his hands and took a step back, afraid to touch her again.

She avoided meeting his eyes. "Good night, Cal."

He climbed into the wagon, grateful for the distance between them. "I hope your first day of teaching is all you dreamed of."

"Thank you."

As he flicked the reins, he was surprised to feel the tremors. By God, the very prim and proper Pearl Jewel had him shaking.

In the barn, he worked quickly, efficiently, grateful for something to do. As he forked hay into a stall, he muttered, "So, Miss Pearl Jewel, you decided to atone for the mistakes of your parents by becoming the most perfect person in the world. You thought that if you were spotless in dress, in manner, in behavior, the good people of Boston would believe that you had risen above your less-than-perfect beginnings and would judge you acceptable in their society.''

He closed the stall and walked outside, glancing up at the stars. A half smile touched his lips as he held a match to the tip of his cigar. She could protest all she wanted, but she couldn't hide one obvious fact. When he kissed her, she'd responded. And not at all like a girl who was repressed by memories of her parents' mistake. She'd kissed him back like a woman. A woman whose actions masked a deep, simmering sensuality.

Chapter Seven

Before dawn, Pearl lay awake, staring at the darkened ceiling. Her sleep had been troubled. Thoughts of Cal McCabe, holding her, kissing her, had intruded like shimmering ghosts, causing her to toss and turn. His kisses didn't disturb her nearly as much as her reaction to his kisses. What had happened to her when he wrapped her in his warm embrace? She seemed to lose herself when he touched her. Certainly last night she had behaved in a most unacceptable way. Like . . . like a wanton.

She struggled to put him out of her mind. But without Cal to fill her thoughts, there was but one thing left.

The day that lay before her.

The enormity of what she had done pressed like a boulder against her chest. She had defied Cal and the townspeople to open a school. Worse, she had rejected their legitimate concerns about timing and location. Her breathing became shallow. She sat up in the darkness. What if no one showed up? What if she had gone to all this time and trouble for nothing? She would be the object of scorn in town. Worse than that, she would be humiliated before Cal and her sisters. She could bear ridicule from the others. What she couldn't bear was the thought of facing Cal in defeat.

Cal. There it was again. That little jolt each time she thought of him.

What if his predictions of danger came true? He knew this land so much better than she.

Oh, sweet heaven, what had she done? She could hear her mother's voice, admonishing her young daughter. *In all things, you should strive for perfection, Pearl. If a thing is worth doing, it is worth doing well.*

Perfection.

With a sigh of disgust, Pearl tossed back the covers and crossed the room to the pitcher of water atop her dressing table. She washed and dressed quickly in the predawn chill, making certain that her hair and clothes were as nearly perfect as she could make them. The gown was simple, as befitted a teacher. Pale pink dimity, with a high neck and long sleeves, and a row of buttons from throat to waist. The hem of the soft flounced skirt brushed the tips of her calf boots. She swept her hair up into a knot at the back of her head and secured it with pins. Almost at once, little tendrils slipped loose to curl around her forehead and cheeks. But try as she might, they wouldn't be tamed. She picked up her shawl and parasol and made her way downstairs.

It was pleasant to have the kitchen to herself for a change. Though she enjoyed having sisters, something she'd never had before coming to Texas, she found their constant chatter unsettling. And when

Carmelita was here, the kitchen became her domain; everyone else was an intruder.

Pearl tossed a log in the fireplace, sending hot sparks flying. With the addition of some kindling, she soon had a cozy fire burning.

She added wood to the stove and placed a pot of coffee on it, then turned her attention to filling a basket with food for the long day ahead.

"You're up early."

At Cal's familiar deep voice, she turned. As always, she felt a quickening of her heartbeat at the sight of him, lounging carelessly in the doorway.

He was dressed all in black, with a gunbelt slung low on his hips. He was freshly shaved, and little droplets of water still clung to his dark hair.

Her gaze centered on his lips. Remembering the kiss they'd shared, she felt a rush of heat that left her dazed. She quickly looked away.

"I couldn't sleep," she confessed.

"Nerves?"

She nodded, refusing to look at him.

"Coffee smells good. Want some?"

"I guess I could try a cup."

He crossed the room and filled two cups, then handed one to her. As their fingers brushed, she absorbed the little tremors.

He continued to stand beside her as she wrapped cold chicken and biscuits in a linen towel and placed them in a basket.

Without warning, he leaned closer, until his lips were almost brushing her temple. "You smell good."

She went very still, fighting the temptation to pull away. Or to turn into his arms. This man was causing her any number of conflicts. "It's probably the lavender soap."

"Lavender? You didn't get that in Hanging Tree."

She laughed. "No. I brought it with me from . . ."

"I thought so. It smells like Boston. Like you."

Did he have any idea how uncomfortable he was making her? She thought about bolting. Instead, she busied herself covering the basket with a linen cloth. That done, she lifted the cup of coffee to her lips and drank deeply.

"Want some breakfast?" Cal asked.

"Who's going to make it?"

"Do you think Carmelita is the only one who knows how to cook?" He crossed the room and placed a blackened skillet on the stove. With the confidence of one who has always taken care of his own needs, he cracked eggs and sliced bread.

"Carmelita told me that cowboys will eat whatever is set in front of them."

Cal nodded. "Deer, steer, bear or rabbit. We don't care if it walks, flies, or crawls on its belly. We'll even eat rattler." He saw Pearl touch a hand to her queasy stomach, and his smile grew. "I'm not bothering you, am I?"

"No. Of course not." She stood in the middle of the kitchen, feeling completely useless around this man.

"I didn't think so. Anyway, I've eaten roots, berries, spices. I've drank water from a mudhole that even the animals wouldn't touch, coffee so strong you could stand on it, and whiskey that would curl your toes. So I guess I can take a chance at my own cooking.''

Soon the air was sweet with the fragrance of eggs and spices. As Pearl watched Cal neatly turn the egg mixture onto a platter, she realized that he'd been teasing her. He cooked the way he did everything—with quiet but complete competence.

Her own feelings of inadequacy grew.

''You might want to get two plates,'' he said as he refilled their cups.

''Oh. Yes. Of course.'' When that was done, she settled herself in the chair he held for her.

She took a small portion of eggs and handed him the platter. She wasn't surprised when he heaped his plate high, added a handful of chilis, then reached for the bread, which he liberally spread with wild-strawberry preserves.

While she picked at her breakfast, he devoured his. She found her gaze drawn to his big hand, curled around the cup. It was a hand more suited to holding a gun or wrestling a steer. Yet that same big hand had held her as tenderly as if she were a delicate flower.

''Carmelita told me that cowboys are a strange breed, always taking off for parts unknown, spending more time talking to their horses than to humans.'' Pearl's tone lowered, as she realized she was revealing far more than she'd intended. ''She said only a fool would ever consider marrying a cowboy.''

Cal chuckled. ''I guess she'd know. Her husband, Rosario, is one of the finest vaqueros in this territory. And those two old fools have been in love for as long as I've known them.''

Pearl laughed then, realizing that what he said was true. She had seen the way the housekeeper seemed to light up whenever her husband brought the carriage for her. Though few words were spoken between them, their love had a language all its own.

"I can see you're not very hungry," Cal remarked.

"I suppose it's because of the nerves that woke me too early this morning."

He surprised her by placing a hand over hers. "It's going to be fine," he said softly.

This time the rush of heat was much more intense.

She pushed back her chair and got to her feet, suddenly needing air. "I think I'll go now. There are a lot of last-minute details to see to."

He scraped back his own chair and stood, towering over her. "I'll bring your horse and rig around before I head out to the north range."

"There's no need, Cal. I can manage."

"I know you can." He stared down at her a moment, then ambled across the room and let himself out.

Minutes later, she heard the sound of his return and made her way to the porch. He helped her into the little rig, then handed up the basket she had prepared.

He studied the stiff way she held herself. "They'll come," he said simply.

"I wish I could be as certain as you are."

"Don't worry."

She swallowed. "Even if they do come, will they come out of a love for learning?" she asked. "Or merely out of curiosity about the Jewel ranch?"

His earlier comments had planted seeds of mistrust in her mind. Though he hadn't mentioned it again, she couldn't forget his disapproval.

"What do you care?" He regarded her carefully. "No matter what brings the children to your school, it's as you said—they'll go away with more knowledge than they brought."

"I suppose so." Pearl picked up the reins.

"I wish you'd reconsider my offer of a rifle, though. I'd feel better if I knew you had some protection out there."

"Protection?" She gave a shake of her head. "All it would do is enrage an attacker. I could never bring myself to fire a weapon. I think it's barbaric."

Something flashed in his eyes, but he said nothing as he stepped back.

She flicked the reins. The horse and rig moved slowly away.

The sky had still been in darkness when Pearl left the ranch house. By the time she stepped from the rig and opened the door to the schoolhouse, the sun was hovering on the horizon, casting the land in a golden glow.

She crossed the room and knelt at the fireplace. With trembling fingers, she held a match to the kindling, shivering until heat and light flared. Soon fire licked along the bark, chasing away the last of the gloom and chill in the room.

She hurried through her chores, eager to have everything in readiness for her pupils. Fetching a bucket of water from the creek, she set it in a corner of the room, along with a dipper. With neat, deliberate strokes, she printed her name on a slate and placed it on her desk. For good measure, she swept the floor and dusted the desks, though they were already spotless.

She walked to the doorway and peered out. There was no sign of a horse or wagon in any direction.

She sighed and struggled to clear her mind of all but good thoughts. It was one of those rare spring mornings, she reminded herself. Though the air hinted of rain and cold, the morning sun had wiped away the last of the shadows from the foothills below Widow's Peak.

Using a rock, she propped open the door to allow the fresh spring air to penetrate the musty cabin. Then she sat down on the step and lifted her face to the sun. She remained that way for several minutes before she gave in to the restlessness that drove her.

She walked through a nearby field and picked a bouquet of bluebonnets and Indian paintbrush. She marveled at the range of colors that swept across the meadow, turning entire hillsides into a rich artist's palette.

She made her way back inside and placed the flowers in a crock of water on her desk.

Desperate to fill the time, she climbed a rickety ladder that led to a small loft. The floor was spread with straw. In one corner was a dusty, faded buffalo robe. Kneeling, she lifted the robe, touching it lightly to her cheek.

Her father had slept here. The realization swept through her with such force that she was rocked back on her heels. As a young man, determined to make his way in the world, he had built a cabin in the middle of a wilderness. Armed with nothing more than his two hands, he had overcome obstacles that would have destroyed lesser men. And had succeeded beyond his wildest dreams.

Her fingers tightened on the robe. *And so will I, Daddy,* she thought fiercely, pressing her face to the faded robe. *So will I.*

She folded the robe carefully and replaced it in the straw, then made her way down the ladder.

Another check outdoors had her heart sinking. The sun was already high overhead. And still there was no sign of a horse or wagon. No children. No parents. No students for her school.

Though she had barely tasted her breakfast, she had no interest in lunch. Ignoring the cold chicken, she took several bites of a biscuit. It stuck in her throat like a hard, cold lump. Even a dipper of water couldn't dislodge it. With a sigh, she set the basket of food aside.

She prowled the room, touching a hand to the desks, running her finger along the spines of her meager supply of books. How vain she had been. She had imagined herself reading to the children, introducing them to fascinating characters and taking them to strange, new places. Places they would never see in their lifetimes, except in the pages of a book.

Oh, how could she have been so foolish? she asked herself. She had seen the reaction to her proposal. "Schoolin's for rich kids," Rollie Ingram had said. And heads had nodded in agreement.

A tear squeezed from the corner of her eye. She wiped it away. She wouldn't cry. Couldn't. For, if she dared to let a single tear flow, she might never stop.

She walked to the door again and stepped outside. The sun had begun its slow arc to the western horizon. And still there was no wagon in sight.

A feeling of melancholy stole over her. What had she expected? She didn't belong here. She would never fit in. This was her father's home. And being his daughter wasn't good enough. She wasn't good enough. She had let him down. Useless. That was what she was. Useless.

She sank down on the step and lowered her face to her hands. Why had she set herself up for such heartache? This wasn't Boston.

Precisely, said an inner voice. She had come all this way to escape the restrictions of her childhood home. To see what it was that had sent her father into raptures whenever he spoke of his home. She had come here to see for herself this raw, primitive land that offered freedom to anyone willing to work hard and pursue lofty goals.

She took a deep breath, fighting to calm the turmoil raging inside her, and lifted her head. She wouldn't let this land defeat her. Nor would she give up on its people.

That was when she saw the wagon rolling toward her. In the back sat half a dozen children. And on the hard wooden seat was Cal, guiding the reins. His horse trotted smartly behind.

They rolled to a stop. At once, the children began leaping down, the bigger ones lending a hand to the smaller ones. Everyone began shouting at once.

"The wagon lost a wheel," five-year-old April Potter called.

"And we started walking back to town," said May Potter.

"It looked like we were going to miss our first day at school," put in June Potter.

All three ducked behind the skirts of Birdie Bidwell, who was positively glowing.

"My folks said they could spare me once in a while, so's I can learn to read and write," she said proudly.

"Travis was in charge, and he said we all had to stay together," said a little boy, who stuck out his hand and added, "My name's Bartholomew Adams. But everybody calls me Bart."

Too overcome for words, Pearl silently accepted his handshake. She had to struggle for composure. She had an overpowering desire to weep—this time, happy tears. Instead, she merely nodded as each child added to the narrative. And all the while her gaze kept flitting up to the wagon seat, where Cal held the reins, silently watching her.

"My pa said I was old enough to be responsible for the others," said the bigger boy, who introduced himself as Travis Worthing. "Besides the townies," he said, indicating the Potter girls and Birdie, "we stopped at a couple of ranches, as well. But then our wheel broke. And I've never fixed a wheel by myself before, so I decided to leave the wagon and have everyone walk back home."

Very wise, Pearl thought, unable to form the words over the lump in her throat.

"But Mr. McCabe came along and said he'd fix the wheel and see that we got to school," added Bart Adams.

"And we all sat in the grass and ate our lunches while Mr. McCabe rode back to his ranch and returned with the tools he needed to fix our wagon wheel." Birdie Bidwell, her curtain of blond hair bobbing for emphasis, nearly ran out of breath as she concluded, "And here we all are, Miss Jewel."

"Here you all are. What an adventure your first day of school has turned out to be," Pearl said when she managed to find her voice. "It's lucky for all of us that Mr. McCabe happened by."

She indicated the door. "If you'd like to go inside, children, find a desk, and I'll be along in a minute."

Chattering happily, the children filed past her. Through the open door she could hear them exclaim at their first glimpse of a real schoolhouse.

Cal climbed down from the wagon to retrieve his horse.

"How did you happen to come upon the children?" She kept her voice low, so that she wouldn't be overheard in the classroom.

He shrugged. "Just crossed their path by accident."

"Accident?" She stepped closer. "You told me you were heading to the north ridge today."

He nodded.

"You're talking to a teacher, Cal. North is that way." She pointed. "There is no way you could have come upon the children. Unless you went out of your way to look for them."

When he said nothing in his own defense, she pressed him. "Were you looking for them?"

He pulled himself into the saddle, still trying to evade the question. "I ... noticed that your schoolhouse was empty."

"You've been watching me?"

"You're alone. Unarmed. And isolated. I see it as my duty to look out for you."

"But if no one had come, you would have been proven right." She stared up at him. "Isn't that what you wanted?"

He winked unexpectedly, and her heart did a series of somersaults. "I didn't want to see all that hard work go to waste. After all, I invested some time and effort, too."

He touched a hand to the brim of his hat. "Better get to work, teacher. Looks like you'll have your hands full with a roomful of students."

With a smile of pure joy touching her lips, she watched him ride off. Then she turned and made her way inside.

Chapter Eight

"Are we going to do sums?" Bartholomew Adams asked eagerly. He had chosen the first seat, closest to Pearl's desk. From his wide smile and pleasant manner, Pearl decided that this boy was happy to attend school. He might prove helpful in stimulating the minds of the other students.

"I don't think there will be time for that today," Pearl said gently. "Perhaps we should settle for getting acquainted, since the day is almost over." She studied the faces turned to her with a mixture of eagerness and curiosity.

"Let's begin with you, Bart. Tell me about yourself. How old are you?"

"I'm eight. But my pa says I'm big for my age. We own a spread over on the far side of Widow's Peak. And every winter, after the crops are harvested and the cattle driven to Abilene, my pa helps out by cutting timber up in the hills, and I stay home with my ma and two baby sisters and try to keep up with the chores."

"I'll bet your folks appreciate your help. Welcome, Bart."

Pearl turned to the bigger boy, who had taken a seat in the back of the row. "How about you, Travis?"

The boy got respectfully to his feet. "I'm Travis Worthing. I'll be thirteen soon, and my pa says I won't have much need for schooling, what with all the chores. I can't come to school every day, but I'll come whenever I can." His voice trailed off as he added, "I'm only here because my ma wants me to master reading and writing."

"That's a fine goal, Travis. You're welcome to come whenever you can manage."

He smiled weakly and took his seat. Pearl realized that he would rather be weeding a field or mending a fence than sitting here in school. She whispered a word of gratitude that his mother valued an education.

She directed her words to the young girl seated in front of Travis. "Tell me about yourself, Birdie."

The girl lumbered to her feet, standing as straight and tall as she could manage. "My real name's Bertha. Bertha Bidwell. But when I was little, I couldn't say Bertha. And the name Birdie stuck. Now I don't even think of myself as Bertha. Just Birdie. I'm almost twelve. My ma taught me how to write a few words, like my name, and my ma's name and such. I can read a few simple things, like Wanted posters. But I surely would like to read whole sentences, and maybe even books." She shrugged. "That's why I'm here. But, like Travis, I won't be coming every day. My folks need me at home to help with the chores. And I lend a hand at Mrs. Potter's place whenever she needs me."

She sat down, and Pearl glanced at the three little Potter girls. They kept their heads bowed, refusing to look her in the eye.

"Well, that leaves April, May and June," she said gently. "Which of you would like to go first?"

The three glanced at each other, then away. It was the youngest, June, who finally scrambled to her feet.

"My name is June Potter," she said in a tiny voice. "I'm five years old."

"Thank you, June. That was very brave," Pearl said.

She glanced at the other two. With reluctance, the middle girl stood. "My name is May Potter. I'm six years old. And my ma runs the boardinghouse in town."

"Welcome, May." Pearl turned to the last sister.

She got slowly to her feet. "My name is April Potter. I'm seven. I don't have a pa."

I don't have a pa.

Pearl realized that this little girl thought those words defined her. As the oldest, she would be able to remember a few things about her father. And feel the pain of loss more strongly than her younger sisters.

"I lost my father, too," Pearl found herself saying tenderly. "And I miss him very much."

The little girl looked at her in astonishment.

"Now," she went on, more briskly, "it's my turn. My name is Miss Pearl Jewel." She held up her slate, so that all could read it. "My home was in Boston, until recently. I'm new to Texas, and there is much I don't know about my new home. So you'll be able to teach me while I'm teaching you."

A current of excitement rippled through the children. It hadn't occurred to them that they might also be teachers.

"I'd like each of you to take up your slate and write as much of your name as you can manage. When you finish, bring it to my desk and I'll check it."

The room fell silent while the children did as they were told. The minutes drifted by as Pearl checked each slate and offered words of encouragement. Then she formed the letters she wanted them to work on before the next class.

The day was quickly coming to an end. Pearl was aware of the long trek these children still had to make, and the chores that would be awaiting them when they arrived at home. Still, she held off the moment when she would send them on their way. Instead, choosing a well-thumbed book from the shelf, she announced, "I'd like to introduce you to something. I thought I'd read from it before we end our first day of school."

In a clear voice she read, "In the beginning God created the heavens and the earth. Darkness covered the abyss, and the spirit of God was stirring above the waters. God said, 'Let there be light,' and there was light. God separated the light from the darkness, calling the light Day and the darkness Night. And there was evening and morning, the first day."

She looked up. The children were staring at her as if she'd spoken a foreign language.

"These are the first words in the Bible," she explained. "Taken from the Book of Genesis, describing the creation. It is my hope that, if you and I persevere together, you will one day read these words for yourself.''

"You mean—'' Birdie's voice was incredulous "—someday I'll be able to read the whole Bible to my ma and pa?''

"That's exactly what I mean.'' Pearl closed the book and set it on the shelf. Touching the books beside it she added, "And the sonnets of William Shakespeare. The words of the world's greatest poets. Once you know how to read words, you can read anything.''

As young as they were, the children seemed to understand the importance of what she had just said. There was an audible sigh from Birdie.

Pearl cast a glance out the window and said, "Now it's time you headed home.''

The children gathered up their slates and made their way to the wagon. Birdie and Bart helped the smaller girls up before climbing into the back of the wagon. Travis pulled himself onto the seat and took up the reins.

"Goodbye, children,'' Pearl called. "I hope I'll see some of you tomorrow.''

"Bye, Miss Jewel,'' came the chorus of voices as the horse and wagon jolted off at a slow, lumbering pace.

Pearl waved until the wagon crested a hill and disappeared from view. Hurrying inside, she looked around at the now empty room. It looked the same as it had yesterday, with the neat row of desks, the shelf of books. The scents of woodsmoke and beeswax and polish were the same, as well. And yet, in the space of a few hours, everything had changed. This wasn't just a deserted cabin now. It was a living, breathing place, filled with the presence of curious children, eager to learn.

She had changed, as well, she knew. She no longer felt useless. She had a reason, a purpose, for each day. She would feed hungry minds. And if she was very lucky, some of them would be forever changed because of what she would do here.

"Oh, Daddy," she breathed. "Can you feel it? Can you feel the new life here in your old cabin?"

Her heart felt filled to overflowing with emotions so powerful she couldn't contain them. All the tears that had been held back throughout the long day suddenly welled up, spilling down her cheeks.

Standing all alone in the middle of her schoolroom, she wept for sheer joy.

Cal peered through the window at the figure seated at her desk. A single lantern at her elbow illuminated the darkness. She flipped through the pages of a book before stopping to write something on her slate.

Cal had taken a detour past the school, expecting to find it in darkness. Instead, she was still here, all alone, miles from home. He felt a rush of emotion. Not protectiveness, he told himself. Anger. Anger at her carelessness. At her refusal to take the proper precautions for her own safety.

But as he studied her, his anger quickly evaporated. He lingered outside another moment, enjoying the sight of her in the lantern's glow. Soft little tendrils of hair had fallen from the neat knot at her nape to drift around her cheeks and forehead. She had rolled back the sleeves of her gown, to keep them from being soiled. Though she was still the model of perfection, she was slightly mussed. And thoroughly appealing.

He strode inside.

"You should have been home hours ago, enjoying Carmelita's special dinner."

Cal's deep voice startled Pearl out of her reverie. With a guilty look, she lifted her head from the book she'd been studying.

"I . . . didn't realize it was so late. Did you say special dinner?"

"That's right. Carmelita planned a celebration for your first day of school."

"Oh, dear. I didn't know. I suppose I've spoiled everything."

"By now, she and Rosario have probably returned to their own ranch. She'll have to hold off the celebration until tomorrow." Cal stepped closer. "I didn't think teachers were expected to sleep at their desks."

"I wasn't sleeping. I was looking for passages to read to my class tomorrow. Something that would stir their imaginations and lift their spirits."

He gave her a slow smile. "I take it you anticipate their return tomorrow."

"Oh, yes. At least some of them." She closed the book and got to her feet. "Oh, Cal. I wish you could have seen their faces when I read to them. It was as though I had held a candle up to their souls."

He studied the expression on her face. He'd never before seen her so animated.

"Suddenly they realized the power of being able to read." She clasped her hands together and, forgetting propriety, twirled around happily, sending her skirts swirling about her ankles.

"They're wonderful children. Bart Adams is a happy, joyful boy. He'll be a delight to teach. And Birdie. So determined to help her family. And eager to learn." Without thinking, she moved closer and dropped a hand on Cal's sleeve.

He felt the heat of her touch, but, except for a slight narrowing of his eyes, gave no indication of it.

"And Travis. Cal, he doesn't think school can help him. He's only here because his mother wants him to learn to read. But once he does, there'll be no stopping him."

She lifted her face to him, her smile warming him as nothing else ever had. "And the little Potter girls. So sweet. So shy. I can't wait to..."

They were mere inches apart, so close that he could feel the warmth of her breath on his cheek. Her hand rested on his arm, and his muscles suddenly tensed beneath her touch. It was all he could do to keep from dragging her against him and savaging her mouth.

Sensing his tension, she paused and ran her tongue over lips that had gone dry. He studied the movement, feeling a tightening deep inside. At once he became aware of the way she was watching him. His heartbeat, always so sure and steady, suddenly became erratic, skipping several beats before starting an unsteady rhythm.

"I suppose I must sound silly, prattling on about the children...."

"No. Not silly at all." God in heaven, he wanted her so desperately, the thought of taking her here, now, had him trembling.

"I never properly thanked you for what you did today, Cal." Feeling suddenly shy, she lifted her hand from his arm.

He could still feel the warmth of her touch through his sleeve. To keep from reaching out to her, he curled his hands into fists at his sides. "Thanks aren't necessary. I'm just glad I could help."

"You did more than just help. You saved me from wallowing in self-pity. I was just about to give in to feelings of despair. I thought there was no hope of seeing anyone come to school." She shot him a dazzling smile and offered a handshake. "Thank you, Cal. I hope someday I can repay the favor."

He glanced at her hand and thought about refusing to touch her. But she'd never understand. She would think he was refusing her offer of friendship, as well.

His big hand engulfed her small palm. He stared down into those smiling blue eyes. And he was lost.

Without a thought to the consequences, he dragged her into his arms and covered her mouth with his.

She gave a little gasp of surprise, but he swallowed the sound as he took the kiss deeper.

There was nothing easy or gentle about the kiss. His mouth moved over hers with a savageness that left her dazed and breathless. His hands moved up her spine, igniting little fires as they pressed and kneaded her flesh through the thin fabric of her gown.

Her breasts were flattened to his chest. He drew her hips to his, alerting her to his full arousal. And all the while his mouth worked its magic, drawing out the kiss until she moaned and moved against him, inflaming him even more.

"Cal, you mustn't...."

"I know." He caught her roughly by the shoulders. "At least my head knows." His touch gentled, his hands making slow, lazy circles around her upper arms and shoulders. "But the rest of me isn't listening."

She thought she could go on like this forever, having him holding her, caressing her. Arousing her. With each touch of his hands, she felt the heat increase, until her flesh was on fire.

"We should go now," she whispered.

"Yes." His gaze trailed the ladder leading to a loft. He thought of lying with her in the straw, listening to the sounds of the night while he made slow, delicious love to her. The thought tormented him, and he lowered his mouth for one more drugging kiss.

She didn't have the power to stop him. Couldn't. The lure of his lips overruled any fear she might harbor.

As his mouth moved over hers, she sighed and gave herself up to the pleasure. This was what she wanted. This mindless passion. This slow, sensual mating of mouth to mouth, tongue to tongue.

As the pressure of the kiss increased, she felt her blood begin to heat, her heartbeat begin to pulse. His arms tightened around her, drawing her so close against him that she could feel the press of his body with every part of hers. His wildly beating heart kept time with hers. The hard, muscled wall of his chest pressed against her breasts. The thrust of his arousal caused a sweet, liquid warmth that reached to her very core.

He lifted his head to press soft butterfly kisses to her temple, her cheek, the tip of her nose.

She sighed, moved by his tenderness.

"We don't have to go," he murmured against her ear.

She froze. Pushing slightly away, she stared up into his dark eyes. "What are you saying?"

"We could stay. Here." He motioned with his head toward the loft.

Pearl shivered at the invitation in his eyes. At the moment, with her defenses weakened, it was too tempting.

"We have to go." She took a halting step backward, and then another. With each step away from him, her common sense flowed back, filling her mind.

She walked toward her desk, praying her legs wouldn't fail her. She scooped up the lantern and led the way to the door, trusting him to follow.

Outside, she breathed in the cool night air and prayed for a return to sanity.

Beside her, Cal McCabe did the same.

Chapter Nine

"We'll do sums this morning," Pearl announced. "I'll give you older children some numbers to work on silently while I help the younger ones with theirs."

School had been in session for a week, and six more children had arrived at various times. But, since none of them could attend daily, the number in the classroom could be as low as three or as high as a dozen.

Pearl was learning to expect the unexpected. Rufus Durfee's two sons, nine-year-old Damon and eleven-year-old Amos, arrived one day in a wagon loaded with goods to be delivered. The boys remained in class until noon, then left to deliver their father's merchandise to neighboring ranchers before returning to school to pick up the other children and return them to their homes.

Millie Potter's three daughters could attend school only when someone from town was willing to bring them. So far, between Travis Worthing, who could manage only a day or two each week, and the Durfee boys, the three Potter sisters hadn't missed a day. Nor had Birdie Bidwell, who counted herself lucky each day she was allowed to return.

The children were thriving. Even those who could manage only an occasional day in the classroom were learning. And so was Pearl. Each day she reminded herself to be content with the little successes.

To teach the concept of addition to the Potter girls, Pearl invited them to sit on the floor in a circle. Then she removed the pretty bouquet from her desk and spread the wildflowers in the center of the circle.

"I'm going to give each of you one flower," she said as she chose three bluebells. "Now, I'm going to add some Indian paintbrush." She plucked two fiery blossoms and added them to the five-year-old girl's bluebell. "Now, June, how many flowers do you have?"

The little girl counted out and replied, "Three."

"That's correct. Because two added to one will make three."

She handed three flowers to May and said, "How many do you have?"

"Four," the little girl said happily. "Three plus one makes four."

"Now, April," Pearl said, "yours is going to be a little more complicated." She gave the girl four flowers.

"That's not hard," April said with a shy smile. "Four and one make five."

"That's correct. But when I take back two, how many are left?"

The little girl counted, while her younger sisters watched with interest.

"Three," April said.

"Do you know why?"

Pearl was pleased when the little girl nodded. "Two from five leaves three."

"That's very good. Now," she said as she stood, "I'm going to give you some simple addition and subtraction to do. And I'll leave the flowers with you, in case you need to work out the sums."

She moved to the far side of the room, where the older children were working with columns of figures.

Seeing the frustration they were experiencing, Pearl turned the project into a game, offering one of Carmelita's cookies as the prize. In no time, the children had their heads bent over their slates, lost in the wonder of numbers. And much to everyone's surprise, Travis, who had shown no interest in doing sums, but an abiding interest in anything sweet, was the first to complete the assignment with no errors.

At lunchtime, the children and their teacher carried baskets outdoors and sat in the shade of an ancient oak.

"Will you look at that!" Bart Adams shouted.

Everyone turned to see Cal McCabe, astride his big black stallion, riding toward the schoolhouse. It was obvious that the children were in awe of this man who ran the legendary Jewel ranch.

"My pa says Cal McCabe can outdraw anyone in Texas." Bart's voice was hushed with admiration.

"My pa said there's no one who'd dare cross him," Travis said in a whisper. "He killed his first man when he was no bigger 'n me."

"Hush, children," Pearl said in her most commanding tone. "I won't permit such talk in my classroom."

Their words had shocked her more than she cared to admit. Cal, a killer? Though her heart denied it, her mind reeled with the knowledge. And a tiny voice inside taunted her with the thought that all along she'd sensed something dark and dangerous about Cal McCabe.

Her heart skipped a beat, and she blamed her heated cheeks on the warm springtime sun. Cal had managed to avoid her since the night they'd shared a kiss. A kiss. Could it be that she had permitted such intimacies with a—a gunman?

At least now, she thought with a feeling of relief, they were surrounded by children. There would be no chance to be alone.

She wondered if Cal had thought the same thing. Was that why he'd chosen such a time to pay a call?

He rode into their midst and slid from the saddle.

"Children, do you know Mr. McCabe?" Pearl asked.

"Yes, ma'am," the children responded in unison.

"I didn't realize this was your lunch hour," Cal said. "I just wondered if you needed anything, since I was in the area."

"Nothing, thanks." She felt a ripple of alarm. He seemed to be making himself at home among the children, with no intention of leaving.

"I...brought enough lunch to share." Pearl opened the basket, revealing several pieces of cold chicken and a little bundle of biscuits. "I always bring more than I can eat, in case any of the children forgot theirs. Would you care to join us?" As she spoke, she spread a cloth in the grass and began enptying the basket.

That was all Cal needed to convince him to stay. He sat in the shade of the tree, with his back against the rough bark, and accepted her offering.

The children sat in a circle around him. Aware that they were watching him warily, he put them at ease by asking them questions about their new school.

"Has Miss Jewel rapped any knuckles yet? Or ordered anyone into the corner as punishment for misbehavior?"

"Miss Jewel wouldn't do that," Birdie Bidwell said, jumping to her beloved teacher's defense.

"How can you be so sure?" Cal bit into a biscuit and winked at the Potter sisters over Birdie's head.

The three little girls blushed and giggled and hid their faces in their hands. It was clear that, despite their almost painful shyness, they found him irresistible.

"'Cause she's the nicest lady I've ever met," Birdie insisted. "Miss Jewel said she doesn't believe in fizz... fizz..."

"Physical punishment," Pearl finished for her.

"That's right. She said she'll never rap our knuckles, or spank us with a tree branch."

"Or beat us with a stick," Bart added.

"No wonder you came back a second day," Cal drawled. "Maybe she's not a teacher at all. Maybe she's a—a fairy godmother."

That sent the children into spasms of laughter. Soon they were laughing and talking, and even volunteering stories about their first days in Miss Jewel's classroom.

"I didn't want to come," Travis admitted to Cal, though Pearl was quite certain he never would have spoken so boldly to her. "My ma made me."

"Are you sorry?" Cal asked.

He shrugged and ducked his head. "No, sir. I like coming here. Sometimes."

"How about you, Bart?" Cal asked.

"I want to learn to read and write. My pa says his grandma was an educated woman. But somehow she got too bogged down in work and babies, and the learning was lost. And now, no one in our family can read. I'll be the first."

There was a note of pride in his voice that had Cal studying the boy with new interest. Then his gaze moved to Pearl, whose cheeks reddened under his scrutiny.

When they had finished eating, shy little April Potter opened a large basket to reveal an entire cake that her mother had sent as a treat.

"Oh, my!" Pearl said, with a trace of wonder. "Will you look at what Mrs. Potter has sent us. Is this a special occasion, April?"

The girl's red curls bobbed up and down as she replied, "Today is Birdie's birthday. And Mama said, since Birdie has been coming over every evening to lend a hand with the cooking, she deserved a nice surprise."

The birthday girl seemed stunned by the gesture. "Now how'd your ma learn that today was my birthday?" she demanded.

April shrugged. "I don't know. Maybe she talked to your ma."

"Well, however she learned," Pearl said with a delighted smile, "I think you should do the honors of cutting the cake and serving it to the others."

"Yes'm." Birdie needed no coaxing, and soon everyone was busy devouring their special treat.

"You can give Mr. McCabe a second helping," Pearl said. "I've learned that he has quite a sweet tooth."

Cal grinned and gave her a mocking bow as he accepted another slice.

For the next half hour, the children were allowed to work off their meal, climbing the tree and hanging upside down from its branches, or chasing each other in a game of tag.

While the children played around them, Cal lounged beside the tree.

"I haven't seen much of you this week," Pearl said softly.

"I had a lot of chores to see to," he muttered.

"Yes..." She looked away, aware of the flush that started up her throat and cheeks whenever he stared at her in the familiar, watchful manner of a hunter. "It's just as well. I...had a lot of work to do here, too. And I work better without interruptions."

He gave her a lazy, knowing grin that told her she hadn't fooled him a bit. "So do I, teacher." He got to his feet, towering over her. As he started to make his way to his horse, he paused and returned to touch a fingertip to her cheek. "But what kind of life would it be without some...interruptions?"

She backed away from his touch as though burned. "Cal, the children..."

"Are busy playing. Besides, there's no rule against touching the teacher, is there?"

She hung her head, wishing he could touch her again, and afraid he might read the invitation in her eyes.

He pulled himself into the saddle. "Thanks for lunch, teacher."

The children shouted and waved as he rode away, and he lifted his hat in a salute before disappearing below a ridge.

Pearl stood watching for several moments, then clapped her hands and summoned her pupils indoors. After a few minutes, they settled down at their desks, ready for another lesson.

"We'll begin our reading," Pearl announced. "Travis, I think you can read first."

She handed him her precious copy of *McGuffey's Eclectic Reader* and walked to the back of the room, where she could listen and observe. Travis stood facing the others. Whenever he stumbled over a word, Pearl would ask him to spell it, and the rest of the class was invited to help him sound it out.

While he read, the others sat with folded hands, enraptured by the story, which, as always, carried a high moral principle relating to God, country or mankind.

Pearl prowled to the window, her thoughts on Cal McCabe. His very presence had a way of making her palms sweat, her heartbeat falter. She seemed to forget everything when he was near. The man was definitely detrimental to her powers of concentration.

But, from what the children had said, the neighboring ranchers had a much different view of Cal from hers. A killer? A gunman?

Her musings were interrupted when a rickety wagon came into view. She recognized it as the one belonging to Rollie Ingram. On the seat beside him was his older son, Gilbert. In the back, wedged between a sow and her piglets, sat Daniel.

Both boys stared hard at the school as their wagon passed. She lifted a hand and waved. Gilbert glanced at his father. Seeing him watching, the boy looked away. In the back, little Daniel began to wave. At that moment, his brother shot him a look. The boy lowered his hand. But he continued watching until they were out of sight.

Pearl felt a pang of loss. She had tried so hard not to think about Gilbert and Daniel. Rollie Ingram had made it plain that his sons would not be attending school. Still, she'd hoped....

"B-E-G-I-N-N-I-N-G," Travis was spelling.

Pearl's head came up sharply. She returned her attention to her class.

"Can anyone help Travis?" she asked.

"Be-gin-ning," Birdie said, pausing for each syllable, as her teacher had taught her.

"That's very good, Birdie. You may finish the story Travis started."

The girl walked to the front of the room and faced the class, reading until the story was ended.

"Birdie, in honor of your birthday," Pearl said, "and because you have made such progress this first week of school, I'm going to permit you to take the

Bible home for the weekend. You may read it aloud to your family, to show them how much you've learned."

The girl's jaw dropped. Her eyes rounded in surprise. When she had finally found her voice, she managed to say, "Oh, thank you, Miss Jewel. I promise I'll take good care of your Bible."

Pearl gave the girl a gentle smile. She had no doubt the precious book would be handled more carefully than a sack of gold.

Pearl dressed carefully for Sunday services, all the while thinking about Cal. Since the lunch he'd shared with her and the children, she hadn't seen him. According to Cookie, Cal had spent the past two nights with their herd on the west ridge. She wondered if his decision to stay away had had anything to do with her, and the kiss they'd shared. At once she dismissed such thoughts as foolish vanity. Cal McCabe had probably kissed hundreds of women in his lifetime. One more wouldn't make any difference to a man like him. After all, she thought as she picked up her shawl and bonnet, he had a ranch to run. He was entitled to stay away as many nights as were necessary. And she had students to see to. They should be her main concern now.

Still, she couldn't dismiss the thought of that kiss. In a way, she actually hoped that was why he was avoiding her. It would be nice to know that it affected him as deeply as it affected her. Though she couldn't imagine a man like Cal McCabe losing sleep over her, or staring into space at the thought of one more kiss.

What utter nonsense, she told herself. If anything, she should be making plans to distance herself from him. She had a reputation to maintain. And the temptation when they were alone would create all kinds of difficulties.

She made her way downstairs and found Jade and Ruby waiting for her in the kitchen. A plate of biscuits lay between them on the table, along with a dish of blueberry preserves.

"Hurry and eat something, *cherie*," Ruby said. "Cal has already gone to fetch the carriage."

So, he was back home, and going with them. Pearl's stomach gave a little hitch, but she blamed it on the blueberries. "I'm not hungry. Maybe by the time services are over I'll find my appetite."

"Come, then." Jade beckoned. "I hear the carriage now."

The three young women walked out onto the back porch. When Cal stepped down to assist them, Pearl couldn't help admiring the way he looked in his black jacket and wide-brimmed hat.

"Good morning," he murmured as he reached for her hand.

The instant they touched, they both felt the jolt. And they both did their best to ignore it.

Avoiding his eyes, Pearl allowed him to help her into the carriage. As she took her seat and drew her shawl around her shoulders, she shivered, despite the warmth of the spring sunshine. On the ride to town, she was subdued, allowing Jade and Ruby to carry the conversation while she pretended to study the passing landscape. But each time she looked up, she found her gaze drawn to Cal's broad shoulders, and the strong hands that held the reins.

In town, Cal hitched the team outside Durfee's Mercantile, then helped the three young women from the carriage. As Pearl brushed past him, he inhaled the fragrance of lavender and felt an involuntary thrill race along his spine.

Lord, but the days were long, he thought. Whether he was alone on the trail, or working alongside dozens of wranglers, his mind constantly conjured up images of Pearl, looking cool and lovely. And the nights were becoming intolerable. Thoughts of her intruded, crowding all other images from his mind. Even in dreams, he had no relief. She was there, brushing her lips over his, while those long, tapered fingers moved over his body, driving him half-mad with desire.

He trailed the three Jewel sisters into the back of Durfee's, and took a seat beside Pearl. And wondered how in the hell he'd be able to pray, when the devil's own temptation was right here at his side.

Chapter Ten

"That was a fine sermon, Reverend Weston." Pearl offered her hand, and was rewarded with a warm smile and a firm handshake.

"Why, thank you, Miss Pearl. I've been hearing fine things about your school, too. Not only from the parents, but from your students, as well."

Pearl walked out of the back room of Durfee's Mercantile wearing a smile of satisfaction.

"You're looking mighty pleased with yourself," Cal remarked. He'd barely heard a word of the sermon. He'd been too aware of the woman seated beside him. Even now, she was too close for comfort.

"It's my first compliment. I hope you don't mind if I savor it awhile."

He grinned. "Not at all. You've earned it. Enjoy it all you like." He paused in the doorway. "Jade and Ruby said they're going to browse in the mercantile for a few minutes. I'll bring the rig around to the front."

When he walked away, Pearl blinked in the warm sunshine. As usual, the little town of Hanging Tree was teeming with life on this late Sunday morning.

Parents and children began hauling baskets of food from carts and wagons to shady spots where they would refresh themselves before the return trip to their ranches. While the women spread quilts in the grass and set out the food, children ran between wagons, playing tag, and the men loaded supplies from the mercantile into their rigs.

Pearl felt a tug on her skirt and looked down to see Daniel Ingram smiling shyly up at her.

"Morning, Miss Jewel," he chirped. "You look pretty."

She knelt until her face was level with his. Despite his shabby clothes and the dirt etched deeply into his skin, his smile was as radiant as a cherub's.

"Good morning, Daniel. Thank you. I was hoping I would see you and your brother in school this past week."

His smile faltered. "So was I. But Pa said school's for spoiled rich kids. He said Gilbert and I are too stupid to go to school anyway. He said we're nothing but useless . . ."

His older brother happened to step out of the mercantile at that moment. Seeing his little brother talking to Pearl, he stumbled forward, balancing a heavy sack of grain on his shoulder. Keeping one hand on the sack, he grabbed Daniel with the other hand and yanked him away.

"Damn it, Daniel, you don't want to rile Pa. Now get away from her."

"Gilbert." Pearl was shocked at his rough language. "A boy your age shouldn't talk that way. Especially in front of your little brother. You should be setting a better example for him.''

"Example?" With a look of disdain, the boy dragged his brother toward their wagon. Just then, the sack of grain slipped from his grasp and fell to the ground. The seams split, spilling grain all over the ground.

From the doorway came the sound of a voice cursing loudly, causing heads to turn.

"Damned lazy, good-for-nothing..." Rollie Ingram bore down on his sons, but not before the two boys dropped to their knees and began hastily scooping up the fallen kernels as though they were precious gold.

While Gilbert and Daniel struggled to retrieve their burden, their father continued raining curses on them. "Damned fools! Can't even watch where you're goin'. You'd best clean it up. Every single grain. I'm not wastin' good money to have you throw it away in the dirt."

Though no one seemed willing to get too close to them, all the adults in town were aware of what was going on. A hushed silence had fallen over the townspeople. Several of the younger children, to relieve the sudden tension, began pointing and laughing at the two Ingram boys groveling in the dirt.

Rollie gave his older boy a vicious kick, then, for good measure, kicked the back of the wagon before tossing down a sack of flour and stomping back into the mercantile for more supplies.

When he disappeared inside, Pearl hurried over and knelt, determined to help the two boys.

Gilbert turned on her with a blaze of anger to match his father's. "Haven't you got it through your head yet? My pa doesn't want you hanging around us. And we don't want you here, either."

Pearl couldn't hide her shock at his unexpected attack.

"Gilbert." She laid a hand on his sleeve. "I know how terrible you feel about spilling—"

He shook off her hand. "You don't know anything. Just go on back over there with the nice respectable folks and leave us be."

She glanced from Gilbert to Daniel. The little boy met her eyes for a moment. Then, hearing a murmur of disapproval from the crowd, he lowered his head and continued scooping up the grain.

As Pearl got reluctantly to her feet, she found herself face-to-face with Rollie Ingram. His mouth was twisted into a leering imitation of a smile. Though it wasn't yet noon, the stench of liquor was strong on his breath.

"You heard my boy, Miss High-and-Mighty Jewel. You got no business botherin' us." He caught her by the shoulder, intending to give her a shove. "Now git."

A big hand clamped over his, squeezing his fingers until he thought they'd break.

Cal's voice was a low rasp of fury. "Don't you ever lay a hand on this lady. Don't even think about it, or you'll answer to me, Ingram."

Rollie's eyes narrowed to little slits. He lowered his hand, and, flexing his injured fingers, took a step backward.

"Didn't know ya'd put yer brand on her, McCabe." He raised his voice, enjoying the fact that he was putting on a show for the whole town. "Should've expected it, though. You and them wranglers must be having one hell of a good time out there at the ranch, now that ya got yerself three new fillies to break in."

Town gossips Lavinia Thurlong and Gladys Witherspoon, as well as several other women, lifted their hands to their mouths to stifle their shocked gasps. The men glanced around nervously.

Out of the corner of her eye, Pearl saw Travis Worthing and Bart Adams shoving their way to the front of the crowd, plainly hoping to witness a juicy fight.

She was aware of the fact that she was completely out of her element. She knew that she was inviting ridicule, standing in the dust of Hanging Tree for the whole town to see, holding tightly to her parasol as though it were a lifeline. But she felt she had no choice. She simply couldn't walk away.

Seeing Cal's stance, feet apart, hands clenching into fists, she acted quickly, stepping between the two men. Facing Cal's wrath was much more difficult than facing Ingram's insults. But she would not permit herself to be the reason for violence.

"No, Cal," she said. "You mustn't do this."

"Step aside, Pearl." His voice was dangerously soft. His eyes were as hard as granite.

"I will not. Let him go."

A low, simmering fury pulsed through Cal. He wanted, needed, a release for it. And he couldn't think of a better one than a good fight. Especially with scum like Rollie Ingram. The man sickened him.

"He insulted your good name."

"It's my name. And my choice not to seek satisfaction. Please, Cal. For the sake of the children, let him go."

Cal's fingers continued curling and uncurling, as he struggled to control his temper. While the crowd watched and waited, he glanced from Ingram to his sons, before finally nodding his head. Pearl was right. Those two boys had been humiliated enough. They didn't need to see their father beaten in front of the whole town.

"If you know what's good for you, Ingram, you'll get out of here as fast as that nag will take you. And stay out."

Rollie Ingram, thanks to the liquor, had an inflated sense of his own power. Instead of being grateful for having been spared a beating, he couldn't resist the chance to gloat. He glanced from Cal to Pearl, then back again, before throwing back his head and giving a roar of laughter.

"Never thought I'd see the day some woman would turn Cal McCabe into a piss-ant."

Then, as the townspeople gasped and began to murmur among themselves, he spat a wad of tobacco, barely missing the hem of Pearl's skirt.

With a muttered oath, Cal started forward, but Pearl placed her hands on his chest, entreating him to hold back.

Gilbert and Daniel, who had been watching the entire scene on their knees, suddenly lifted the gaping sack of grain into the back of the wagon.

Rollie pulled himself up to the seat and snarled, "Git in or git left behind."

The two boys scrambled to climb aboard as their father cracked a whip and the horse and wagon lurched forward.

The crowd of townspeople fell silent, sickened by what they had witnessed. Some felt cheated because there had been no fight, no sense of satisfaction. Others were simply saddened by what they'd seen. One by one, they began to drift away.

Without a word, Cal helped Pearl into the waiting carriage.

As she settled herself, she said, "I'm sorry, Cal. I know I overstepped my bounds. But I thought, as a teacher, I had to set an example of forgiveness for my students."

"Forgiveness?" He bit off the word with a tone of contempt. "A bully like Rollie Ingram doesn't understand anything except strength. What you see as a virtue, he sees as a weakness. Remember that, and be warned, Pearl. There will be nothing but grief for anyone Ingram suspects of being weaker than himself."

The ride home was the longest of Pearl's life. Though Jade and Ruby attempted to engage them in conversation, she and Cal exchanged not a word. And from the way he gripped the reins, Pearl knew that his anger had not abated.

When the carriage rolled to a stop at the front door of the ranch house, Cal climbed down and offered a hand to the women.

Ruby and Jade hurried inside, to escape the sun's heat.

Pearl placed her hand in Cal's and wished there was something she could say to make amends.

"My heart goes out to the Ingram boys," she began. "Their father's behavior is despicable. And he has forbidden them . . ."

Cal ignored the heat of her touch and concentrated on cooling his temper. It would take a heap of chores to erase the fire that still burned in his gut. Maybe he'd ride to one of the line camps, and spend a few days working from dawn to dark. Hard, demanding work might do it. Then again . . .

His head jerked up. "What did you just say?"

"I said," she repeated patiently, "that little Daniel, and even Gilbert, as hardened as he may pretend to be, couldn't take their eyes off the schoolhouse when they passed by the other day."

"Passed by?"

"With their father." She lowered her parasol, intending to climb the front steps. "In his wagon."

Cal's hand clamped around her arm, stopping her in midstride.

"What day was that?" he demanded.

She was surprised by the strength in his grasp. "Cal, you're hurting me."

Instead of loosening his grip, he caught her by the other arm and nearly shook her in frustration. "What day did you see them?"

"Friday, I think." She paused a moment, then nodded. "Yes. Friday afternoon."

His tone hardened. "And you never thought to mention it?"

"No, I..." She lowered her gaze, uncomfortable beneath his burning look. "I simply forgot."

"You forgot? You forgot to mention that Ingram was trespassing on Jewel property?"

"I'm sorry. I had other things on my mind." She pushed free of his grasp and rubbed idly at the crushed fabric of her sleeve. "But I don't think it's the trespassing that has you upset. It's the fact that it was Rollie Ingram."

"You bet it is." His eyes narrowed in thought. "There have been some thefts lately."

She stiffened. Her head came up. "Thefts?"

He nodded. "Farm implements. Brood cows. And now a sow and her litter."

"A...sow?" Pearl's heart fell. "Oh, Cal. Where?"

"The west line camp. Lester Miller sent a message with one of the wranglers yesterday." Seeing the look of dismay on her face, he said, "Now what?"

"There...was a sow and piglets in the back of Rollie Ingram's wagon."

Though his expression never altered, there was a subtle change in his tone. "You're sure?"

She nodded.

He gave a sound of disgust. "If you had told me sooner, I could have confronted Ingram with it."

"But what's to prevent you from going to him with what you know now?"

"He'll just deny it. And call you a liar. By now, the piglets are probably gone, sold for whatever they could fetch, so that he could buy whiskey and supplies in town."

Pearl felt her heart sink lower with each revelation. Rollie Ingram had been very drunk. And loading his wagon with expensive supplies. It would seem that he hadn't been able to wait to spend his newfound wealth.

"And the sow?" she asked.

"Most probably butchered."

"Oh, Cal. I'm so sorry."

But Cal wasn't listening. He was unaware of Pearl's distress. Unaware of the guilt that hung like a boulder around her heart.

He turned away from her and climbed to the seat of the carriage. In the barn, he unhitched the horses. And all the while he brooded about Rollie Ingram's bold intrusion on their land.

He had to put a stop to this immediately. Unless he made an example of Rollie Ingram, this would merely be the first of many such invasions of the Jewel ranch by outsiders.

He checked his guns, then saddled his horse. As he rode away, he was forced to admit the truth to himself. He was looking forward to the coming confrontation.

The Ingram ranch was little more than a shack surrounded by scrub and tumbleweed. The herd, a few dozen head of scrawny cattle, ranged across dry gulches and the foothills of Widow's Peak foraging for food.

The first thing Cal noticed when he rode up was the wagon parked behind the shack. Two horses lolled in the afternoon sun, pulling on tufts of grass. A sure sign that Rollie was home. And probably drinking, or he'd be out in the fields, tending to chores.

Cal rode around to the back and slid from the saddle. Dried blood in the grass caught his eye. There'd been an animal butchered. He touched a hand to the blood, rubbing it between his fingers. No more than a day or two, he calculated. Rollie had been in a hurry.

The door to the shack was thrown open. Little Daniel Ingram stood in the doorway.

"My pa wants to know what you're doing here."

"Does he?" Cal took a step closer. "Why doesn't he do the asking?"

The boy shrugged. "He sent me."

"I can see that." Cal's eyes narrowed. "Is he too drunk to stand up?"

Daniel flinched, then stepped aside as Cal pushed past him, muttering, "Guess I'll just see for myself."

What he saw, as his eyes adjusted to the dim light of the cabin, sickened him.

Rollie Ingram lounged in the only chair in the room. A room cluttered with filth. Animal hides. Saddles. Farm implements. Tools. Even chickens. All probably stolen, and littering every inch of the dirt floor. The air was fetid with the stench of waste, both animal and human.

Gilbert crouched over a small fire, cooking something in a blackened skillet. When he turned, he bore testimony to a savage beating. One eye was swollen shut. His nose and mouth were bloody, and his cheek was a raw open wound.

Cal felt something begin to stir deep within him. Something so dark, so dangerous, he had struggled to keep it locked away, buried beneath layers of pain, for years. For he knew that if it was ever to surface, it would take over his senses and destroy all that he'd worked so hard to build. Calling on all his willpower, he tamped it down and struggled to bank the fire that simmered in his soul.

"So, Ingram. I see you found a way to work off your anger."

Rollie slid a glance over his older son. "Made sure the damned fool wouldn't waste any more grain." He tipped the jug in his hand and drank deeply, allowing a river of whiskey to run down his chin and the front of his shirt.

"Why didn't you just kill him?" Cal's voice dropped to a soft, dangerous level. "Then you'd be sure he'd never make another mistake." He paused for just a fraction, then added, "Or are you afraid you'd have no one left to do your dirty work?"

"There'd still be one left." Rollie pointed the jug at his younger son. "So Gilbert will take his beatings like a man, if he knows what's good for him. Or I'll run him off and let Daniel take his place."

So that was what kept the older boy imprisoned in this hellhole. The knowledge that, without him, his younger brother would suffer his fate. Cal's hatred of Rollie Ingram threatened to choke him.

The object of his fury lifted the jug and drained it, then sat back, studying Cal through narrowed eyes.

"State your business and get off my property, Mc-Cabe."

"I came about a sow and her litter." Out of the corner of his eye, Cal saw Daniel's mouth open. A quick shake of Gilbert's head had the little boy looking away.

"A sow and her litter?" Rollie stroked his chin, as if in thought, then said, "Naw. I ain't in the market for one."

"That's good. Because I'm not selling. I've come here for satisfaction for the one you stole."

"Stole? You think I stole your pig? You got witnesses, McCabe?"

"You were seen driving your wagon across Jewel land. With a sow and piglets in the back of the wagon."

"You want to search my land, you go right ahead. But you won't find a sow or her litter."

"I'm well aware of that. But if I have to, I'll send my wranglers to every ranch in the territory. How hard do you think I'll have to look before I find ranchers who'll swear you sold them some fine piglets? As for the sow, unless I miss my guess, that pork Gilbert is cooking came from the Jewel ranch."

"You're guessing, McCabe. But you got no proof. So git. And don't come back without the marshal."

Cal took a step closer. In the gloom he saw Rollie's hand tighten on the handle of the jug. With one hand, he unbuckled his gunbelt and let it fall to the floor. "I don't need the marshal. This is between you and me, Ingram."

Despite the liquor he'd consumed, Rollie moved with amazing agility. He rolled to one side and smashed the jug against the edge of a small table. The jagged shards of glass he held in his hand glinted in the firelight.

"Oh, I've been itchin' for a chance like this, Mc-Cabe." He circled, slashing out with the broken jug, laughing each time Cal danced back. "You think you're so much better'n me. Wormin' your way into Onyx Jewel's good graces. Protected by his army of wranglers. And now livin' high on the hog in that fancy house."

"There are no wranglers now, Ingram." Cal waited, biding his time, giving Rollie a chance to throw the first punch. He could feel the blood pumping. Could taste the adrenaline flowing. And still he waited, knowing that if he baited Ingram enough, he would strike like the snake he was.

"It's just you and me, Rollie. If you're man enough to fight fair."

"Fair?" Rollie laughed and slashed out with the broken jug.

Cal darted back, but Rollie managed to rake the razor-sharp edges along Cal's arm, drawing thin streaks of blood that quickly soaked his sleeve.

"Funny," Rollie muttered. "Your blood doesn't look any different than Gilbert's. All you little pissants bleed the same way."

Emboldened by his initial success, he moved in closer and slashed out again. This time Cal was ready for him. He caught Ingram by the wrist and twisted until he cried out in pain. The shards of glass fell to the dirt floor of the shack.

"You broke it!" Rollie shrieked. "Broke my damned wrist!"

"I hope so."

Enraged, Rollie landed a fist in his opponent's face. Blood spurted from Cal's nose, drenching the front of his shirt.

"I've been praying you'd do that," Cal muttered as he tasted blood.

His first blow to Ingram's chest sent the burly man staggering backward. Cal followed with a blow to Ingram's chin that loosened his teeth.

Rollie pulled a knife from his boot and made a dive toward Cal. Before he could plunge the blade, Cal moved aside, and the blade landed harmlessly in the wall, embedded so deeply into the wood that it couldn't be removed.

Desperate, Rollie bent double and plowed his head into Cal's midsection, sending both men to the floor, where they continued raining blows on each other. The air was filled with grunts, sighs, moans, and the thudding of fists hitting flesh.

"Gilbert," his father commanded, "git my rifle."

"Not if you value your life, boy," Cal said sternly.

Gilbert remained where he was, backed up against the wall, out of the way of the fighting, his arm around his younger brother's shoulders. Both boys watched in silence as the bloody fight continued.

"Did you hear me?" Ingram bellowed.

"He heard. And he understands the rules. This is between you and me," Cal said as he landed a blow to Rollie's face that was followed by a spurt of blood. "And this time, you're not dealing with a helpless boy. Let's see how you handle a real fight. With a man."

"A man, is it? Is that what that prissy eastern schoolmarm tells you when you're kissin' her?" Rollie's high-pitched laughter was cut short by a blow to his jaw from Cal's fist.

"Oh, you'll pay for—" Rollie's head snapped backward. His eyes rolled back in his head before the lids closed. His fist, which had been poised to strike again, dropped heavily to his side.

Cal felt a moment of disappointment. He was just getting started. He'd hoped to be able to work off all the layers of anger and frustration, to calm the storm of emotions that still roiled inside him. Instead, he'd have to settle for half a fight.

"Next time," he muttered as he staggered to his feet, "I hope you're stone-cold sober, Ingram. So I can have the satisfaction of beating you to a pulp."

He bent and picked up his gunbelt, then retrieved his hat, which had fallen off. As he was straightening, he saw the look of horror on the faces of both boys, and heard the unmistakable click of a revolver.

There was no time to draw his gun. Instead, he whirled and swung the gunbelt out in a wide arc, knocking the pistol from Rollie's hand. The bullet discharged into a wall directly behind Cal.

He swore and caught the man by the front of his shirt, dragging him to his feet. This time he pounded

Ingram with his fists until, gasping for air, Rollie collapsed into a heap.

"Thanks, Ingram," he muttered as he fastened his gunbelt and pulled on his hat. "Now there won't have to be a next time."

Chapter Eleven

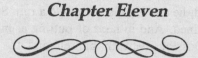

Cal leaned against the outer wall of the Ingram shack and sucked fresh air into his starving lungs. It was a relief to breathe freely again after experiencing the fetid air inside the cabin.

When he straightened, he noticed Gilbert and Daniel watching him warily. The younger brother seemed always to be standing in the shadow of his older sibling. And always Gilbert had one arm around Daniel's shoulder, as though shielding him from the cruelties of the world.

"You'll be wanting to take back the pork," Gilbert said matter-of-factly.

Cal shook his head. "I would, if it would teach your father a lesson. But the only ones who would be punished would be you and your brother. I'm sure you'll make good use of it."

He could read the relief on the boy's face. Reaching into a pouch he wore tucked in his shirt, he tossed some money to Gilbert. "Put this where your father can't find it."

The boy's eyes went wide with stunned surprise. "Why?"

Cal shrugged. "Just in case you find yourself in need."

He watched as Gilbert stuffed the money deeply into his pocket.

Cal pulled himself into the saddle. Without another word, he nudged his horse into a run. Suddenly he felt drained. And in need of putting as much distance as possible between himself and the Ingram ranch.

With a sinking heart, he realized that there had been no satisfaction in beating Rollie Ingram. It hadn't changed a thing. He still harbored a deep, simmering hatred of the bully, who would continue to take out his anger and frustration on those who were smaller and weaker. Ingram was still a thief who would steal whenever he thought he could get away with it, because he was too lazy to earn his own keep.

As the miles stretched out, Cal realized something else. No matter how far he rode, he could never get away from the Ingrams. They were too deeply imprinted on his mind and heart. And seared into his very soul.

Pearl shoved open the door to her school. Setting her lantern on her desk, she hurried to light a fire on the grate. Soon the chill had been chased from the little cabin, and she began preparing for a new day. But, though she struggled to concentrate on the lessons she had prepared, she found her thoughts returning again and again to Cal.

She had seen him ride off in the direction of the Ingram ranch, and return hours later. From her window she'd been able to make out what appeared to be blood on his shirt. But instead of coming inside to clean up, he had remained in the bunkhouse until he rode out again, sporting a duster and bedroll. That could mean only one thing. He intended to be gone for some time.

She was fairly certain he had confronted Rollie Ingram. But there were still so many questions she wanted answered. Had Ingram admitted to the theft? Had Cal demanded restitution? And Rollie's sons— were they willing parties to the theft?

Oh, why had he left without a word? Now she would just have to be patient until he returned from wherever he had gone.

Carmelita's words came back to her. *Only a fool would ever lose her heart to a cowboy. They are like the tumbleweed, traveling where the wind carries them, never putting down roots.*

She hadn't lost her heart. She was merely... distracted.

It was just as well that he had left for a while, she thought. Cal McCabe was a most unwelcome distraction. With him gone, she could spend all her time thinking about her students.

But as she began to write on her slate, she found her mind drifting time and again to thoughts of Cal. Of his unexpected kindnesses. And his sudden bursts of fury. He was not an easy man to know. Or to like. There were things he kept hidden from the world. Perhaps, she thought, it would be best if they were never uncovered. For she was uneasy about the things she might find.

She was grateful when the sounds of a horse and wagon broke the morning stillness. While Travis unhitched the horse and tethered it, the other children climbed down from the back and made their way to their desks, filling the classroom with happy chatter, scattering the last of her uneasiness.

Today there were eight children in attendance, since the Durfee boys, Damon and Amos, had joined Bart, Birdie, Travis and the three Potter sisters.

"Miss Jewel?"

At the sound of Birdie's voice, Pearl turned.

"Yes, Birdie?"

The girl held out a parcel, wrapped carefully in a square of muslin.

"What's this?"

"Your Bible," she said shyly. "My ma didn't want my hands soiling it."

"Why, this is a beautiful cover, Birdie. Please thank your mother for me. It's so pretty, I believe I'll leave it on for everyone to see."

The little girl glowed under the compliment.

"Did you read a passage to your parents?" Pearl asked.

"Yes'm." Birdie stared at a spot on the floor. "Ma cried. And Pa kept clearing his throat. They said hearing their daughter reading from the Bible was the best gift they'd ever had. They thank you kindly."

Pearl found a lump in her own throat when she realized how much pleasure had been derived from such a simple act. She turned away to busy herself at her desk. "Take out your slates, children. We'll begin with—"

At the sound of another wagon, she looked up in surprise. Before she could push back from her desk, the door was opened and Rollie Ingram strode in, followed by his two sons.

Rollie's face still bore the ravages of his encounter with Cal. Now Pearl had no more doubts about whether or not they had tangled. Her hand went to her throat in a gesture of surprise, and she experienced a sudden rush of fear. Had he come here looking for Cal? But the fear was quickly erased when Rollie gave her an almost jovial smile.

"Mornin' Miss Jewel. Thanks to Cal McCabe, I've seen the light."

"The . . . light?"

"Of knowledge, so to speak. I've decided my boys ought to attend your fine school with the other children."

He stepped aside to reveal his two sons, and gave them a shove when they held back.

"Oh, Gilbert." Pearl covered her mouth to stifle her revulsion at the sight of his bruised and battered face. "Whatever happened to you?"

"Fell from his horse. Landed on a rock." Rollie gave a sly wink. "The boy's just naturally clumsy. Always fallin' and hurtin' himself. Sports a new cut or bruise every day. Don't you, boy?"

Gilbert kept his gaze averted as the children in the classroom set up an audible ripple of whispers and giggles. "Yes."

"What's that? Speak up, boy," Rollie growled, grabbing his son's arm and pinching.

"I said yes, sir."

"That's better." Rollie turned to Pearl. "Now, I've let my boys know that I expect them to behave themselves in your school." He puffed up his chest self-importantly. "They know they'll answer to me if I hear they misbehaved."

Pearl had already witnessed how he "disciplined" his sons. The memory of him kicking Gilbert while the boy was on his hands and knees, scrambling to retrieve the fallen grain, was deeply imprinted on her mind. She hadn't swallowed his story about the boy falling from his horse. She had her own idea about how Gilbert had come by his latest scars. "I'm sure we'll have no trouble."

"Good. Good." Rollie rubbed his hands together and studied Pearl for a long moment.

She felt a chill race along her spine and had an overpowering urge to cross her hands over her chest and turn away from his scrutiny.

Rollie sauntered to the door, obviously pleased with himself. "I'll be back to pick up my boys before supper. You see they stay put till I git here."

As the door closed behind him, Pearl released the breath she'd been unconsciously holding. That man made her skin crawl. But she had to put aside her feelings for him and concentrate instead on his sons.

She'd feared trouble. Instead, she had two new pupils. She wondered just what Cal had said to convince Rollie Ingram to permit his two sons to attend school. Whatever it was, it had done the job.

"Come, Daniel and Gilbert." She led the younger boy to a desk beside her youngest students, May and

June Potter. Gilbert was directed to take a seat beside Amos Durfee.

The children seemed reluctant to share space with the ragged-looking Ingram boys. Daniel and Gilbert looked equally uncomfortable, refusing to look at the people around them. Though the two Potter girls kept their thoughts to themselves, and scooted over to make room, Amos Durfee had no intention of suffering in silence. "Don't want him near me," he said as Gilbert started to sit down.

"That's enough, Amos," Pearl said sharply.

"He's a thief," Amos protested. "My pa said him and his pa stole a whole shipment of flour last winter and then sold it in a neighboring town."

"Did you see the theft?" Pearl asked.

"No, ma'am. But everybody said—"

"Then what you are repeating is malicious gossip."

"Everybody knows who did it," Amos insisted. "I don't want to sit next to a thief."

"I will not permit such talk in my classroom. Now, Gilbert . . ." Pearl started to point to a desk, but then she felt a tug on her sleeve. "Yes, Birdie?"

The girl said shyly, "I don't mind if he sits beside me, Miss Jewel."

Pearl wanted to hug the girl. With a gentle smile, she said, "Thank you, Birdie. Gilbert, you may take this desk."

He slid into the desk beside Birdie, all the while keeping his gaze averted.

"Here, Daniel." Pearl handed the little boy a slate. "I'd like you to form any letters you know. When you're finished, bring this to my desk and we'll go over them."

"Yes'm." He bent over the slate, deep in concentration.

Pearl gave the rest of the children their assignments, then paused beside Gilbert's desk. "Can you read?" she asked softly.

He shrugged, avoiding her eyes. "Some."

"Why don't you come up to my desk and read?" Seeing the question in his eyes, she explained, "Just so I know what you're capable of."

When she was seated at her desk, she handed Gilbert a simple reader. He began to read aloud, rarely faltering, even over unfamiliar words. At the sound of his voice, deeper than that of the others, several heads came up. Pearl fixed each student with a look that commanded them to return their attention to their work. But, though they kept their gazes averted, she was aware of their continued interest in this boy, who seemed so different from all of them. It wasn't just his reputation, his shabby clothes, or the cuts and bruises on his young body. He was a commanding presence, though she couldn't figure out why. True, he was big for his age. Bigger even than Travis Worthing. His arms already showed the beginnings of muscles. But it wasn't his size that set him apart. Perhaps it was his attitude—a deep-seated anger that seemed to have robbed him of his childhood, combined with a stoicism in the face of his harsh existence. And one other thing. A surprising intelligence.

"Thank you, Gilbert." She reached for the book. "How is it that you read so well?"

"My ma taught me. Before she died."

"She was a very fine teacher."

Pearl thought, for just a moment, she saw a light come into his eyes. But just as quickly, when someone snickered, it was extinguished, and the sullen curve of his lips returned.

"You may take your seat," she said. "Daniel, have you finished your letters yet?"

"Yes'm." The little boy hurried to her desk and presented his slate.

Pearl couldn't hide her astonishment. Though the letters were crudely written, they were all correct. And at the bottom of the slate Daniel had printed his name.

"Who taught you this?" she asked.

"My brother," he said proudly.

"Gilbert?"

He nodded. "He taught me how to make my letters in the sand, with a stick." His voice lowered. "You won't tell Pa?"

She glanced over his head to where his older brother sat, his hands shoved into his pockets, his gaze fixed on his desktop. Then she returned her attention to Daniel. "Your father wouldn't like it if he found out Gilbert is teaching you?"

"No, ma'am."

"Thank you, Daniel. You may return to your desk." To the class she called, "We'll work on our sums now."

While the younger children worked on simple addition, the older ones were given columns of figures to add. As she walked among them, helping, encouraging, Pearl found herself mulling over what she'd learned. It would appear that Rollie Ingram had indeed had a very sudden change of heart. Despite the fact that he had previously disapproved of his sons learning, he had dragged them to school today.

Hadn't he said that his encounter with Cal had caused him to see the light?

Her heart began to slip free of a heavy burden as she continued moving among the children, offering praise and encouragement. It was the start of a new week. And the dawn of a new day for the children of Hanging Tree. And especially for the unhappy sons of Rollie Ingram.

"It's such a lovely spring day, I think we'll take our lunch outside," Pearl announced.

The children scampered to the back of the room to retrieve the baskets their parents had prepared for them. Seeing that Daniel and Gilbert had none, she picked up her basket and said, "I'd like you two to sit beside me. I have more than enough food to share."

"We don't need anything," Gilbert said. When his little brother opened his mouth to argue, he added firmly, "We had lots to eat this morning, before we set out for school."

"I'm sure you did." Pearl chose a grassy spot beneath a tree, where she spread out a cloth, then began unpacking the basket. She unwrapped several slices of sourdough bread piled high with thinly sliced roast beef.

Without a word, she handed one to Daniel and another to Gilbert. Before the older boy could protest,

Daniel bit into the sandwich and rolled his eyes heavenward.

"Ummm… Gilbert's a good cook, Miss Jewel," he managed to say around a mouth filled with food. "But he sure can't make anything that tastes like this."

"You do the cooking?" Pearl asked the boy beside her.

"Yes'm." He ducked his head and decided to follow his little brother's lead by tasting the teacher's lunch.

Pearl watched as they devoured their food in a couple of bites. She broke her last sandwich into several more pieces and placed them in front of the boys. Then she unwrapped a mound of flaky biscuits that had been split and drizzled with honey, and blessed Carmelita for always sending too much food.

"I could never eat all this," she said, setting the tempting confections down.

Daniel was the first to taste them. And, Pearl noted, Gilbert didn't reach for one until he was satisfied that his little brother had eaten all he could. Then he reached for a biscuit and ate it slowly, savoring every crumb.

Pearl opened a jar of lemonade and took several sips before silently passing it to Gilbert. He seemed startled that she would share even this, but, without a word, he drank, then passed it on to his brother.

"That was just about the best food I've ever eaten," the little boy said as he wiped his mouth on his ragged sleeve.

"I'm glad you enjoyed it. Now you may run and play with the others for a few minutes, until it's time to return to the classroom."

"Play?" Daniel asked.

"Climb the tree or play a game of tag." She paused, and realized with a start that the little boy had no idea what play was. Quickly composing herself, she called, "April, May and June. Would you like to play a game of tag with Daniel?"

"Yes, Miss Jewel," they said in unison.

"Fine. But first, you'll have to explain the rules."

"We take turns being It," April said firmly. "Whoever is It has to tag the others. And no running beyond the tree, or past the schoolhouse. Whoever is tagged first has to be It next."

Soon the four were joined by the others in a rollicking game of tag.

"Wouldn't you like to join them, Gilbert?" Pearl asked.

The boy stood alone beneath the tree, watching in silence.

"No, ma'am."

"Then perhaps you'd help me." She packed the remains of their lunch in the basket and handed it to him. "Come along."

The boy followed her into the cabin.

"You can put the basket over there," she said, indicating a spot in the corner of the room. "And then, if you wouldn't mind, I could use a hand with some firewood. Though the sunlight is warm enough outside, there is a chill in here, don't you think?"

He shrugged. "I suppose."

He made his way to a pile of logs outside and returned carrying an armload that would have staggered some men.

Pearl watched in astonishment as he lowered the logs to the floor and, with an economy of movement, began to toss several on the fire.

When that was done, he stood watching her at her desk. When she looked up, she realized his gaze was centered on the little vase of wildflowers there.

"I picked them on my way to school this morning," she said. "They're pretty, don't you think?"

He nodded. Moving closer, he touched a dirty hand to one tiny bloom. "My ma used to like wildflowers."

"I'll bet you picked some for her," Pearl said.

His voice lowered, as though he were talking to himself. "They used to make her smile. Sometimes, when she was sad, they were the only things that would do it." He looked up. "I still bring flowers to her grave sometimes."

Pearl touched his hand. "That's nice. I visit my mother's grave, too. And bring her flowers."

At once he pulled back, as though offended by the touch of her. "What other chores do you want me to do?"

She sighed. Whatever spell had come over him for a moment, it was broken now. His sullen pout returned, along with his characteristic anger. She would have to remember not to touch him. Maybe he feared that all grown-ups would hurt him as his father did.

"Nothing else, Gilbert. You've been most helpful. Thank you."

She crossed the room and called out, "Time for class, children."

Within minutes, the boys and girls had returned to their desks and settled into their routine. But as Pearl worked, she had a sense that there was much more to Gilbert Ingram than the image he showed the world.

Chapter Twelve

"How many of you studied your spelling words?" Pearl asked.

Most of the hands went up.

"If you would line up in the front of the room, we'll start our spelling bee." Pearl turned to Daniel and Gilbert. "Since you boys weren't here last week, I'll excuse you. You may remain in your desks. But I'll ask you to try to write the words on your slates, in order to see how many of them you know."

Pearl started off with simple words for the younger students, then moved gradually to more difficult words as the younger children were eliminated from the competition. Soon, only Birdie and Travis Worthing were left.

"The word is *honor*," Pearl said. "Travis?"

The boy frowned. He knew it was one of those tricky words, but he just couldn't picture it in his mind.

"*O-N-E-R*," he said slowly, pausing at each letter.

"I'm sorry. That isn't correct." Pearl turned to Birdie. "If you get this one, you'll win our spelling bee, and win another chance to take the Bible home for the night.''

The girl nervously chewed on her lip. How she would love to bring home the Bible again, and see that light in her mother's eyes. But she was hopelessly lost on this word.

As she twisted her hands together, she glanced across the room and saw Gilbert Ingram turn his slate so that she could read what he had written.

''H-O-N-O-R.'' She mouthed the letters without even being aware of what she'd said.

''That's correct.'' Pearl was delighted. ''I didn't expect any of you to know that the *H* is silent in this word. Congratulations, Birdie. You've just won our spelling bee, and the chance to take home . . .''

Birdie was vehemently shaking her head. ''I can't do that, Miss Jewel. I didn't win.''

''But you did.''

''No, ma'am. I didn't have any idea how to spell it. It was Gilbert. He knew the word and showed me on his slate.''

Surprised, Pearl said, ''Gilbert, would you please bring your slate up here.''

The boy did as he was told.

As he stood beside Birdie, he whispered, ''Why'd you tell? I did it for you, so you'd be able to win.''

''But I don't want to win that way,'' she said softly. ''It isn't fair.''

''But winning's important to you. And I just wanted to pay you back for letting me sit next to you today.''

"You don't have to pay me back, Gilbert. I don't mind sitting next to you. Really I don't," she insisted. "In fact, I . . . liked it."

Pearl overheard their whispered conversation as she checked the list of words. Amazingly, Gilbert had spelled every one correctly. Her mind raced as she fretted about how to handle this.

"Do you know the meaning of this word, Gilbert?" she asked softly.

He shrugged. "Honesty, I guess. Respect."

"You wouldn't know about that!" Amos Durfee shouted. "You may be able to spell it, but you'll never have it!"

Pearl shot the boy a look that silenced him. Then she turned to Gilbert.

"All of us can find ways to practice this word in our daily lives. Birdie just showed us the finest example of honor. Taking home the Bible meant a lot to her. But her honor, her integrity, meant more. And she knew that she hadn't earned the right to the prize. She could have chosen to say nothing. No one would have been the wiser. But she chose the nobler path, and admitted the truth."

"But she didn't do anything wrong," Gilbert argued. "I was the one who cheated."

"Answer me this, Gilbert," Pearl said gently. "If a man steals, and then sells his stolen goods to one who knows they were stolen, aren't both men guilty?"

When he said nothing, she said, "By allowing you to help her win, Birdie knew that she was guilty of cheating, also."

"I would never do anything to hurt Birdie. I just wanted to help her," he protested. "As for me—" he hung his head "—it doesn't matter. Everybody knows what I am."

"What you are," Pearl said, catching him by the chin and forcing him to look up into her eyes, "is a fine young person who wanted to help a friend. And that is admirable. But the finest gift you can give yourself, and your friend, is honor. Our honor, our good name," she said, allowing her gaze to move over each student for emphasis, "is our most precious possession. Be very careful not to ruin a man's name by idle gossip. Or the same might happen to you one day."

Amos Durfee flushed and looked away. Several of the other students did the same.

"Now," Pearl asked, "what am I to do with the prize?"

"Why not give it to Gilbert?" Birdie pleaded. "You said he got every word right."

"So he did." Pearl held out the Bible. "I believe you just won our spelling bee, Gilbert."

The boy looked dumbstruck. "I—I've never won anything before."

"Would you like to take home the Bible? You could read it tonight to your little brother and your father."

At the mention of his father, Gilbert's smile faltered. "I—don't think I'd better do that."

Pearl placed the book in his hand. "It's your prize, Gilbert, to do with as you please. Just see that it's returned in the morning."

She turned away. "Now, class, we'll have a final reading before it's time for dismissal."

Gilbert walked to his desk beside a beaming Birdie. And for the first time anyone could remember, he managed a half smile before turning his head away.

"Remember to study your new list of spelling words," Pearl called as her students climbed aboard Travis Worthing's wagon and headed home.

"We will. Goodbye, Miss Jewel," Birdie called. Her gaze slid from her teacher to the tall boy who stood framed in the doorway of the school. She waved.

Though Gilbert didn't return the wave, his eyes betrayed him, watching avidly until the wagon dipped out of sight beneath a ridge.

"I'm sorry you have to stay on our account," he said as Pearl returned to her desk.

"I don't mind. I often stay late to prepare for tomorrow's lessons." She began to stack the children's slates for cleaning. Glancing up, she said, "Would you boys care to help me?"

"Yes'm," Daniel replied with an air of excitement. He would do just about anything to please this pretty woman who reminded him of a princess.

Pearl handed him a rag and the pile of slates and said, "Why don't you take these outside and wipe them clean? Then you can return one to each desk."

The little boy accepted them eagerly.

"Gilbert," she said, "you can toss out that bucket of water. I'll fill it with fresh water from the creek in the morning. And then, if you don't mind, I could use another pile of logs for the morning fire."

He picked up the bucket and headed outside.

Within minutes, Daniel was back.

"I'm all done, Miss Jewel." The little boy placed the last slate on a desktop and made his way to her desk.

"So am I," Gilbert announced, turning away from the wood he'd piled neatly beside the fireplace.

Pearl couldn't help smiling at their efficiency. It was obvious that they found these chores simple compared with those they were called upon to do at home.

"Now you've earned the right to do something that pleases you." She glanced around. "You may explore the school, if you'd like. Or go fishing down by the creek."

Daniel glanced toward the crude ladder leaning against the far wall. "Is it all right if we explore the loft, Miss Jewel?"

She nodded. "I don't mind. In fact, I'll go with you."

She followed the boys up the ladder and knelt in the straw.

"What's this?" Daniel asked as he lifted the buffalo robe.

"A remnant of my father's early years here in Hanging Tree. This little cabin was his first home."

"Your pa lived here?" Gilbert stared around at the crudely built cabin. "I thought he was born in that big house."

She laughed at the surprised look on his face. "I guess that's what a lot of children think. But my father was just a poor, struggling cowboy with a dream. He wasn't much older than you, Gilbert, when he started carving out a life for himself, here in the wilderness." She looked around the tiny loft and said, "I wonder what things he had to face all alone out here."

"Indians, I'll bet," Daniel said.

"And outlaws," Gilbert added.

"Not to mention loneliness and fear and hunger," Pearl mused. "Visiting this place gives me a new appreciation for all my father went through in his lifetime."

She made her way to the ladder. "You boys stay up here as long as you like. I still have a few things to do at my desk."

As she worked on her lessons, Pearl could hear the sounds of whispering coming from the loft. It was pleasant, she thought, to hear the sounds of life in this cabin. Of all her father's dreams, that would have been his fondest. To find a woman to share all this, and fill their home with children.

But the dream had been shattered when his young wife died after the birth of their firstborn, Diamond. And though he loved other women who bore him children, he had died before his family could be united.

How it must have pained Onyx Jewel to know that he was unable to persuade any of the women he loved to share this life. What bittersweet irony that now, after his death, his daughters had come together to share what they had never shared during his lifetime.

Absorbed in her thoughts, she didn't hear the approach of the horse and wagon. When the door was thrown open, her head came up sharply.

"Mr. Ingram. You caught me by surprise."

"Mr. Ingram." He smiled, showing tobacco-stained teeth. "I like that, teacher. It shows the proper respect." He seemed highly agitated, and he reeked of whiskey. His gaze swept the room. "Where are my boys?"

"Up here, Pa," came Daniel's muffled voice.

"What you doin' up there?" Rollie demanded.

"Just looking around. Miss Jewel said we could."

"Well, git down here. Now." A cruel, feral glint came into his eyes. "I got a surprise for you."

When his sons descended the ladder, he was holding his pistol flat in his hand, rubbing it with the other hand, the way a man might caress a beloved treasure.

"What's the surprise?" Daniel asked.

Behind him, Gilbert stopped short, watching his father with a cautious look. It was plain that he'd experienced his father's many moods, and that he knew that this particular mood signaled trouble.

"Me and your teacher are going on a little journey," Rollie said.

"Journey?" Pearl scraped back her chair and started to rise, but Rollie leveled the gun at her. She sank back down and weakly gripped the edge of her desk.

"That's right. See, I did a little figurin'. And I figure the only way Cal McCabe could know that I stole his sow and her litter was if you told him about seein' us passin' your school."

"Pa..." Gilbert's words died as his father swung toward him with a look of pure hatred.

"Shut up, boy." He turned back to Pearl, and when he spoke again, his slow, even drawl was more frightening than his snarl of anger. "Everybody thinks I'm lazy and stupid. But I got a brain. A brain that tells me that every man has a weakness. And I've decided Cal McCabe's weakness is you, Miss High-and-Mighty Jewel. So I'm going to use you to lure McCabe up into the hills."

"But why?" she managed to ask through a throat clogged with fear.

"'Cause nobody beats up Rollie Ingram and gets away with it. Cal McCabe is going to pay. Only first, before he dies, he's going to suffer. And there's no better place to inflict pain than up there, where I'm king of the hill." He laughed—a shrill, high sound that scraped across her nerves, sending a shudder through her. "Nobody knows those hills like me. Not even McCabe." He motioned with the gun. "Now move, prissy little schoolmarm. I got the wagon all loaded and ready for our adventure."

Pearl couldn't stand. Her legs were trembling violently. Instead, she tried to reason with him. "You can't do this, Rollie."

"Oh, now it's Rollie, is it? What happened to Mr. Ingram?"

"Respect has to be earned," she said in her most imperious tone.

He threw back his head and laughed. "Oh, I'll earn your respect, all right. Before this is over, Miss High-and-Mighty Jewel, you'll call me whatever I tell you to call me. And you'll do whatever I want to save your miserable life and that of McCabe." His laughter died, and his face took on the look of a cruel, sadistic madman. "Now move."

She forced herself to stand and assume a rigid, proud pose. "I will not go with you. If you must, shoot me now."

"Well now, how noble . . ." His lips curled into an evil grin as he toppled her desk, sending her books and slates, and her vase of flowers, crashing to the floor. "Oh, I'll shoot you, all right. But I won't kill you. Not yet. I intend to keep you alive for a long time, teacher. 'Cause you're the bait that'll lure McCabe into my trap." He aimed the pistol and fired, just missing her foot by a fraction, sending splinters of wood flying through the air.

Pearl's heart nearly stopped, then began racing so hard she feared she might faint.

"The next one won't miss. And I won't take time to bind your wounds. You'll just have to live with the pain. And bleed all over that pretty gown." He waved the gun. "Now move."

"What about your boys?" she asked.

"They know how to git home. The walk'll do them good."

"Pa," Gilbert pleaded, "you'll have the whole town after you."

"Let them come. I got enough bullets stashed to hold off an army. It'd be worth fightin' the whole town just to kill McCabe."

He jammed the gun in Pearl's ribs. She lifted her skirts and started toward the door. When she didn't move quickly enough, Rollie grabbed her by the arm and hauled her roughly outside, knocking desks and benches aside in his haste. "Now git up there, and let's git movin'."

Daniel started to cry, and Rollie turned and swung his hand in an arc. Before he could connect with the little boy's face, Gilbert had stepped between them, taking the blow meant for his brother. A blow that snapped his head to one side. His father grabbed him by the front of the shirt and dragged him close. The boy didn't flinch as his father snarled, "Are you ready to fight me, boy? 'Cause if you are, you'll answer to my gun."

Gilbert spoke not a word, but his eyes were as hard and angry as his father's. Rollie gave him a shove that sent him sprawling.

"See that you go straight home. And stay there. That'll give me plenty of time to git where I'm goin'. When McCabe comes lookin' for his lady, you tell him I took her to the hills. Tell him I'll be waitin' for him. Then you just sit tight, if you know what's good for you."

"This time he'll kill you," Gilbert said quietly as he began to pick himself up from the dirt.

The father caught him by the shirtfront and hauled him to his feet, then dealt him a punch to the stomach that sent him to his knees.

With a cruel laugh, Rollie climbed aboard the wagon and flicked the reins. Over his shoulder he called, "I guess I know who you'll be cheerin' for. But I'll be the one returnin' from the hills, boy. And when I do, you and me are going to find out once and for all just what you're made of."

Chapter Thirteen

"**P**a's done it this time. He's going to kill Miss Jewel, isn't he?" Daniel's tears rolled down his cheeks, mixing with the dirt and grime to form muddy little rivers.

Gilbert watched as the wagon disappeared over a ridge. His hands were balled into impotent fists at his sides. He wanted to cry, too, but figured he was too big for such things. Besides, it would only add to his little brother's woes.

He should have known, he thought, berating himself. All that talk of Pa's this morning about taking his sons to school and proving they were as good as the other kids. It was all a lie, so Pa could get even with Cal McCabe for that beating.

The worst part of it was, he'd wanted to believe his father. Even though Rollie Ingram had never once kept a promise, or treated his sons with a scrap of kindness, Gilbert had hoped and prayed that this time would be different. When would he learn?

"If you think people hated us before," he muttered, "just think how they're going to treat us after this. We won't be able to show our faces in town ever again. As soon as Pa gets back, we'll have to go up into the hills to hide, and start over in some other place.''

"It's not our fault," Daniel whispered, the tears falling faster.

"It's never been our fault. But that didn't stop people from hating us just 'cause we're Ingrams.''

"What are we going to do, Gilbert?" his little brother asked between sobs.

The older boy shrugged. "If we do as Pa said, Mr. McCabe will walk right into Pa's trap and get himself killed. But if we disobey, Pa will surely fly into a rage and kill Miss Jewel." Not to mention what Rollie Ingram would do to his son if he dared to disobey him.

In his young life, Gilbert had been forced to make many decisions. In order to survive, he'd shouldered far more responsibilities than most boys his age. But this time he felt completely lost. No matter what course he chose, someone would suffer. Maybe the best course of action would be to do nothing. To run and hide and prepare for the inevitable.

"We'd better get started," he said.

"We're just going home?" Daniel asked through his tears.

"What else can we do?" Gilbert passed a hand over his face, more scared than he cared to admit.

As he made ready to close the cabin door, his gaze fell on the Bible on his desk. For almost a minute, he'd actually thought about taking it home and reading it aloud to his father. What a joke.

And then he thought about the word that had won him the prize.

Honor.

He could still see Miss Jewel's pretty face as she'd lectured the class on the meaning of the word. There had been a light in her eyes. The kind of light he used to see in his ma's eyes sometimes, when his pa was gone, and the tension in their little cabin had been replaced by a few moments of peace. Then she would talk about her life before. Before she'd recklessly pulled up stakes in St. Louis and agreed to be Rollie Ingram's bride. Before their love had somehow become buried beneath a mountain of lying and cheating and cruelty. There had been love and laughter in her childhood home, she'd told her eldest son. And music and religion and books and poetry.

And dignity.

Her eyes had fairly glowed when she talked about her very proper, churchgoing father, and the delight he took in his lovely wife and only daughter. That life had seemed, to Gilbert, as much a fairy tale as the stories she'd spun for the younger children, stories about kings and castles. Especially when she'd talked about her hopes and dreams for their future. A future far different from the life she'd settled for with Rollie Ingram.

"You'll build your own life one day," she had told him. "A life of goodness and honor."

There was that word again. *Honor.*

"Come on," Gilbert said, catching hold of his little brother's hand. "We've got a long walk ahead of us. It'll be dark before we get even halfway to the Jewel ranch."

"The...Jewel ranch? We're not going home?" Daniel asked. When his older brother shook his head, he whispered, "You know you'll have to face Pa's fists when he comes back."

"Won't be anything new," Gilbert said matter-of-factly. "And at least I'll know, while I'm taking a beating, that it's for doing something right."

Pearl gripped the hard seat of the rickety wagon and struggled to calm her pounding heart.

If she were Diamond, she thought, she would have a gun tucked away in her boot. If she were Jade, it would be a jewel-handled knife. If she were Ruby, she would have all the guile, all the cleverness, of a born scoundrel. But, as usual, she berated herself, she had none of their survival instincts. Instead, she was useless. Helpless.

Oh, Daddy, she thought. *There have been so many times in my life when I've felt alone and afraid. But never like this. This time, I'm to be the cause of Cal's death, as well. And, oh, it weighs heavily on my heart. Help me, Daddy. Help me to at least face my fate without being a coward.*

The mere thought of her strong, brave father brought a rush of feelings. Hadn't she just speculated on the harshness of his early days in this very place? Surely he'd faced far more desperate situations than this. What would he have done? she asked herself. What would he have advised her to do?

At once the answer came to her. She could hear her father's voice. *You have a fine mind, Pearl. The good Lord means for us to use all the gifts we're given.*

She wasn't completely helpless. She would use her mind to fight Rollie Ingram.

First, she needed to mark the route they were taking, so that, if she managed to escape, she would be able to make her way to safety.

She began to note unusual rock formations, small pools, distant buttes. She reminded herself that, though they were putting miles between themselves and the schoolhouse, they were still on Jewel land. She was not alone. Somewhere nearby were wranglers tending the herds. On the far perimeters of the ranch were line camps, with men patrolling them to keep out intruders and to round up stray cattle.

The thought brought her a measure of comfort.

If she could get Rollie Ingram to fire his gun while still on Jewel land, someone might hear and investigate. But how to pull it off?

She had to incur his anger. And force his hand.

She felt the panic begin to rise within her as she plotted and schemed. Did she dare risk the broken bones she might incur by jumping from the speeding wagon, in order to tempt Rollie to fire his gun? And if she succeeded, would she also survive the gunshot? Or would he kill her here, and then use her dead body as bait to lure Cal to his death?

Oh, why did she have to be cursed with a mind that insisted upon looking at a problem from all angles? For once, she would simply do what she had to, and forget the consequences.

Clutching her hands together tightly, she gritted her teeth, shut her eyes, and leaped from the wagon.

The ground was hard, and she hit it with such force that for a moment she saw stars flashing through her brain as she bounced, rolled, then came to an abrupt halt in the midst of prickly bushes. With a little moan, she opened her eyes. As her vision cleared, she saw Rollie struggling to halt the lathered, snorting horse, which had been running at a full gallop.

Scrambling to her feet, she lifted her skirts and started to run, all the while expecting to hear the sound of a gunshot rumbling across the hills. She wondered what it would feel like to be shot. Bracing herself for the pain, she kept her eyes on the goal. Up ahead was a small gully. If she could make it there, she would at least have a chance.

Her dainty kid boots hadn't been made for running over hard-packed earth and slippery rocks. Several times she had to struggle to remain upright. But, though she lost her balance, she continued running, until a body suddenly hurtled through space, tackling her and dragging her to the ground.

"Thought you could git away from old Rollie, did you?"

He straddled her, pulling her hands roughly behind her, pressing her face into the dirt. She was breathing hard, but had the satisfaction of hearing him suck in several wheezing breaths as he tied her hands behind her. Dragging her to her feet, he shoved her ahead of him, toward the wagon.

"Haven't figured out if you're just plain stupid, or if you thought you were bein' clever," he muttered. "Either way, you just sealed your fate."

He tossed her into the back of the wagon and shocked her by shoving up her skirts and tying her ankles. When he was finished, he gave her an insulting leer. "Sorry there isn't more time, teacher. I'd like to see what else you're hidin' under these skirts."

She fixed him with a look of disgust. "You'll have to kill me first."

"That can be arranged," he said with a harsh cackle.

Still laughing, he climbed up on the seat of the wagon and cracked the whip. The horse took off at a run.

In the back of the wagon, Pearl gave in to feelings of self-loathing. She had hoped to force a gunshot that would alert someone to her plight. Instead, all she'd done was to make things worse. She couldn't even see the landmarks they were passing. Now she could only stare at the sky. And pray that Cal wouldn't fall into this evil man's trap.

Cookie scrubbed the last of his pots and pans and tucked them away in the chuck wagon. Tomorrow he planned to take supper to the wranglers handling the big herd up on the north range. Though he enjoyed cooking for the hands in the bunkhouse, his greatest pleasure was cooking on the trail.

He idly rubbed his sore leg. The knee was stiffening up, giving him more trouble than he cared to admit. That always meant a change in the weather. He'd have to hide his pain from the Jewel sisters, or they'd start fussing over him and start talking about hiring someone to replace him. So's he could "start enjoying the life of leisure he'd earned.'' Ha! He bit down on the stem of his pipe. They just didn't understand. This was the only life he wanted. And he intended to die cooking for the wranglers. Hopefully somewhere out on the trail. With his boots on, and his stew simmered to perfection.

He pulled a flaming stick from the fire and held it to the bowl of his pipe, puffing until the fragrance of tobacco stung the night air and a rich cloud of smoke encircled his head.

Just as he dropped the stick back into the fire, he saw two unfamiliar figures emerge from the gathering darkness. He reached for his rifle and took aim.

''Who's there?'' he demanded.

The figures halted, and then the taller one stepped forward.

''My name's Gilbert Ingram.''

''Rollie Ingram's boy?''

''Yes, sir.'' He drew the smaller figure into the circle of light. ''And this is my little brother, Daniel.''

''You boys are a far piece from home.'' Cookie's hands tightened on the barrel of the rifle. He'd heard rumors about the Ingrams. Not a decent one in the bunch. And though the little one looked scared, and not a bit dangerous, the bigger one was already a head taller than Cookie, and the look in his eye wasn't exactly peaceable.

''What do you want?'' he asked.

''We're looking for Mr. McCabe,'' Gilbert said.

''He ain't here.''

Both boys looked crestfallen.

"Where is he?" Gilbert's hand tightened on his brother's shoulder.

"Up on the north range."

"When will he be back?"

Cookie shrugged. "Didn't say. Just said he'd be gone for a while." And when he saw the murderous look in Cal's eye, Cookie hadn't pressed. The bloody clothes and battered face had told him enough. Cal had been in a fight. And from the looks of him, Cookie would have hated to see his opponent. Cal McCabe was just about the toughest brawler the old man had ever seen in his lifetime. There weren't many who could best him in a fight, fair or otherwise.

"We have to find him."

Cookie heard the note of urgency in the boy's voice. "Why, son?"

Gilbert shrugged. "It's ... real important. In fact, it's a matter of life and death."

"Whose death?"

"Our teacher. Miss Jewel."

Cookie nearly bit off the stem of his pipe. Setting down the rifle, he pulled the pipe from his mouth and shook the burning tobacco into the fire, then dropped the pipe into his shirt pocket. Having used those precious moments to compose himself, he turned to the intruders.

"Now, boys, maybe you'd better start at the beginning, and tell me everything."

Daniel and Gilbert exchanged looks. Gilbert took a deep breath. And started talking.

When he was through, Cookie raced to the bunkhouse, shouting orders as he burst through the door.

Within minutes, a dozen wranglers were dressed and saddling their horses.

"One of you will ride to the north range and alert Cal to what's happened. Another will head to town and find the marshal. The rest of you will fan out in search of Miss Pearl," Cookie called.

"I'd like to ride with the wranglers," Gilbert said.

Cookie gave a vehement shake of his head. "Don't need no kids getting in the way. You'd best go on home now."

"But I know the hills around here. And I know how my pa thinks."

Cookie considered for a moment, then shook his head. "Nobody knows these hills better'n Cal Mc-Cabe. Besides, son," he added, trying to soften his words, "I don't think Cal will take kindly to an Ingram riding along, once he hears what happened."

As the boy turned away, Cookie dropped a hand on his shoulder. "I hope you understand, son. Miss Pearl is a very special lady." Especially to Cal McCabe, thought Cookie. Though the old man hadn't said a word to anyone else, he had his suspicions about Cal's black moods lately. He'd be willing to bet money that Pearl Jewel was the reason. If what he suspected was true, the last person Cal would want to see was the son of the man who'd just kidnapped the woman he loved.

For the next few minutes, the corral was alive with the sounds of men's voices, cursing and grumbling as they pulled themselves into saddles and took off with a thunder of hoofbeats.

As the dust settled, the old man began limping toward the ranch house, to break the news to the women. Miss Jade and Miss Ruby would be devastated. But at least they'd have each other. Miss Pearl, on the other hand, was being forced to face her terrors alone.

Shivering in the chill of the night, Gilbert watched the old man limp away, then glanced at his little brother. Seeing the way his eyes were closing, he urged him to climb onto his back.

"You can't carry me all that way," Daniel protested.

"It's the only way you'll make it. Come on," Gilbert commanded.

The little boy did as he was told, locking his thin arms around his brother's neck.

As Gilbert turned away from the bunkhouse, he gave a last hungry look toward the empty beds inside. The lingering odor of Cookie's stew, and the warmth of the lantern's glow, made an inviting picture.

The boy turned resolutely away and started out on foot toward the lonely, distant cabin. It would be midnight before the journey was complete. And though their only meal had been the food shared by Pearl at lunchtime, they would be too exhausted to do anything more than tumble into their blankets, hungry and cold. And desperately afraid.

Chapter Fourteen

Darkness had fallen, and still the horse and wagon continued across the hills. Pearl had long ago lost all sense of direction as Rollie Ingram followed a trail that twisted and turned, at times tumbling down rock-strewn gorges, other times splashing through swollen streams. But this much she knew—they had been climbing steadily for some time now.

At last the horse came to a halt. She could hear the scrape of Rollie's boots as he made his way to the back of the wagon. But instead of helping her out, he fumbled around in the darkness until he located a lantern.

He struck the match and held it to the wick, then walked some distance away. The sound of his footsteps grew faint, then gradually grew louder as he returned.

He began removing the provisions from the back of the wagon—some filthy blankets, an empty bucket, several half-filled sacks, an armload of rifles.

Once more he disappeared, then reappeared, this time to cut the ropes binding her ankles before hauling her roughly to her feet.

"Well, now, teacher, let's see how you like your new classroom," he drawled as he shoved her ahead of him.

She blinked in the light of the lantern. They appeared to be in a large cavern, tall enough for both man and horse to stand comfortably. Here and there were rocky outcroppings, and the sounds of creatures slithering away from the light.

With her hands still bound, she glanced around nervously.

Seeing the fear in her eyes, Rollie taunted her. "There's a big black she-bear makes her home in the back of the cave. But if yer nice and quiet, she'll probably leave you alone." Enjoying her terrified reaction, he gave a negligent shrug of his shoulders. "And if she should decide to have you for lunch, it'll be no loss. I just need you around long enough to lure McCabe up here. After that, you're no good to me. As soon as I've finished with him, you'll be dead anyway, so I don't care how you meet your death."

He lifted the lantern high and threw back his head in a cackle of shrill laughter. She had a sudden impression of his cruel face in the blaze of light. His yellow teeth glinted in a wide, dangerous smile. His eyes gleamed like the very devil's.

"Had you going there, didn't I, teacher? Bet you got all weak in the knees, just thinkin' about that old bear." He ambled toward the mouth of the cave, and for a moment, Pearl was terrified that he was going to leave her all alone in the darkness.

He came back leading the horse and wagon, then set the lantern on a shelf of rock and hung a hide at the mouth of the cave to prevent the light being seen by passing riders.

That done, he returned to her side and tossed down a dirty blanket, commanding tersely, "Sit."

"Why?" she demanded.

Her haughty tone and manner caused him to bristle. "Woman, around here, I'm the teacher and you're the pupil. I make the rules. And you follow them without question. Now sit."

She did as she was told, and was forced to endure in helpless rage as he bound her ankles. When he was assured that she couldn't escape, he wrapped the second blanket around himself and lay down on the hard ground.

"What are you doing?"

"Goin' to sleep, teacher. You'd better do the same. If my plan works, tomorrow should prove to be a long and interestin' day."

Within minutes, the cave was filled with the sound of his snoring.

Despite her weariness, Pearl kept a silent, watchful vigil. How could she sleep, knowing what this monster intended to do? She struggled to hold back the wave of helplessness threatening to swamp her. It was bad enough that she was hobbled like a calf at branding. But being trapped in this primitive place had magnified all her fears about Texas, until they began nibbling away at her very sanity. She imagined evil, slimy creatures and feral animals, fangs bared, lying in wait for her to let down her guard.

Oh, Daddy, she thought, with a trace of desperation, *tell me how to survive. At least long enough to warn Cal of the dangers.*

Almost at once, a feeling of calm began to take hold of her frayed nerves. For the moment, Rollie Ingram was no threat. He was sleeping as peacefully, and as noisily, as his fictional bear. She was as yet unharmed. And Cal McCabe was no fool. When he discovered what Rollie had done, he would come, not only armed, but probably with his wranglers and half the town in tow.

That thought soothed her fears, and her eyes began to close. Determined to fight sleep, she forced her lids to open. And prayed that the oil in the lantern would last until morning light.

Cal reined in his mount on a ridge overlooking the herd. Taking a pouch of tobacco from his pocket, he rolled a cigarette and held a match to the tip. He filled his lungs, then blew out a cloud of smoke.

A sliver of moon and a million glittering stars hung in the midnight sky. It was a scene that always soothed him. And yet tonight he had to fight a feeling of restlessness.

He'd volunteered to ride herd tonight, so that the others could sleep. He had a need to be busy; to keep from dwelling on all the thoughts that were swirling around in his mind.

It wasn't just Rollie Ingram, though he'd been agitated since their fight. It was something else. Something vague and intangible that tugged at the corners of his mind.

Pearl. It was always Pearl who crowded his thoughts. From the first day he saw her, he'd had to fight the impossible attraction. And now he was beginning to feel things he had no right to feel about Onyx Jewel's daughter. Onyx had trusted him to look out for the ranch and everything on it. That certainly included the prim and proper Pearl. But the things Cal had been thinking lately were about as far from proper as one could get.

He knew that marriage was out of the question. There was no way he'd ask a lady like Pearl to be saddled with a cowboy pledged to a life in this harsh land. From the looks of her, Pearl wouldn't last a year in Texas. And when she'd had enough of this life, she deserved to be free to walk away, with no regrets.

Still, at the thought of Pearl, he felt as agitated as a stallion downwind of a mare in season. Damned if he didn't want her more than he'd ever wanted anyone or anything. And that was the hell of it. He was a man who'd become accustomed to getting everything he'd ever wanted. Onyx had taught him that. And now he'd gone and lost his heart to the one thing he could never have.

With an angry oath, he filled his lungs one last time before tossing the butt aside.

Suddenly his head came up sharply at the sound of a horse, approaching at a run.

Making out the silhouette of one of his top wranglers, he was about to lecture him on the danger of pushing his horse to the limit. But before he could say a word, the wrangler called out, "Trouble, Cal. Cookie told me to hightail it out here. Rollie Ingram's setting a trap for you, as revenge for the beating you gave him.''

''Yeah?''

Cal started to smile, but the smile faded when the wrangler continued, ''To make sure you'll agree to fight, he's kidnapped Miss Pearl.''

Marshal Quent Regan stepped off the porch of Doc Prentice's infirmary and headed toward the jail. It had been a fairly quiet night, since there were few cowboys in town. Just one shooting, and it hadn't been over a woman or a card game, but rather over whose horse was fastest. Liquor had a way of doing that to normally peaceable ranchers. Doc had removed the bullet, and his patient was more concerned about how to face his wife after such foolishness than he was about the pain he'd endured.

Quent studied the darkened buildings as he ambled through the silent town. He'd grown accustomed to working through the night and going to bed when most men were just starting their chores.

He turned at the sound of a galloping horse. At this time of night, it always signaled trouble.

''Marshal.'' Horse and rider pulled up short beside him, spewing dust. ''Rollie Ingram's gone crazy. Stole Miss Pearl Jewel away from her schoolhouse.''

''That no-good Ingram again.'' Quent's face turned grim. ''Where's he taken her?''

''Up into the hills beyond the Jewel ranch. Wants to force Cal McCabe into a gunfight. Cookie sent the wranglers out to notify Cal and start a search.''

"Then I won't be needing a posse." The marshal was already heading toward his office. "I'll get my gear and join you as soon as I wake my deputy."

It was a good bet that Deputy Arlo Spitz's wife would have the news all over town before the chickens were up.

And it was a better bet, Quent thought, that Cal McCabe wouldn't rest until Rollie Ingram was dead. He only hoped Cal was in time to shoot him before he had a chance to hurt that fine lady, Miss Pearl.

In the thin, pale light of dawn, Cal knelt on the rocky ground and peered at the wagon tracks. Though it had cost him considerable time, he'd returned to the schoolhouse, in order to pick up Rollie's trail.

Now, with the help of the morning light, he could begin his quest. With a furious oath, he pulled himself into the saddle and began to follow the tracks. But as he followed them into the hills, he was puzzled. The horse and wagon had stopped abruptly. There were footprints. Small, feminine footprints. Had Pearl escaped? He leaped from the saddle and followed on foot. Larger prints, made by a man's boots. Running. And here . . . He knelt. A scuffle. God in heaven. A delicate little lady like Pearl had fought that brute. He felt the bile of fury rise up to choke him. When he caught up with Rollie Ingram, he would make him pay dearly. And if he had harmed Pearl in any way, the man would pay with his life.

He mounted and took off at a run. All his thoughts were focused on Pearl. And the half-forgotten words of his childhood prayers fell from his lips.

* * *

Pearl's head bobbed, waking her from a fitful doze. For one brief moment she felt disoriented. Then she remembered where she was. Fear sliced, cold and sharp, through her veins. How could she have given in to sleep? All through the night she had pulled and tugged on the ropes, until her wrists and ankles were raw and bloody. But her feeble efforts had been to no avail. She was still bound. Bound and helpless.

Assured that Rollie Ingram was still sleeping, she glanced toward the covered entrance to the cave. A thin ribbon of morning light pierced the gloom. So soon, she thought with a feeling of dread. The night had flown by so soon.

"Well now…" Rollie yawned, stretched, and sat up. "Ain't this cozy? Just you and me, teacher." He crossed the space that separated them and squatted down in front of her. "Still feelin' high and mighty?" He cackled at his own joke. "Just look at you. Why, your pretty gown is all soiled, and your face is dirty. And I do believe that's blood on your wrists." He grabbed at her, twisting her bound arms painfully. "Been workin' on those ropes, I see. Well, it won't do you any good. You're not gettin' free. Not till I do what I came here to do." His eyes glittered with madness. "First I'm going to shoot Cal McCabe. And I hope I don't kill him with the first shot, 'cause I don't want him dead right away."

"What do you mean?" she asked in horror.

"Didn't I tell you?" He laughed again. "I do want McCabe dead. But first I want him to suffer." He took hold of her hair and yanked her head back so hard, tears sprang to her eyes. That only made him laugh harder. "See, I figure the best way to do that is to force him to watch while I have a little fun with his lady. And then, when I'm done, why, McCabe can die a nice slow death. One bullet at a time. And afterward, when I'm tired of you, you can die, too. But if you ask real nice, I'll make it fast." He ran a finger from her throat to her heart, all the while enjoying the look of revulsion that crossed her face. "With one bullet, right here."

He was pleased to see the way she cringed at his touch. "One of them innocent, untouched females, huh? That makes it even better."

He shuffled to his feet and pulled some food and a flask from one of the sacks on the floor of the cave. He ate quickly, then washed it down with whiskey.

"I'd offer you some," he said with a satisfied grin, "but there's no need to waste good food on someone who hasn't long to live. Besides, I've got work to do. By the time McCabe gets here, I'll have a whole army of guns ready for him."

Pearl listened to the sound of his footsteps as he moved around outside. The sounds grew louder, until they seemed to come from directly above. Glancing up, she saw a rope snake down from a hole in the roof of the cave. A few minutes later, Rollie slid down the rope.

"Got a little surprise for your hero," he said with a grin.

He picked up several rifles, blew out the sputtering lantern and strolled from the cave.

For a moment, Pearl had a glimpse of the morning sunlight glinting off rocky peaks. Then the hide was dropped back into place. And she was left in darkness, except for the thin stream of light from the top of the cave.

Cal urged his horse into the swollen waters of Poison Creek. On the opposite bank, he knelt and studied the marks of the wagon before pulling himself back into the saddle.

The morning sunshine had given way to dark, rolling clouds. The air tasted of rain. He shivered inside his duster and worried about Pearl. How was she handling the cold? The fear? The thought of her at the mercy of Rollie Ingram tore at him, causing him to whip his mount into a run.

He'd give Ingram credit, he thought as he urged his horse up the steep rocky side of the mountain. He'd covered his tracks well enough that the average wrangler wouldn't be able to follow. But Ingram had left just enough signs of his passing to guarantee that someone with Cal's reputation for tracking wouldn't miss them. That way, he would have Cal to himself, without the backup of the wranglers who had fanned out in either direction.

"Suits me just fine," Cal muttered aloud.

So he and Rollie both knew this wasteland. And both of them knew something about fighting and survival. But he had one thing even Rollie didn't have. A fierce determination to save the woman he loved.

Love. It hit him with the force of a blow. He loved Pearl more than life itself. If he was too late, if she died, his own life wouldn't be worth a thing.

Why had it taken the work of a madman to show him the truth?

And what if he had come to the realization too late?

He swore, loudly, savagely, as he guided his mount ever higher into the mountain wilderness.

Chapter Fifteen

Cal was grateful for the thunder rumbling off in the distance. It masked the sound of his horse's hoofbeats.

The path he was following had been climbing steadily for some time now. Though it was narrow, it was wide enough for a horse and cart. He couldn't make out any tracks, but he was certain Rollie had come this way.

Suddenly he reined in his mount and listened. Had there been a cry? Or had it just been the sound of the wind? The storm was definitely moving closer, raising a din. But he was a man who had always trusted his instincts. And right now, he could feel a prickling along his scalp. Despite the rising wind and the rumble of thunder, that had been Pearl's voice, cut off in midcry. He was certain of it.

The thought of Rollie Ingram's cruel hands touching her, hurting her, had sweat trickling between his shoulder blades. With no further thought to his safety, he slid from the saddle. Cradling his rifle, he crept forward, through the gathering darkness. Aware that Rollie planned an ambush, he swung his gaze from side to side, searching for anything suspicious. All he could see was what appeared to be a sheer wall of rock on either side of a narrow path. In a break in the rock was a drop-off that plummeted hundreds of feet to a granite ledge below. There seemed to be no place for a man to hide. Let alone a woman, a horse and a cart. Unless...

He felt a chill along his spine. Of course. These mountains held dozens of caves. He peered through the blackness to find an opening, but in the darkness, he saw only shifting shadows.

The first shot rang out from his left, missing him by inches. He turned and fired instinctively, but a second shot, from the opposite direction, had him dropping to the ground.

He heard a cackling laugh that could only be Rollie Ingram's. "Got me an army, McCabe. Think you can fight an army?"

Instead of a reply, Cal fired in the direction of the voice.

"That was close. But you can't fight us all, McCabe." A second later, another shot rang out, from a third location, sending dirt flying directly beside Cal.

How many men did Rollie have in his employ? And how had he managed to entice anyone to work for him? How could a man like Rollie Ingram pay gunfighters?

"Drop your weapon, McCabe." Rollie's voice carried across the hills. "Or I'll have my army cut you to pieces."

Cal realized that, just as the bullets had come from different directions, so had Rollie's voice. He came to a sudden conclusion. The only army Rollie had was himself. And a clever arrangement of rifles.

Despite the danger, Cal stood. "Go to hell, Ingram," he shouted as he fired in a circle, sending bullets spraying in several different directions.

He heard Rollie's savage oaths as he was forced to dodge the gunfire.

After long moments of unexpected silence, the hide was lifted, revealing the entrance to the cave.

"Looking for us?"

Cal spun around. Inside the cave, in the glow of a lantern, he could make out the image of Pearl, bound and gagged. Beside her was Rollie, holding a pistol to her temple. Behind them, a rope twisted and turned, and Cal realized just how Rollie had managed to slip out of the way of his bullets.

"Drop the rifle," Rollie commanded. "If you want the woman to live."

Cal did as he was told, tossing aside his weapon.

"You don't need to hurt her, Rollie." Cal's voice was pure ice. "This fight is between you and me."

"So it is," Rollie shouted. "But it's not a fight. We had our little fight, and you won. This is a game. A game of chance, McCabe. And this time, I intend to win. See, I've learned to never play unless I can stack the deck in my favor. Now—" he motioned with his pistol "—step into my saloon. We're going to have us some fun."

Cal took several steps forward, without ever taking his eyes off Pearl. What he saw caused a terrible pain around his heart.

Her hair had pulled loose from its neat knot, and it hung in tangles around a pale face. Her gown was dirty and bloodstained, and the sight of the blood had his jaw clenching. God in heaven, if Rollie hurt her...

"That's close enough!" Rollie shouted. "Now raise those hands high!"

When Cal lifted his arms, a shot rang out. He gasped, then muttered a savage oath. His right arm dropped limply to his side, blood spurting from a gunshot wound to his shoulder. The staggering pain brought him to his knees, where he grasped the wounded arm in a vain attempt to stem the flow of blood.

"That's my first ace in the hole. That'll prevent you from pulling a hidden gun or knife on me, McCabe." Rollie was shouting with glee. "See, I know that's your gun hand."

Pearl's gag prevented her from crying out. But she whimpered at the horrible sight of Cal's pain, and began to sink to her knees.

Rollie hauled her roughly to her feet. "Uh-uh, little lady. You ain't fallin'. You're going to stand straight and tall, so our hero can see you real good. And if you don't, I'll have to shoot him again. Understand?"

She blinked the tears from her eyes and nodded, then forced her trembling legs to hold her upright.

"That's real good." He glanced over at Cal with a sly smile. "See how quick our teacher is learnin'? And that's just the beginnin'. I'm goin' to teach her things she never dreamed of. And you know the best part of all?" He gave a shrill laugh and stepped closer, until he was standing directly over Cal. "The best part is knowin' you'll be watchin'. And can't do one thing about it."

He raised his gun again and took aim at Cal's leg. "Just so's you don't think about runnin'."

He fired at point-blank range. The bullet slammed into Cal's thigh with such force it sent him backward, where he lay in a widening pool of blood.

Rollie stepped close and caught Cal by the hair, forcing his head up. "Don't you go fainting on me, hero. You stay awake for the entertainment I got planned."

Cal's glazed eyes focused on the man standing over him, and he managed to say through clenched teeth, "I'll stay...awake. And you'd better do...same. Because I'm going...kill you, Ingram."

"Looks like I'll be the only one doin' any killin' today." Smug with success, Rollie swaggered across the cave and said, "Now for the best part. The teacher and me are going to have some fun. And she knows that if she fights me even a little, I'll be forced to shoot you again. Isn't that right, Miss High-and-Mighty Jewel?"

Pearl gave the slightest nod of her head.

Rollie lifted a knife to the gag, cutting it away. "I said, isn't that right?"

"Yes." Though her lips trembled, and her throat was clogged with fear, she managed to speak.

"I think I prefer the sound of 'yes, sir' better." He prodded her with his pistol.

"Yes, sir." She nearly choked on the words.

"Good. That's very good, teacher." He cut the ropes at her wrists and ankles, and teasingly lifted her skirt to her knees. "Look at this, McCabe. Take a good look. I'm going to let you watch it all."

He straightened and ran a finger along the high, modest collar of her gown. "I always wondered what that pretty white skin would look like. You keep it covered up so much, it teases a man's mind."

He saw the look of revulsion on her face and laughed. Without a word, he caught both sides of the gown and tore it to the waist, revealing an elegantly embroidered chemise beneath. "Now I'm about to uncover all those secrets you've been hidin', teacher."

With her gown torn away, hanging only by the cuffs at her wrists, Pearl lowered her head and folded her hands over her breasts.

Across the cave, Cal struggled, through layers of pain, to sit up. He had to get to her, to save her from this brute. The thought of her pain and humiliation was greater than any gunshot. As he eased himself up against the wall of the cave, the effort cost him dearly, and he closed his eyes a moment, fighting to remain conscious.

"Untie those pretty ribbons!" Rollie bellowed.

When Pearl hesitated, he turned and pointed the pistol at Cal. "I'll give you to the count of three, teacher. And then I start shooting our hero again."

"Don't shoot him again. I'll do anything you want." Tears streamed down her cheeks as Pearl lifted trembling hands to the ribbons of her chemise.

"That's better." With a chuckle, Rollie turned back to watch.

As soon as he turned away from Cal, a gunshot rang out, reverberating inside the cave. The smile died on

Rollie's lips as something hot and sharp pierced his back. For a moment, he seemed merely shocked. Then, as the pain of the bullet sank in, his mouth contorted in a snarl of rage.

He turned. And saw the gun in Cal's hand.

"A good gunman always carries a spare in his boot," Cal managed to say between clenched teeth. "And you were wrong about the gun hand. I learned to shoot with either hand when I was just a boy." His voice took on a dangerous edge. "I had a good teacher, Rollie. He was a monster, just like you."

"Now you've done it, McCabe. I'm going to have to kill you." Feeling sick to his stomach, Rollie closed his eyes for a moment against the pain, and leaned heavily against a rock. When he opened them, and lifted his own gun to take aim, he discovered that the corner of the cave where Cal had been lying was now empty.

With a look of panic, Rollie staggered to the entrance of the cave.

Outside, thunder rolled directly overhead, signaling the beginning of a ferocious storm. Rain began to fall on the mountain, making the rocks slippery.

Seeing a trail of blood, Rollie lumbered into the night, determined not to be denied his chance at revenge.

"Go ahead!" he shouted into the wind and rain. "Crawl away like a coward! But I'll find you, McCabe. And when I do, I swear this time I'll kill you."

Lightning flashed as Pearl ran, crying, to the mouth of the cave. In her hand was Cal's discarded rifle.

Though she didn't know how to fire it, she clung fiercely to it.

In that instant, Rollie caught sight of Cal, leaning heavily against a rock, struggling to pull himself into a standing position. An evil smile curled Rollie's lips. He lifted his gun and took aim.

"No! No!" With a strangled cry, Pearl ran at him, wielding the rifle like a club.

He fired, but the shot went wild as he lifted his hands to stave off her attack. In that instant, a gunshot rang out, echoing and reechoing across the mountains.

Pearl froze. Rollie stiffened, and his hands shot out, clutching wildly at her torn gown. Then, slowly, his hands opened. He tumbled backward, disappearing over the edge of the ravine. Without even waiting to see what had happened to him, Pearl raced to Cal's side. Just as she reached him, he fell to the ground in a bloody heap, holding a hand to a fresh wound in his chest.

A sob was torn from her lips, and she dropped to her knees beside him.

"Cal. Oh, sweet heaven, Cal. Please don't die. Please. You mustn't. I love you so. I . . ."

He made no reply. The storm struck in all its fury, filling the night with a howling rage. Oblivious of the stinging rain drenching him, Cal lay as still as death.

Pearl's tears mingled with the rain as she struggled with what appeared to be an impossible task—getting the unconscious form of Cal out of the storm and into the shelter of the cave.

Finally she tore the hide from the entrance. With great effort, she managed to roll Cal onto it. Using the ropes that had once bound her, she attached it to his horse's stirrups. With murmured words of encouragement she urged the horse into a slow walk, dragging Cal's lifeless form behind. Once they were safely inside the cave, she rolled Cal onto a pile of dry blankets.

Despite the blankets, the shock of his injuries had him shivering violently.

Gathering twigs and wood scattered around the inside of the cavern, she used the flame of the lantern to build a fire. Then she knelt beside Cal to probe his wounds.

Using Rollie's knife, she cut away Cal's blood-soaked clothes. The bullet to his thigh, fired at point-blank range, had gone right through his flesh, leaving a gaping wound that was bleeding profusely. She tore her petticoats and made a tourniquet to stem the flow of blood. She whispered a word of thanks for Rollie's ample supply of whiskey as she poured a liberal amount on the wound, then bound it securely.

She turned her attention to his other wounds. He had taken a bullet to the chest and another to his shoulder. Both bullets were lodged somewhere deep in muscle and sinew, and the thought of removing them had her feeling faint.

"Not now," she told herself sternly. If ever she had needed courage, this was the time. Though she was sickened by the thought of the pain she was about to inflict, she must remember that it was necessary to begin the healing process. Cal had risked his life for her. The least she could do was swallow her fears and do all that was necessary to pull him through this terrible time. He would die from the loss of blood unless she saw to his needs immediately.

She lifted Rollie's knife and held the blade to the flame until the steel gleamed red-hot. Then she touched the blade to Cal's flesh and began to probe.

He moaned—a low, terrible sound that had her eyes going wide with fright. Biting down on her fear, she probed deeper. And felt the scrape of metal. With quick, nervous movements, she slipped the blade below the bullet and lifted. As soon as it was removed, she poured a stream of whiskey on the raw, bleeding flesh.

Cal hissed in pain, and his left arm swung out convulsively, catching Pearl a bruising blow. With a little cry, she caught his arm before he could swing again, and held it by his side. Even now, despite the seriousness of his wounds, he displayed incredible strength, and she was forced to use all her energy to subdue him. Within moments, his arm went limp, and she realized that he was once again unconscious. Working feverishly, she managed to bind his chest, then repeated the process for the wound in his shoulder. Then she wrapped him in blankets.

Though she was exhausted from her efforts, she found the strength to flee the cave. Dropping down beside a boulder, she retched until the fear and nausea abated. Then, drained, she lifted her face to the pouring rain, allowing the icy sting to revive her.

Coward, she thought, berating herself. All her life it had been the same. She was a useless, gutless coward.

She straightened and then, head bent against the storm, began gathering as much wood as she could find. It would be necessary to keep the fire going all through the night. For she had felt Cal's hands. They were as cold as ice.

All the while she worked, one thought kept going through her mind. Somewhere out in this night could be a madman, determined to kill them both. For the truth was, though she had seen Rollie Ingram fall, she hadn't seen him die. And until she had the chance to glimpse his dead body, she could not let down her guard.

That was just one more fear she would have to deal with.

Chapter Sixteen

Wind howled across the mountaintop and swirled through the opening of the cavern, sending sparks from the fire dancing toward the roof of the cave.

At once, Pearl's head came up. She had been kneeling beside Cal for so long, she had actually begun to doze.

His mere presence brought her comfort. Though she feared for his safety, and her own, she felt stronger just knowing Cal was with her.

She shivered in her thin gown and hurried across the cave to cover the entrance with the hide. She was reluctant to shield their fire from view, since she had hoped to use it as a signal to anyone who might be searching for them. But the cold wind gave her no choice. Besides, she reasoned, the storm had probably forced everyone to seek shelter. If the marshal and the wranglers were nearby, they couldn't see anything through the drenching downpour. They would have to wait until the storm passed.

She added another log to the fire and began rummaging through Cal's saddlebags. It was plain that a cowboy carried with him everything necessary for survival along the trail. There was a packet of dried meat, matches and a flint for fire, as well as a hunting knife. In his bedroll was a change of clothes, along with a skillet and pot and some small pouches containing tobacco, bullets and a mixture of coffee and chicory.

Next she went through the supplies that Rollie Ingram had brought. It was obvious that he'd planned on a prolonged siege. There were half-filled sacks of flour and sugar, as well as a generous supply of whiskey, matches and tobacco.

She quickly pulled on Cal's spare shirt and pants, leaving her wet, blood-soaked gown in a heap. Sitting cross-legged beside the fire, she tied up her damp hair and nibbled some hardtack, her first food since her capture.

Cal moaned in his sleep. At once, she knelt beside him. Touching a hand to his face, she felt a jolt of alarm. Sweet heaven. He was as cold as ice. She began to massage his hands, his arms, his shoulders. The physical act of touching him, of caring for his needs, brought her a measure of comfort. But, though she rubbed his flesh until she ached from exhaustion, his skin was still cold to the touch.

She pulled the covers over him and watched the uneven rise and fall of his chest as she listened to his labored breathing.

Tears stung her eyes as she thought about the pain he'd been forced to endure. How could any human inflict such pain on another? What deep well of courage did Cal possess, that he could withstand such torture? And all for her sake. That thought brought no solace, only guilt.

A shudder rippled through him. And then another. Shock. She felt a moment of panic, then took firm control of her emotions. This was no time to be frightened. This courageous man had risked his life for her. She could do no less.

She lifted the blankets and climbed in beside him, determined to warm him with her own body. Drawing her arms around his shoulders, she cradled his head against her breast and murmured words meant to assure herself as much as Cal.

"Hold on. Please hold on, Cal. Don't leave me now. We've come so far together. Just hold on a little longer. In the morning, when the storm has passed, the wranglers will be here to take us home. Home. Think of it. Oh, Cal, hold on. Just a little longer. Please."

Those words became a litany, as the storm continued to savage the countryside. Inside the cave, another sort of storm raged. But through it all, Pearl continued to hold tightly to the man in her arms. And pleaded with heaven to bring them safely through the night.

Pearl awoke to a strange, muted silence. Though the wind still gusted occasionally, sending a sound like the spray of sand against the outer wall of the cave, the thunder and lightning seemed to have dissipated. The wind had stopped howling, and the rain, as well. But there were no familiar morning sounds. No birds chirping. No light footfalls of deer, no pounding of mustangs' hooves racing along the trail.

Though the embers of the fire still glowed, the temperature in the cave had dropped considerably. She sat up, shoving her hair from her eyes. In the chill of the morning, she could see her breath.

Slipping from the covers, she tossed another log on the fire. Then she strode to the mouth of the cave and pushed aside the covering. She blinked in surprise. Snow was falling so hard it was impossible to see beyond a few feet. To her dismay, the ground was already covered with a fresh snowfall. In places, the mounds had drifted to the height of a boulder.

Snow? In April?

She brought a hand to her mouth to cover her gasp of alarm. Hadn't Carmelita warned her that springtime in Texas was like nowhere else? At some other time, the sight of all that pristine whiteness would have taken her breath away. But now, her only thought was of Cal. How would she ever be able to get him to safety now? Worse, how could any of the wranglers get through this blizzard to continue the search for them?

Trapped.

She felt her heart plummet, and with it, the hopes that had sustained her throughout the long night. There would be no rescue. At least until the storm ended and the snow melted. If they were to survive, it would have to be up to her.

She swallowed back her fear. Courage, she told herself. This time, she would have only herself to depend upon. And she would be up to the task, she vowed. For Cal had already given enough. She would do all in her power to see that he wasn't required to give his life, as well.

During the day, the temperature continued to drop. The wind picked up, sending occasional gusts of snow spraying against the outer walls of the cave. Though Pearl pressed a wet cloth to Cal's lips and begged him to drink, he gave no response. He remained unconscious. And the chills that had gripped him earlier seemed even more pronounced.

Pearl was forced to don Cal's boots and duster in order to search the snowdrifts for fallen logs. It was imperative that she keep the fire going day and night.

Once the cave was warm and snug, and she had set aside a supply of logs, she added his duster to the pile of blankets that covered Cal's body. Then, desperate to warm him, she settled in beside him and drew him once more into her arms.

Day and night blurred together as she held him close and struggled to hold her fears at bay.

Pearl stirred. She had been dreaming of a fire. A raging forest fire that was engulfing everything in its path. With her eyes closed, she could feel the heat of the fire. Suddenly her lids snapped open. She touched a hand to Cal's forehead. She gave a gasp of alarm. He was burning with fever. His skin was as hot as a flame.

She slipped from the covers and tore a strip from her discarded petticoat. Dipping it into the snow, she began to bathe his fevered flesh.

As she worked, her lips moved in a silent prayer. "Please, Cal," she whispered, "You've been so strong. Don't give up now. Fight this. Live, Cal. Please fight to live."

She pressed the cold cloth over his face, his neck and chest, the corded muscles of his arms and shoulders. As she did, she examined his wounds, changing the dressings and liberally washing them with whiskey to see that they didn't fester.

That done, she lay down beside him once more and wrapped her arms around his waist, clinging to him as if to life itself, and willing him to heal.

When Pearl awoke again, it appeared to be late afternoon. A glimpse outside confirmed her worst fears. It was still snowing. In places, the drifts were taller than a horse.

She paced back and forth, wondering how long they could survive in this place. If Cal was well and strong, she realized, there would be no need to worry. But their survival depended entirely on her. And with each new surprise, she felt more and more inadequate.

After tossing another log on the fire, she knelt beside Cal and began to sponge his fevered body. But as she began to remove the dressings that covered his chest, his hands closed over her wrists. She glanced at his eyes. They were still closed. But a low moan of protest issued from his lips, and he held her in a death grip as he muttered unintelligible words of torment.

She struggled, but that only caused him to tighten his grasp. With an oath, he dragged her against his chest.

"Cal." She struggled to keep the fear from her voice. "Please, Cal, you're hurting me."

At the sound of her voice, his struggles ceased. At once, his fingers loosened their grip. She pulled free and staggered to her feet, drawing deep drafts of air into her lungs. Even in his state of unconsciousness, he was strong enough to snap her bones as though they were twigs. But he had heard her. Though he remained locked inside his mind, he had responded, no matter how feebly.

She rubbed the feeling back into her bruised wrists, then knelt and began once more to change Cal's dressings. But this time she was prepared to do battle if necessary.

As she worked, she crooned to him in a low voice, hoping to wake him from the deep sleep that held him in its grip. But, though she whispered words meant to reassure him, he remained in that other world. Fighting demons that only he could see.

Cal lay very still, trying to clear his jumbled thoughts. He could recall Rollie Ingram's voice as he'd shouted into the storm-filled night, and the sight of Rollie pointing his pistol.

And then another vision intruded. Pearl, completely oblivious of her own safety, attacking Rollie with an upraised rifle. Little fool. He clenched his teeth together so hard they ached. Hadn't she known Rollie couldn't miss at such close range? He began to sweat as he remembered squeezing off a frantic shot, the sound echoing across the hills. Dear God. Had he been in time? Or had Rollie succeeded in taking her life?

He wondered how he would manage to go on living if she was gone. If his life had been empty before, it would now become meaningless. Yet he clung to a glimmer of hope. It seemed that he had heard her sweet voice, calling from a great distance. But that could have been his mind, playing a cruel trick.

He tried to stir, and felt a heaviness against his chest. At once, his eyes snapped open, and he found himself staring at the most wonderful sight he'd ever beheld.

Pearl lay curled up beside him, one arm thrown protectively across his chest. But this was a Pearl he'd never seen before.

Her golden hair was unbound, falling seductively over one eye, then spilling across his naked chest. Gone was the spotless gown. In its place were his rough shirt and a pair of his pants, tucked into boots that were far too large for her feet.

He watched the steady rise and fall of her chest, and experienced a rare sense of peace. She was alive. And apparently unharmed. He tried to touch a finger to her cheek, and was surprised to feel a stab of hot, burning pain all the way up his arm and across his shoulder.

He stared in wonder at the dressings and then, slowly, gradually, began to remember. But, though he could recall the wounds to his shoulder and thigh, he had no recollection of a wound to the chest.

He glanced around the cave, trying to sew together a patchwork of memories. Rollie was nowhere to be seen. Did that mean he was dead? Or had he merely escaped? And Marshal Quent Regan and the wranglers. Were they on their way? Or had they somehow become lost? He gave a long, deep sigh. There were too many missing pieces.

He wondered about the unusual silence. Except for the hiss and snap of a log on the fire, and the occasional gust of wind outside, there were none of the usual, familiar sounds.

He decided that it would all come back to him later. Right now, it was enough to know that Pearl was unharmed, and here with him. As long as she was safe, he would relax his guard.

Within minutes, he was fast asleep.

Pearl awoke abruptly. Had she merely dreamed it, or had Cal stirred?

She got to her knees and pressed a hand to his forehead. His flesh was cool to the touch.

Swallowing the lump in her throat, she closed her eyes and whispered a prayer of thanks. When she opened her eyes again, she found Cal staring back at her.

"Oh, thank God," she breathed. "I've been so afraid for you."

"For me?" He was surprised at how difficult it was to speak. His throat felt as though it had been tangled in barbed wire. "Why would you be afraid for me?"

"Because you were shot. And I thought . . ."

He touched a finger to her cheek. "Tears? For me, Pearl?"

She blinked and struggled to stem the flow. But the tears fell faster. "I couldn't bear to see you hurt. And when Rollie shot you in the chest—"

He pressed a hand over her lips to still her words. "When did that happen?"

"When he followed you outside into the storm. Afterward, I tried to stop him, but it was too late. He'd already fired his gun."

Cal nodded. "I remember now. He would have killed me if you hadn't attacked him with my rifle."

She shook her head, and the tears fell faster now, as she was reminded once again of her inadequacy. "I didn't save you, Cal. You saved yourself, by firing at Rollie. I don't even know if he's dead or wounded. As soon as he toppled over the ravine, I hurried to see if you were still alive."

It was plain that these few moments of exertion had cost him. He closed his eyes weakly. "And am I? Still alive?"

"Oh, Cal . . ." She pressed her cheek to his.

He tasted the salt of her tears, and thought it the sweetest flavor in the world. It was his last conscious thought before he drifted back to sleep.

Chapter Seventeen

Pearl lifted her head and shivered in the chill of the cave. The only light came from the glow of embers.

Slipping from the warmth of the covers, she hurriedly tossed a log on the fire and waited until flames began to lick along the dry bark. Then she turned and made her way to the mouth of the cave. Lifting a corner of the hide, she peered into the midnight blackness. The swirl of snowflakes kissed her cheeks. At once she drew back and returned to the bed she shared with Cal.

As she slipped in beside him, she touched a hand to his forehead. Feeling his cool flesh, she felt a welling of gratitude.

"Is that a smile?" The sound of his rough voice startled her. He was watching her in the glow of the fire.

"Oh, Cal. I'm just so relieved that your fever has passed. You really had me frightened. I've never removed a bullet before, and I was afraid . . ."

He shifted to face her, though the movement had him hissing with pain. "Did you say you removed a bullet?'' He probed the dressings at his shoulder and chest.

"Two of them, in fact. I had no choice. I'm sorry...."

"Sorry?" He threw back his head and laughed, but the laughter was cut short by a stab of pain. "You're sorry you removed the bullets and saved my life?"

"Of course not." She stiffened and pulled away. "I'm just sorry I had to cause you such pain."

He knew her well enough by now to realize that her haughty words were a cover for nerves. His own tone softened, and he laid a hand over hers until she relaxed once more. "You didn't cause my pain, Pearl. Rollie's bullets did that. But you did save my life."

She felt her pulse begin to accelerate. A strange heat began to radiate through her veins. If it were possible, she thought, she would be content to lie here, just like this, beside the man she loved, with his hand on hers, for the rest of her life.

The man she loved. A long, deep sigh rose up from deep inside her. Gathering her courage, she lifted her other palm and closed it over Cal's, sandwiching his hand between both of hers.

"I suppose you're wondering why I'm sleeping here beside you, Cal." She licked her lips, which had suddenly gone dry, and forced herself to continue. "You needed all the blankets, because you were in shock, and trembling violently. But when that wasn't enough, I had to warm you with my body, as well. And then..." She shrugged and squeezed his hand. "It just seemed the most natural thing in the world to continue to lie here beside you." She turned her head. "I hope you don't think me too bold."

When he made no reply, she felt her heart catch in her throat. Dear heaven. He must be scandalized by her behavior.

"I'm sorry." She sat up, shoving the hair from her eyes. "If you'll feel better, I'll . . ." The words died in her throat.

His eyes were closed; his breathing was slow and steady. He had drifted back to sleep.

With heat staining her cheeks, she rolled to her side, grateful that she had been spared this humiliation. But it brought her no relief. For she was forced to face another dilemma. Now that he was beginning to heal, and she no longer had to fear for his life, she would have to deal with a new, and very different, fear. Cal was no longer a patient to be tended. Now that the crisis had passed, he was a man. A strong, virile, flesh-and-blood man. A man whose mere presence had her thinking about things that were highly improper. And wishing for things far beyond her reach.

Courage, she warned herself as she began to slip into that twilight state between sleep and dreams. So far, her courage had not failed her. She had no doubt it would see her through the next trial, as well.

Cal awoke to the sounds of muffled footsteps and something heavy being dragged across the floor of the cave. Still clinging to the dregs of sleep, he started to reach for his gun and found, to his amazement, that even that simple movement had him clenching his teeth in pain.

He opened his eyes to see Pearl, wearing his duster and boots, struggling with a heavy log. Once she had managed to get it in out of the cold, she rolled it onto the fire, where it soon leaped into flame.

"Is that how you got me in here?" he asked.

She turned. Wiping her hands on her britches, she hurried to kneel at his side. "I should have rolled you like a log. It would have been simpler. How are you feeling this morning?"

"Like I wrestled with a bear. And the bear won." His gaze burned over her. "That's a mighty fancy gown, ma'am."

For the first time, she smiled, and his heart took a jolt before settling down to its normal rhythm.

"I didn't think you'd mind if I borrowed your clothes, since you had no use for them."

He gave her a crooked grin. "That's another thing I'd like to talk to you about, ma'am. I noticed I'm naked. Did you have something to do with that?"

To cover the flush that crept over her cheeks, she lifted a hand to his forehead and made a great show of probing for a fever. He reached up and covered her hand with his, stilling her movements. He felt the way her pulse leaped at his touch.

"How did you get me inside this cave? As I recall, Rollie and I shot at each other quite a distance from here."

"I . . . managed to drag you in, with the help of that hide hanging in the doorway, and your horse. You went for a sleigh ride, but I'm afraid you didn't get to enjoy it."

Though it cost him a great deal of pain, he lifted both hands to cup her face. "You're an amazing woman, Pearl Jewel. And a very inventive one, I might add."

She shook her head and pulled away, alarmed at her reaction to his touch. "I just did what I had to."

"From the looks of things, I'd say you did much more. How did you manage those logs?"

"I rolled most of them inside. One or two had to be dislodged with the help of your horse and some ropes. The snow made everything more difficult."

"Snow?"

She nodded. "The storm turned into a blizzard. Judging by the size of the drifts out there, it might be days before anyone can get to us."

Now he understood the unnatural silence.

"You mean—" his gaze burned over her "—we're all alone up here, with no hope of being rescued anytime soon?"

"That's right."

He shot her a wicked smile. "I can't think of anyone I'd rather be lost in a blizzard with than you, Miss Jewel."

She turned away and busied herself with the fire, aware that her heart was pounding. She had begun to think the same thing herself. "Are you hungry?"

It was several seconds before he replied. "Starving."

"I found some dried meat in your bedroll. And a couple of hard biscuits, if you'd like."

When he made no response, she turned to him. Once again, his eyes were closed and his breathing was slow and steady. She knelt beside him, watching and listening for long moments. It was the sweetest sound, the most endearing vision, in the world. And one that she'd hoped and prayed for. There was no sign of pain in his relaxed features. This strong, brave man, who had risked his life for her, was truly healing.

Assured that Cal was still deep in sleep, she ventured outside once more, this time in search of game.

She knew it was pointless to carry Cal's rifle, since she didn't have the vaguest idea how to fire it. But she carried his hunting knife tucked into the waistband of her britches and, for luck, his pistol in her pocket.

She remembered hearing the gurgle of a brook nearby. Now, following the sound of rushing water, she located the swollen stream. It was teeming with fish. But how to catch them? She returned to the cave and looked over her meager supplies. Stuffing her torn petticoat into an empty bucket, she made her way back to the stream. Within an hour, having used the sheer undergarment like a net, she returned to the cave with a bucket of wriggling fish.

Soon the little cave was filled with the mouth-watering aroma of fish grilling in a blackened skillet, biscuits browning over the fire and coffee bubbling.

As she began to eat, Pearl felt her spirits restored and her courage renewed.

"You're looking very smug, Miss Jewel."

At the sound of Cal's voice, she looked up, then hurried to his side. "Are you hungry?"

"Starving. What smells so wonderful?"

"Fish. There's a stream nearby just brimming with them."

"Is that so? And how did you manage to catch them?"

"My petticoat." The minute the words were out of her mouth, she felt her cheeks grow hot. "I mean, I used it as a net and filled a whole bucket with fish."

"Now what would the good people of Hanging Tree think if they learned that their teacher went fishing with her petticoat?"

She flushed and looked away until she heard the deep rumble of his laughter. Oh, it was such a wonderful sound. She realized at once that he was teasing her, and she joined in the laughter.

"They might be even more shocked to learn that I've been spending my days tending a naked man."

He caught her hand. "I've been meaning to talk to you about that...."

"We'll talk later." She pulled free and returned to the fire. Filling a tin plate with biscuits and fish, she handed it to Cal. "Right now, I think you need to eat something if you're ever going to regain your strength."

He accepted the plate and took several bites before setting it aside. "That's all I can manage right now."

She knelt beside him and lifted his head until it was pillowed on her lap. Then she held a steaming cup of coffee to his lips. He drank, long and deep, before refusing more.

Over the rim of the cup, he muttered, "You'd better be careful, Pearl. I might learn to like this kind of treatment."

She merely smiled, pleased that he had managed to eat and drink. But when she started to get up, he caught her hand, holding her still.

"I definitely intend to get my strength back."

"Oh?" She knew he could feel the way her pulse was hammering.

"Um-hmm. And when I do, there are some things we're going to have to talk about."

Her heart did a series of somersaults, but she managed to say calmly, "Your little talk will have to wait until you're stronger." She stood and moved around the cave, then picked up her petticoat.

"Going fishing again, teacher?"

She nodded. "One of us has to see about supper."

He closed his eyes, too exhausted to do more than offer a weak smile. "And one of us has to keep this bed warm."

By the time the day had ended and the first stars had begun to glitter in the evening sky, Cal had awakened several more times. Each time, he managed to eat and drink a little more, adding to his growing strength.

Pearl, too, noticed the renewal of both her energy and her spirits as the day wore on. The frequent treks to the stream, struggling through waist-high snowdrifts, added color to her pale cheeks. Her relief at Cal's recovery, and the knowledge that she could provide them with food, put a sparkle in her eye.

Now, as night swiftly stole over the land, she sat beside the fire, huddled inside Cal's duster. The only thing she wore beneath it was her chemise. Her gown, which she had washed in the stream until all the blood had been removed, was draped over a rock to dry. Cal's shirt and britches, as well as his tall boots, had become thoroughly soaked, and were now drying by the fire.

She ran her fingers through her tangled hair to smooth it, then pulled it over one shoulder and began to plait it into a fat braid.

Across from her, Cal lay in the shadows, eyes narrowed in concentration. It was the sweetest torture to watch her long, delicate fingers as they wove the strands of hair. He imagined those fingers moving over him, touching him. He experienced a wave of heat that left him weak.

He watched as she stood and removed his duster. The contours of her lithe young body were clearly visible beneath the opaque fabric of her chemise, which revealed more than it covered.

The heat became an inferno.

She tossed several logs on the fire to keep it burning through the night, then lifted the covers and slipped in beside him. With an economy of movement, she rolled onto her side. Soon her breathing had become soft and easy.

Cal lay awake, watching the shifting shadows of the fire paint stark, vibrant pictures on the wall of the cave. His hands were balled into tight fists. But this time his tension was not caused by pain. This was a very different tension. One that had his entire body vibrating with need.

The miracle that had brought them so far would be nothing compared with the miracle needed to get him through the night. For the need to touch her, to hold her, was so strong, it threatened to tear apart all his hard-won control.

Chapter Eighteen

Pearl stirred. She'd been having the most delicious dream. In it, she was safe in her father's arms. They had come through a perilous journey, and he was boasting of his pride in her courage. His words warmed her and she smiled, stretched—and froze.

It hadn't been a dream. At least not all of it. She was indeed encircled in a man's arms. But it wasn't her father's tender embrace. Her eyes opened. She found herself staring into the warm, fathomless depths of Cal's gaze.

"Good morning." Watching her awaken had been the sweetest pleasure of his life.

"Good morning." Embarrassed, she started to shift away, but his arms tightened, holding her still. She avoided meeting his eyes. "You'll be wanting some breakfast. I imagine you're hungry."

"I am hungry." His gaze moved over her face, enjoying the flush that stole across her cheeks. "But it isn't food I'm hungry for, Pearl."

His lips hovered just above hers, and she knew that if she moved only a fraction, she could taste them. That thought had her heartbeat racing. Did she dare?

She reached a tentative hand to his chest. His heart was pounding as erratically as her own. And his eyes were positively devouring her.

"You aren't going to recover your strength unless you have food."

"Don't you know that man can't live on food alone?" He traced the outline of her lower lip with his finger, and she held her breath at the intimacy of his touch. "I've been feeding my soul."

"Cal..." She opened her mouth, and he slipped his finger inside for just a moment, before pulling it back.

She gasped at the intimacy of such boldness. Her gaze flew to his face while he idly traced his thumb around her lips, all the while studying the shifting moods reflected in her eyes.

He was aware of her shock, her surprise, and her grudging acceptance of the situation. But he was also aware of the gradual warming in her voice, in her eyes. The slow awakening of passion.

"I've been lying here, watching you sleep. It was a vision that filled me with peace. Having you here, Pearl, and knowing you're safe, has done more to heal my wounds than any food or medicine."

He lowered his head and brushed her lips with his in the merest whisper of a kiss. For several moments, they remained so, lips touching, moving apart, then touching again, with the gentleness of a snowflake.

The silence of the morning surrounded them, with only the soft hiss of the fire in the background.

Pearl sighed, and gave herself up to the pleasure of his kiss. But just as she began to relax in his arms, he changed the angle of the kiss and took it deeper. His hands moved along her back, igniting tiny fires along her spine.

She started to pull back, but he was ready for her. His arms tightened, drawing her firmly against him. He nuzzled the sensitive hollow of her throat, until she sighed and arched her neck, giving him easier access.

Her blood was beginning to heat, pulsing through her veins like liquid fire. A fist seemed to close deep inside, causing a different kind of heat, heat that radiated through her body until she felt a burning need to toss aside the covers and cool her heated flesh.

"Cal—" Whatever she'd been about to whisper was cut off by a hard, demanding kiss.

She clutched at him and, as her hands made contact with his skin, her arms slipped naturally around his waist. Their legs tangled. And suddenly she realized that the body pressed to hers was naked. And thoroughly aroused.

"Cal. No. Stop." Confused, dazed, she pushed against his chest and strained to break free of his embrace.

He lifted his head. "You want this, too, Pearl. You can no longer deny it."

"No." She shook her head, then said more firmly, "No." She took a deep breath, filling her lungs, then sat up, shoving her hair from her eyes. "I can't think. I . . . need some time."

Without giving him a chance to argue, she slipped out from under the covers and began to pull on his pants and shirt and heavy boots. Grabbing up his duster, she flung it over her arm and reached for the pail and the torn petticoat.

In the blink of an eye, she was gone, swallowed up by the mounds of snow outside the cave.

Cal fell back against the blankets, berating himself. How could he have been so callous? Pearl was a lady. A sheltered, innocent young lady who had never been exposed to such treatment. When would he learn? He had no right to even touch her. She had to preserve her honor, to save herself for a man who could offer her a proper courtship. A man who would marry her and provide her with a bright future and the respect she deserved.

He wished with all his heart he could be that man. But he knew he was only fooling himself. All he would ever be was a cowboy. And not even a respectable one. For, despite his success, he was a man with a dark past. A past that still haunted him in the darkest recesses of his mind. And brought him shame.

Pearl sat on the banks of the stream, huddled miserably in the folds of Cal's duster. The beauty of the day, with the brilliant sunlight glittering like diamonds on the pristine snow, was lost on her. The schools of fish that churned the water, filling the flimsy petticoat netting, barely caught her eye.

All she could think of was Cal. The way he tasted—dark and mysterious. The way he made her feel when he held her—beautiful, alluring, seductive. It didn't matter to Cal that she felt shy and confused. In Cal's arms, she became someone new. She was no longer the prim and proper Boston lady, who constantly fretted over the way she looked, the image she presented to the world. With Cal, she could be herself or, if she chose, become someone quite unlike herself. That was his charm. He brought out all the hidden traits she had never even known she possessed.

How she wished she could tell him, show him, how special he was to her. But she was afraid.

"Oh, Daddy," she said aloud. "I love Cal. But I'm so afraid of these strange new feelings churning inside me. Help me, Daddy. Please help me."

In her mind's eye, she could see that day she had walked proudly beside her father on the streets of Boston. *As always, she was dressed in her finest gown. Her father, too, looked as fine as any eastern gentleman. But when two men came to blows over an argument, and others in the street stood aside to watch, her father stepped between them, without a thought to his own safety. When the scuffle ended, twelve-year-old Pearl asked, "Aren't you ever afraid, Daddy?"*

She could still hear his words. *"The person hasn't been born who hasn't had to face down fear, Pearl. But dealing with that fear brings freedom. When you're older, you will be free to choose the path you will walk. There will be many fears to face along that path. But face them you will. Then, and only then, will you be truly free. Cherish that freedom, Pearl. And know that I will always support your choice. For your freedom to choose is a precious gift."*

Suddenly she gave out a laugh of pure delight and leaped to her feet. With her arms lifted to the heavens, she raised her face to the sunlight. "Oh, Daddy!" she cried. A smile split her lips and brought a fresh new light to her eyes. "How could I have been so blind?"

The answer had been there all along. With Cal, she'd found freedom. The freedom to be, or do, anything she chose.

She strode into the frigid waters and gathered up the ends of the petticoat, dumping the wriggling fish into the bucket of water. With a light heart and a spring to her steps, she picked up the bucket and headed back to the cave.

Cal had managed a few tentative steps around the cave. He'd located his pouch of tobacco, and lay back amid the blankets, a wreath of smoke curling over his head.

He'd come to a decision. Even though he would have liked a few more days to gather his strength, it was time to head home. They might be heading into another storm, but that was the chance they had to take. Despite a lingering weakness, he could sit a horse. Whatever pain and discomfort he was forced to endure, it would be nothing compared to this. For the truth was, it would be impossible to remain here, trapped in this cave with Pearl, and not touch her. And if he touched her again, they would both be lost.

He forced himself to look away as she entered.

"I've caught more fish," she announced. "I'll start your breakfast."

"There's no rush." He tossed his cigarette into the fire. "I'm not hungry."

"That's not what you said a little while ago." She turned and started toward him, shedding his duster as she walked. It drifted to the floor of the cave and lay in a heap.

Annoyed that he still hadn't looked at her, she kicked up a foot, sending a boot flying. It landed across the cave with a thud.

That got his attention.

He watched in amazement as she did the same with the other boot. It bounced off one wall and dropped to the ground.

After watching it fall, he turned his attention to Pearl. But this wasn't the Pearl he'd known these past few months. Her walk had slowed to a flowing, sensuous dance. Her hips were swaying in a most seductive manner. And there was a gleam in her eye that he'd never seen before.

"I needed time to think," she announced. "And I've come to a decision."

"So have—"

His words were cut off in midsentence when he saw her wiggling out of his pants. They dropped to the floor of the cave. She stepped out of them and continued moving toward him, wearing nothing but his shirt and a flimsy chemise that barely covered her nakedness.

By the time she was kneeling beside his bedroll, her fingers were already on the buttons of her shirt.

He reached up and caught her hands, holding them still. "Have you lost your senses?"

Instead of giving him a haughty reply, she merely smiled. In a breathy voice, she whispered, "I think I've just found them."

"I don't understand."

He started to release her, but she caught his hands and lifted them to her mouth. The press of her lips against his rough palms was so erotic, he felt as if all the breath had left his lungs.

"I was wrong, Cal. Wrong to run from what you were offering. It's what I want, too."

"No." He shook his head in denial. He wouldn't listen to this. Couldn't. "I'm glad you ran. It gave us both time to clear our heads. And I realize now that I was being selfish, Pearl. I would take your virtue, your honor, and would give you nothing in return."

"Nothing? Oh, Cal, you have so much to offer," she murmured.

Before she could argue further, he placed a hand over her mouth to stop her. "Don't you see? If I allow this to happen, I'll be no better than Rollie Ingram."

"Oh, Cal . . ."

She spoke the words on a long-drawn-out sigh, and he closed his eyes against the pain. His only consolation was the knowledge that he was doing this for her own good. Whatever embarrassment she was suffering would soon be forgotten.

In the silence that followed, he opened his eyes, only to discover that she had completely unbuttoned the shirt and was slipping it off her shoulders.

"What the hell do you think you're doing?"

She lifted a corner of the blanket and began to crawl in beside him. "I'm going to lie here with you until you get over your shyness."

"My shyness?" His jaw dropped in surprise.

She nodded and snuggled close. "That's the only reason I can think of for your sudden bout of conscience."

He sat bolt upright, holding her at arm's length. "My sudden bout of conscience, as you call it, is common sense. It appears than one of us needs to be sensible about this."

"I don't want to be sensible. All my life I've been sensible. I've always been blessed, or cursed, with the need to see every side of an issue. In my whole life, I've never done anything for the sheer joy of it. Right now, I want to show you how much I love you."

At the dazed look in his eyes, she laughed. It was a clear, tinkling sound that wrapped itself around his heart and began to squeeze, until he couldn't breathe.

"You love me, Pearl?"

"Of course, silly. And you love me, whether you care to admit it or not."

"I do?" He gave her a lopsided grin that sent her heart spiraling out of control. Suddenly he leaned toward her and framed her face with his hands. "Oh, Pearl. I do. Truly I do."

His admission had tears springing to her eyes. She quickly blinked them back and touched her lips to his. "You see? That wasn't so hard to admit, was it?"

The first touch of her lips was like the kick of a mule. While he absorbed the shock, he ran his hands down her neck, her shoulders, along the top of her arms.

Soft. She was so incredibly soft. Her skin as pale as that of some imaginary goddess. But she was warm. And real. And his for the taking.

A second shock wave rumbled through him at the realization.

He had no right.

"Pearl." He drew her a little away, forcing her to meet his eyes. "You don't know anything about me."

"I know that you're a good man. A man my father loved and trusted. A man I love and trust, as well."

"You don't know anything." His voice frosted over. "I wasn't always good. In fact, until I met your father, I didn't even know how to be good and decent. I was a man on the run."

She thought of what Travis had once said at school. *I've heard that Cal McCabe killed his first man when he was no bigger'n me.*

"It doesn't matter, Cal. What happened before doesn't mean a thing to me. The only thing that matters is that I love you. And I want to show you how much."

He could see her heart in her eyes when she looked at him, and he felt his own heart responding with a fresh burst of love.

He lifted his hands to her hair and watched as the silken strands sifted through his fingers. And all the while, he watched her eyes, loving the way they warmed and softened as they stared into his.

"Do you know what you're doing?" he whispered.

She lifted her hands, clutching his wrists. "Oh, Cal. I've never been so sure of anything in my life."

He drew her into his arms and pressed his lips to her temple. "There'll be no turning back. I'd never find the strength to stop once we've started."

Even though he was offering her one last chance to refuse, he knew it was futile. He would have crawled across these mountains to have her. Or ridden blindly through a hail of bullets. Still, he held his breath, knowing the power she wielded. One word of refusal from her lips and he would be banished forever from paradise.

In reply, she turned her face until their lips were touching. Against his mouth she whispered, "No more protests, Cal. Just love me."

"Dear God." The words were less a sigh, and more a savage oath. But then his tone softened as the enormity of her offer began to sink in. He muttered once more, almost like a prayer, "Dear God."

Chapter Nineteen

For long moments, neither of them moved. Neither spoke. Then, almost against his will, Cal pressed her closer. His mouth moved slowly, lazily over hers, nibbling, tasting, until her lips parted. His tongue tangled with hers, teasing her, tempting her. With a sigh, she gave herself up to the pleasure.

His lips feathered over her face, pressing light kisses to her forehead, her cheeks, her closed eyelids, the tip of her nose.

"Oh, Pearl." He whispered her name like a caress, and she suddenly knew what it felt like to be cherished.

With his tongue, he traced the curve of her ear, pausing to nibble and tug before darting inside, sending her heartbeat climbing.

She gave a delighted little laugh and clung to him as he ran wet kisses down her throat and across her shoulder. Suddenly her laughter turned to a moan of pleasure as his lips moved lower, to the soft swell of her breast. The thin fabric of her chemise was no barrier as his mouth, his tongue, worked their magic.

He lowered her to the blankets, and she twined her arms around his neck, drawing his head down for another drugging kiss.

Outside, a breeze scattered snow across the walls of the cave, making a sound like sand pebbles. Birds, exiting the shelters they had sought during the storm, began a chorus of song as they snatched food before the next onslaught. But inside the cave, there was only the hiss and snap of a fire. And the muted sound of breathing as two people lost themselves in the wonders of love.

Cal struggled to bank his needs. Needs that had been building until they threatened to overpower him. He was determined to draw out every taste, every touch, every pleasure, in order to make her first time as memorable as possible. It was, after all, the only thing he could give her.

He ran soft butterfly kisses over her face, her neck, her shoulders. His fingers followed suit, tracing every line and curve of her body. And with each touch he felt her grow more tense, her breathing grow more shallow.

He wouldn't allow himself to think about the future, and what would happen when they returned to the ranch. Nor would he permit himself to brood about what had happened in the past, for it was too late to change it. Instead, he would think only about now. This moment. This woman. And the love he felt for her.

As her blood heated and her body pulsed with need, Pearl shut out all fears, all uncertainties. The world beyond this cave no longer mattered. There was only this man. And the love she felt for him. She wouldn't think about this momentous thing they were sharing; it was enough to know that she trusted Cal to lead her.

Trust. There had been so little in her life. But she knew that Cal would never betray her trust.

He felt the gradual change in her. Before, there had been fear. And so he had moved slowly, easing her fears, leading her, with tender kisses and whispered words of endearment, to a new plateau. But now, as he felt her gradual release, he was free to lead her higher still.

His touch unlocked all her inhibitions, allowing her to explore all the passion that had been lying dormant, awaiting this moment. He could see it in her eyes, taste it on her lips. Hot. Hungry. Pulsing with need.

He kept his eyes on hers as he reached for the ribbons of her chemise. As the fabric parted, he allowed his gaze to roam her body.

"Pearl, you're even more beautiful than I'd dreamed."

With great tenderness, he bent to her, feasting on her breast until the nipple hardened. Her sigh of pleasure became a moan as he moved from one breast to the other.

He struggled against taking her too high, too fast. But he wondered how much longer he could exert such control. The needs he'd denied for so long were struggling to be free. Soon, he knew, the dam would burst and they would both be swept away by the tide of emotion.

She longed to touch him as he was touching her. She brought her arms around his waist and felt his muscles contract violently at the first touch of her fingertips.

At his moan of pleasure, she grew bolder, tracing her fingers along his body as he had touched her.

His fingers tangled in her hair as he drew her head back and covered her mouth in a savage kiss. For a moment, she stiffened, feeling a flash of fear at the change in him. Then the fear was swept away by her own newly awakened passion.

So this was what he had struggled to keep from her. This dark, passionate side of him that he had kept hidden until now. Exulting in her newly discovered power, she leaned into him, running her lips and fingertips over him, exploring him as he had explored her.

Cal's body was alive with need. For so long, he had struggled to hold back. But now, with Pearl's passion unleashed, his own senses burned with an all-consuming desire that could no longer be contained.

Oh, the things he wanted to teach her. Not just freedom from the restrictions that had held her prisoner for a lifetime. It was so much more. He wanted her to experience the wild, free flight of a bird, soaring high across the mountain peaks. To taste passion, in all its delights. To give in to the madness, the insanity, of following wherever he led, not out of fear, or a sense of duty, but out of love.

Love. That was what he wanted for her. For himself. A banquet of love.

With exquisite tenderness, he feasted on her lips, her throat, her breast, moving his tongue across the nipple until it hardened. With great care, he moved to the other, until she writhed and moaned with pleasure, her hands fisting in the mound of blankets beneath her. And still he held back as, with lips and teeth and fingertips, he moved over her, drawing out every moment of pleasure.

Heat rose between them, clogging their throats, making their bodies slick with sheen. And still he gave her no release from the needs that were building, building, until they threatened to drive them both mad.

Pearl had slipped into a world of touch and taste and exquisite pleasure, where thought no longer mattered. All that mattered was Cal. The feel of his rough, callused fingers against her flesh was more heavenly than the finest silk. The taste of him was as dark and mysterious as this cave. The touch of him was as wild as the land that had nurtured him.

She trembled and shuddered as he slid along her body, moist flesh to moist flesh, taking her on a wild and reckless ride.

He had thought he was teaching her. But he was the one being taught. From the first touch, the first kiss, he had been imprisoned by primitive needs begging for release.

He felt her stiffen as his lips moved over her. And then she cried out his name as she reached the first crest. He gave her no time to recover as he moved upward, tracing his lips along her body.

It didn't seem possible that she could want more, but as he entered her, she wrapped herself around him, clinging to him as if to life itself.

He filled himself with her, breathing in the fragrance of icy streams and evergreen, and knew that in springtimes to come, he would always think of her. And be warmed by the memory.

Needs ripped through his last shred of control, and he found himself teetering on the brink of madness. He forgot how to be gentle. His kisses were rough, almost savage; his touch was bruising.

"Pearl. Look at me," he commanded roughly.

Her lids snapped open. Her gaze focused on him.

"I want to see you," he whispered savagely. "Only you. And I want to see myself in your eyes."

Together, they began to climb. She moved with him, matching his strength, his rhythm, with an incredible strength of her own.

For Pearl, time seemed suspended. Cal's heartbeat became her own. His sighs, his moans, became her own voice.

He murmured her name, or thought he did, as they reached the crest. Their bodies shuddered convulsively. Suddenly they seemed to break free of the bonds of earth and found themselves soaring. It was a journey like none they had ever taken before.

Pearl felt as though she had touched the sun and it had exploded inside her. She felt Cal follow her inside the sunlight, and together they burst into tiny fragments.

He was part of her now. And she was part of him. Together they had shared something special, something wondrous. Something they could never take back. And from this moment on, their lives would be forever altered.

Damp with sheen, still joined with Pearl, Cal continued holding her. He never wanted to let go. Slowly, languorously, he pulled the blankets over them, then rolled to his side and cradled her against his chest.

As he bent to kiss her, he tasted her tears.

"Dear God, I've hurt you."

"No." She touched a hand to his cheek to reassure him, then allowed it to linger there, loving the feel of his rough, scratchy growth of beard against her palm. "These are happy tears. You could never hurt me, Cal."

But she knew, even as she spoke the words, that they weren't true. Now that she had given him her heart and her body, Cal McCabe was the only man who *could* hurt her.

She nudged aside such thoughts. Right now, all that mattered was that she and Cal were together. And for a little while, there would be no ranch chores, no teaching chores, to come between them. She found herself wishing they could remain lost in this cave forever.

"I could fix some food now," she murmured against his lips.

"Not yet." He kissed her, slowly, lazily, while his fingers played with her hair. "Do you know how long I've wanted to hold you like this?"

"How long?" She sat up, taking no notice of her nakedness.

"Since you stepped off that stagecoach in Hanging Tree, all buttoned up to here—" he ran a rough finger around her throat, and she shivered at the intimacy of the touch "—and holding that ridiculous parasol."

"Ridiculous!" She pushed away in indignation, but he caught her and, with a laugh, dragged her close.

"And all I could think about was mussing that perfect hair, and unbuttoning that gown so I could see the cool, pale skin you kept covered up." With his finger, he circled one breast, then the other, watching her eyes begin to darken with renewed passion.

"And all I could think about was the way you were always frowning when you came near me," she said with a laugh. "You looked so fierce you frightened me."

"That was no frown." His hands had begun exploring the slope of her waist, the curve of her hips. "That was just a look I used to cover my lustful thoughts."

"You're frowning now." She traced a finger over the furrow between his brows.

"Then I guess..." He pulled her down on top of him. "I'd better admit what I'm thinking."

She leaned up on her elbows and surprised him by pressing her lips to his chest, then running moist kisses across his stomach. She heard his sudden intake of breath as she moved seductively lower.

"Why, Cal McCabe..." She gave a sly grin. "You don't need to admit a thing. It's obvious what you're thinking."

Her hair fell forward like a curtain, and he plunged his hands into it as she moved over him. He groaned, but soon there were only sighs of pleasure as, once more, they slipped into a world that only lovers know.

"Would you like that food now?"

The two lovers had drifted back to sleep and awoken to find the fire burned to embers and a bitter wind beginning to blow outside the cave.

Cal answered with a deep, possessive kiss. As he struggled to sit up, Pearl heard his hiss of pain.

"I think you'd better take it easy," she said with a tender smile. "All that...activity may have opened up your wounds."

"It's the first exercise I've had in days. And, woman," he said with a growl of pleasure against her lips, "I have no intention of giving it up for the sake of a few bullet holes."

"Men," she said with mock exasperation. "That's what I'd expect from a naked cowboy who has just come back from the dead and found himself sleeping with a very prim and proper schoolteacher."

"Prim and proper?" He gave a roar of laughter. "You certainly had me fooled."

"Show a little respect," she said as she scurried from the blankets and rolled a fresh log onto the embers. With the help of some kindling, she soon had a roaring fire.

A short time later, the cave was redolent with the wonderful fragrances of biscuits, fish in a skillet, and coffee bubbling over the fire.

Cal leaned his back against his saddle and sipped coffee while Pearl filled a plate with food. Then she sat cross-legged in the blankets and fed him.

"You'd better be careful," he warned. "I might learn to like this."

"Enjoy it while you can," she said with a laugh. "As soon as your strength returns, I'll expect you to do the same for me."

His hand snaked out, closing around her wrist. With ease, he dragged her into his arms. "Now, what was that about my strength?"

"Cal, you're going to spill this plate of food."

He took the plate from her hand and set it aside, then pulled her down on top of him and ran his hands lightly along her body. Her laughter died as he claimed her lips. With a moan of pleasure, she clutched his waist and moved over him until, lost in pleasure, they had completely forgotten their meal.

"Just how strong are you feeling?" she whispered against his lips.

"I was just about to show you."

The second storm struck during the late afternoon. The few brief hours of sunshine disappeared as storm clouds darkened the sky, turning daylight into night. The wind picked up until it became a roar. By morning, the mountains were covered with a fresh snowfall.

It continued for three days.

They were the happiest days of Pearl's life. With each passing hour, she found herself wishing the storm would continue. She knew it was an irrational wish.

There were people worried about them. And for that she was truly sorry. But she had never known such peace, such contentment, in her whole life.

Waking up in Cal's arms was the greatest of pleasures. The warmth of his love had brought her to full bloom. She felt completely unselfconscious with him. And their lovemaking had taught them much about each other. She now saw a gentle side to Cal that he never showed to the world. And he'd discovered a playfulness about Pearl that she had kept carefully hidden.

He loved the way she awoke, all soft and sleepy-eyed in his arms. And she blossomed under his teasing laughter.

His strength was improving with each day. Although he hadn't ventured outside as yet, he could walk around the cave, and had taken over simple chores, such as tending the fire and cooking the fish Pearl managed to catch.

He taught her how to line the floor of the cave with evergreen boughs for warmth. More of the boughs were placed beneath their bedroll, to soften and cushion. The fragrance of evergreen filled the cave, lifting their spirits.

One evening, after another meal of fish and biscuits, Cal rolled a cigarette and held a flaming stick to the tip. Exhaling a cloud of smoke, he grumbled, "I'm so tired of fish, even Rollie's horse is beginning to look like a candidate for supper."

"Don't you dare," Pearl called from across the cave. "We'll need him to pull that cart when we leave here."

She had managed to repair her torn gown, and pulled it on, smoothing down the wrinkled skirt. Without a petticoat, the gown hugged her curves in a most seductive manner. Her hair hung long and loose, and she tied it back with a faded ribbon. All in all, Cal realized, she made a striking picture.

"What makes you think that storm is ever going to let up?" he asked teasingly.

"Would you mind if it didn't?" She walked toward him, and he felt his throat go dry. Would it always be like this? he wondered. Would his heart stop every time he looked at her?

"Woman, as long as you're here with me, I wouldn't care if the storm lasted all spring and summer."

He had pulled on his pants and boots, but had shed his shirt so that Pearl could wash and mend it. He pulled her into his arms and cradled her against his naked chest. "You feel so good here. So right."

"I was just thinking the same thing." She smiled up at him, and his arms tightened around her.

"Maybe we'll turn in early tonight," he whispered against her temple.

"I thought you were going to mend that harness." She touched a hand to his rough, scratchy beard.

He grinned. "There's always tomorrow."

As they started toward the bedroll, Cal suddenly froze.

Pearl looked up in alarm. "What is it? What's wrong?"

In one swift motion, he thrust her behind him and reached for his rifle. Striding toward the mouth of the cave, he waited, all his senses alert.

Had that been only the wind? Or had he heard someone approaching? It could have been an animal. But he trusted his instincts. The prickling at the back of his neck had him tensing.

He waited. And heard it again.

With his rifle cocked and ready, he took aim at the hide covering the entrance to the cave.

It moved inward. And into the circle of firelight stepped a giant, clad in fur, frosted with snow.

Pearl let out a cry of terror, before covering her mouth with her hand.

But as Cal's finger reflexively closed over the trigger, she launched herself against him, shouting, "No, Cal. Don't shoot. It isn't what you think."

Chapter Twenty

For the space of a heartbeat, no one moved. No one spoke.

Then, before Cal's disbelieving eyes, the giant began to topple. The snow-laden fur dropped to the floor of the cave to reveal Gilbert Ingram, holding his little brother, Daniel, on his shoulders.

"What in the hell—?"

Pearl placed a hand over Cal's mouth, to halt the savage oath, then hurried forward to draw the two shivering boys toward the fire.

"Quick. They need blankets, Cal," she cried.

Cal peered out into the darkness for any sign of their father. Convinced that they were alone, he crossed to the bedroll and removed two blankets. He watched in silence as Pearl draped one around each boy. Then she set about filling two cups with strong, hot coffee, which she handed to them. From the blackened skillet, she removed the last of the fish and biscuits, then watched as the boys quickly devoured every bite.

It was evident from the condition of their boots, wrapped with snow-matted fur, that they had been walking for many hours. Still, they seemed surprisingly calm. They were shivering, and their teeth were chattering. But after only a few bites of food and sips of the hot liquid, they were able to answer Pearl's questions.

"What in the world are you doing here?" she demanded. "How did you find us, when no one else could?"

"Right from the start, Gilbert thought about this cave. He figured Pa might bring you here," Daniel said matter-of-factly. "That first night, when we reached your ranch, he tried to tell your cook he could help. But I guess he was just too upset to listen." The boy turned to Cal. "Besides, the old man didn't think you and your wranglers would like having an Ingram along."

Cal nodded, too surprised to find his voice.

"But the storm . . ." Pearl began.

"It did set us back a little," the boy admitted. "As soon as it let up, Gilbert and I started out, figuring we could get here in about a day. But we weren't counting on another storm. That set us back a bit more."

Pearl tried not to smile at his low-key description.

"We had to take shelter a couple of times," Daniel admitted.

"Shelter?" Pearl repeated.

"Yes, ma'am. There are a couple of deserted shacks Gilbert knew about, and a cave or two."

Pearl couldn't hide her amazement. "How could you get through snowdrifts that are taller than you?"

"Gilbert's been tracking since he was my age," Daniel said proudly. "He knows his way through anything."

Gilbert, who had not spoken a word, drew an arm around his little brother and stared at the floor of the cave.

"If Gilbert doesn't track, we don't eat." Daniel glanced up and, seeing the way Pearl and Cal were watching him, explained, "Sometimes Pa's gone for a month or more. Gilbert takes care of himself and me."

"I can see that," Pearl said dryly.

"Speaking of your father," Cal put in quickly, "has he returned home?"

Gilbert's eyes widened. "No, sir. Is he alive, then?"

Cal watched the boy carefully. He was convinced Gilbert wasn't playacting. He really didn't know what had happened.

"The last we saw of your father, he was shot, and tumbling over a ravine."

The boy digested the news thoughtfully, without emotion. Then he nodded. "Pa's survived worse. He's probably waiting out the storm in a cave nearby."

Pearl shot a nervous glance toward Cal, and saw the way his eyes narrowed in thought.

"Why did you come here, boy?" he demanded.

Gilbert avoided his eyes. "It was our pa who took Miss Jewel. Daniel and I decided it was our responsibility to find her, and bring her back safely if we could."

"Even if it meant standing up to your father?" Cal asked.

Gilbert hung his head. "Yes, sir."

"Why?" Cal demanded.

The boy lifted his head and met his steely gaze. "Miss Jewel lectured me on the meaning of honor. I . . . wanted her to know I was paying attention."

Pearl felt tears sting her eyes at his quiet admission. "Well." She turned away to hide her emotions. "We'll have to make up a bed for you boys. I expect you're feeling exhausted."

She made a nest of evergreen boughs, then covered them with a blanket. Leading the boys to it, she waited until they lay down. Then she covered them with the furs they had worn when they arrived.

She noticed that, as they fell into sleep, they curled up together, with Gilbert's arms protectively around his little brother.

"I must say." She cleared her throat, struggling to swallow the lump that was threatening to choke her. "They're very brave little boys."

"Or very foolish," Cal muttered. He had opened a pouch, and was counting his bullets.

"What does that mean?"

"It means they could have perished in this storm. And no one would have found them until the snows melted."

"Maybe they didn't think they had much to lose," she said in their defense. "From what I've seen, their lives have never been easy. I can't even imagine surviving with a father like Rollie Ingram."

Cal said nothing. But there was a frightening look in his eye as he systematically cleaned his rifle, checking every part, before loading it.

Pearl glanced at the bedroll. "Will you be coming to bed soon?" She wanted—needed—to feel his arms around her, holding her, keeping her safe.

He shook his head. "I won't be sleeping tonight. In fact, from now on, we'll have to take turns sleeping and keeping watch."

"Then you think Rollie Ingram will be back?"

He didn't say a word. But she knew, from the set of his jaw, what he was thinking.

As she crawled between the covers, she realized with a sinking heart that their paradise had just evaporated, like a misty, half-remembered dream. Reality had returned. And with it, the gnawing terror that, somewhere in the night, a killer watched and waited.

"That was a fine breakfast, Miss Jewel," Daniel announced.

"I'm afraid that's the last of the fish," she remarked as she passed around a plate of biscuits. "I'll have to go back to the stream and catch more."

"I don't think I could take another meal of fish." Cal drained his coffee and idly rubbed the wound at his shoulder. "It's all we've had since we got here."

"I could catch us a rabbit or two," Gilbert offered.

Cal shook his head. "I don't want to risk a gunshot."

The boy nodded. "I understand. But I don't need a rifle." He pulled on his boots, then draped a fur throw around his shoulders and tucked a knife into the waistband of his trousers. "I'll be back soon."

As he exited the cave, Pearl turned to Daniel. "How can your brother hope to catch anything without a gun?"

The little boy smiled. Now that he'd had a good night's sleep, and plenty to eat, he was feeling even more talkative than usual.

"Gilbert can do anything."

Pearl knelt down beside him. "You think the world of your brother, don't you?"

"Yes, ma'am. If it weren't for Gilbert..." His words faded, and he turned away. But not before Pearl saw the way his lips quivered.

She dropped an arm around his shoulders. "He's a very brave boy. And so are you. I still can't quite believe that the two of you found us when no one else could."

"Gilbert's the best tracker in all of Texas," the little boy boasted.

"How about your father?" Cal asked.

The boy looked away. "Pa knows these hills. He hides out in them sometimes, when the law is after him. But even Pa doesn't know the land the way Gilbert does. My brother could show you a wildcat's lair, or a wolf's den. He can climb to an eagle's nest, or dig down with one hand and come up with a prairie dog's pups. When he says he'll come back with game, you can trust he will. Thanks to Gilbert, we've never gone hungry."

True to his word, within a few hours, Gilbert returned to the cave with an armload of game. There were four rabbits, which he skinned and tossed into a pot, along with an assortment of spring vegetables, which he'd found under the snow. From his pocket he removed a handful of plants.

As he crumbled the leaves and tubers and tossed them into the stew, Pearl asked, "What are they, Gilbert?"

He shrugged. "My ma used to know their names. Things like feverfew and spear. I only know they taste good in stew and soup. And sometimes I use them for healing."

Pearl breathed deeply and smiled. "Whatever they're called, they smell wonderful." She reached into the sack of flour and brought out a small measure to start her biscuits.

"Why don't you let Gilbert make some flat bread?" Daniel asked.

"You bake, too?" Pearl turned to the boy, who was setting out the rabbit skins to dry.

"Yes'm. Ma taught me." With deft strokes, he mixed flour and melted snow and made a batter, which he dropped into the hot skillet. In no time, he had made half a dozen flour tortillas.

Pearl shook her head in wonder. "Is there nothing you can't do, Gilbert?"

He merely shrugged and picked up the hides. In a corner of the cave, he pounded them with a rock until they were softened. Then he laid them out once more to dry.

While he worked, Cal began to mend a harness, while Pearl plied needle and thread to repair Cal's shirt.

While she worked, she said, "This might be a good time to work on our sums." She pointed to a small stick. "Daniel, I'll call out some numbers. Why don't you write them in the sand and see if you can add them up?"

The little boy brightened. "Yes'm. I'd like that."

"Gilbert, do you think you can do the sums in your head?"

The older boy nodded.

The hours seemed to fly by as Pearl drilled the boys in their sums, and then engaged them in a spelling bee. And all the while, the wonderful fragrance of rabbit stew permeated the little cave, filling it with a special warmth.

As they sat down to eat, Pearl was astonished to see Gilbert and Daniel join hands and bow their heads. After an awkward moment, she and Cal followed suit.

"We thank Thee," Gilbert said aloud. He lifted his head and added sheepishly, "I'm afraid that's all I remember of Ma's prayer."

The murmured words had brought a dryness to Pearl's throat. She glanced toward Cal and saw that he, too, had been moved by the boy's simple blessing.

"That's all you need to say." She touched a hand to Gilbert's arm. "The Lord knows what's in your heart."

After only a few bites, Pearl declared, "I can't remember when I've eaten anything so good. Gilbert, this is a feast."

The boy blushed at her praise.

"I told you," Daniel chirped. "Gilbert can do anything."

"No, I can't." Gilbert touched the knife at his waist. "I spotted a deer while I was out. But he was too far away. If I could have used a rifle..." He shrugged. "Maybe he'll come back to the stream tomorrow. If he does, I'll be waiting for him. Then we'll have a real feast."

"Rabbit stew is good enough for me," Cal said casually. "Especially when it's this good."

His simple compliment brought a smile of pleasure to the young boy's face. Seeing it, Pearl thought how much a boy like Gilbert would treasure the approval of a man like Cal McCabe.

"I believe I'll have a few more of those spices," Cal remarked. He glanced up. "How about you, Pearl?"

"I'd like that." She held up her plate, causing Cal's jaw to drop.

Without a word, he tossed several of the strong spices into her stew and watched as she enjoyed every bite.

After dinner, Cal rolled a cigarette and ambled to the mouth of the cave, where he stood staring into the darkness. Across the cave, Pearl and Daniel heated snow over the fire and washed up the few battered tin dishes they'd used. Then, not wanting the pan of warm water to go to waste, Pearl said, "Would you care to take a bath, Daniel?"

"A...bath?" The boy seemed not only surprised, but repelled, by the suggestion.

"Yes. A bath. Don't you ever take one?"

"No, ma'am." He glanced to where his older brother was busy tanning the rabbit hides. "Like Pa said—what good is a bath? I'll just get dirty again."

"That's true." She struggled not to laugh, though a smile tickled the corners of her lips. "But sometimes it just feels good to get all warm and clean. And while you're bathing, I could wash and mend your clothes.''

"But what would I wear to sleep in?'' he asked innocently.

"I'll wrap you in a blanket,'' she assured him.

"I...guess so,'' he said reluctantly. "As long as you think I should.''

"I think you'll enjoy the experience,'' she said with a smile.

She brought him a blanket and draped it around him as he removed his clothes. Then she showed him how to wash himself, using a scrap of fabric from her petticoat and soap from Cal's saddlebag. When he was finished, he held up his hands proudly.

"Look, Miss Jewel. All clean.''

"Indeed you are.'' She studied his shining eyes. "But there's one more thing.'' Leading him to the pan of water, she soaped his hair, then rinsed it off using a tin cup.

Amid squeals of laughter, he allowed her to wrap a corner of the blanket around his head so that he looked like a hooded monk.

"There now,'' she said, drawing him onto her lap and wrapping her arms around him. "Didn't I tell you you'd enjoy it?''

"Yes'm. But you didn't say it would tickle.'' He peered across the cave at his older brother. "Gilbert, you ought to try it. You'd like taking a bath. It's fun.''

"I think I'll leave the fun for you,'' the older boy said with disinterest.

Hearing him, Cal tossed out the dirty water and added fresh snow to the pan before setting it over the fire to warm. With a wink in Pearl's direction, he said casually, "It's my turn. I've been hoping for a chance to clean up."

Gilbert turned to study Cal, who removed his shirt and picked up the soap. As soon as the melted snow had heated, he began to wash. When he'd finished, he said, just as casually, "Think you could rinse my hair, too, Miss Jewel?"

She felt her cheeks begin to redden as she set Daniel on the bed of furs and moved to Cal's side. He bent over the pan of water and allowed her to rinse the soap from his hair.

Was it just her heightened senses? she wondered. Or was washing this man's hair the most purely sensual thing she'd ever done? With each touch of his scalp, with each caress of his hair against her palm, she longed to draw him into her arms and hold him close. But with the boys watching, she forced herself to show none of the emotions she was experiencing.

When she was finished, Cal shook his head like a great shaggy dog, then ran his fingers through the damp strands.

"Ah, now that felt heavenly," he said aloud. And it was clear that he meant every word. He glanced up. "How about you, Gilbert? Want to take a turn?"

The boy swallowed. It did indeed look inviting. And if Cal McCabe was willing to wash, maybe it wasn't such a silly waste of a man's time.

"I . . . guess so."

"If you'll undress," Pearl said, "I'll wash your clothes along with Daniel's."

"What would I wear?" he asked in embarrassment.

She was about to suggest the other blanket, but Cal came to the rescue. "Why not wear my shirt tonight? In the morning, your clothes will be dry."

"You...wouldn't mind?" the boy asked, awestruck.

"Help yourself." Cal held the shirt out to the boy, who, after a moment's hesitation, accepted it.

Just as his little brother had, Gilbert undressed beneath a blanket, and washed himself. Then, allowing Pearl to rinse his hair, he turned away and dressed in Cal's oversize shirt.

As he buttoned it, Cal remarked, "In no time at all, you'll be able to fit into all my clothes, boy."

Gilbert made no reply. But the look of pride on his face spoke volumes.

Pearl heated water over the fire and scrubbed the filthy clothes until, after several rinses, the water ran clear. Then she laid them out over rocks in the cave to dry.

In the silence of the night, Cal rolled a cigarette and held a flaming stick to the tip, inhaling deeply. He leaned his back against his saddle, while a wreath of smoke curled over his head.

Humming a little tune from her childhood, Pearl moved about the cave, emptying the pan of water, pouring the last of the coffee into a cup, which she shared with Cal.

"Thank you," he muttered as he drank, then handed it back.

For a moment, their eyes met and held.

Though Daniel's lids were heavy, he battled the desire to sleep, forcing himself to watch every move Pearl and Cal made. Snuggled into the cocoon of his blanket, he gave his older brother a smile.

Gilbert, feeling warm and content, as well, asked, "Why aren't you sleeping?"

"I don't want it to end," Daniel whispered. "It feels so good."

"Yeah." Gilbert gathered the little boy close. Against his temple he muttered, "Like home used to feel. When Ma was alive."

Hearing them, Pearl felt her throat constrict. She was forced to turn away, to hide the sudden tears that filled her eyes.

Cal, too, heard. And clenched his hand into a fist at his side, before busying himself with the task of mending the harness.

Chapter Twenty-One

Sunshine found its way around the edges of the hide, poking fingers of light into the darkened cave. Pearl yawned, stretched, and sat up. For a moment, her heart seemed to stop, when she didn't see Cal standing guard at the entrance to the cave.

But one glance at the roaring fire told her that he had been watching over them while they slept. Moments later, as if on cue, he stepped inside, his arms piled high with logs.

"Morning, sleepyhead," he called cheerfully.

"You're happy this morning. You must be feeling stronger."

"Strong enough to take on that deer." He glanced to where Gilbert and Daniel were just waking. "Feel like having a partner along to track this morning?"

Gilbert's eyes widened. "Yes, sir."

"Well, then, as soon as we've had some breakfast, we'll see what we can find."

The boys dressed quickly, admiring their clean, mended clothes. They gathered around the fire for a meal of leftover stew and biscuits, washed down with hot coffee.

A short time later, as Cal and Gilbert prepared to depart, Cal took Daniel aside.

"Do you know how to handle a pistol, son?"

The boy nodded. "Gilbert made sure I learned a long time ago."

Considering that the boy was only six, Cal's eyes narrowed thoughtfully. Then he handed over his gun. "While we're gone, I want you to stand guard at the entrance of the cave. If you see anything suspicious, fire a shot. That'll be our signal to come running."

The little boy said solemnly, "Yes, sir."

"You won't forget?"

"No, sir." He glanced at his beloved teacher. "I'll look out for Miss Jewel."

"Good boy." Cal turned to Pearl and touched a hand to her cheek. "We won't be long."

"I know." She placed a hand over his and waited the space of several heartbeats, until she became aware of the way the two boys were watching.

Cal turned away. Within minutes, he and Gilbert had disappeared into the sun-dazzled snow.

While they were gone, Pearl shook out their blankets and rolled them up, setting them to one side. Then she cut fresh evergreen boughs and scattered them over every inch of space, filling the cave with the fresh, sweet fragrance of a pine forest.

When the cave had been made as comfortable as possible, she prepared fresh biscuit dough and set it by the fire to rise.

Daniel crouched near the entrance of the cave. "Umm...it sure smells good in here," he said, breathing deeply.

"Yes, it does. Funny." Pearl paused to brush a strand of hair from her eye. "I never would have believed it, but I guess just about anyplace can be made to feel like a home."

"Yes'm." Daniel turned, fixing his gaze on the snowy approach to the cave, as Cal had instructed. "As long as it's got the right people in it."

Within a few hours, Gilbert and Cal returned, carrying a buck between them. They dropped the heavy burden at the entrance to the cave. Then Gilbert reached into his pocket and removed a tiny bundle of fur.

"What's that?" Daniel asked excitedly.

"A coyote pup," Gilbert said as he cuddled the prize close to his heart.

After a series of whimpers, a small pink tongue reached out and licked Gilbert's neck, and the boy ran a finger gently over the fur until the whimpering ceased.

"Can I see?" Daniel asked.

Gilbert knelt down and held the tiny pup in both hands.

"Oh." Pearl dropped to her knees beside him and watched as Daniel petted him. "Where did you find him?"

"Down by the creek. Probably born in the blizzard. His mama was dead nearby. He was shivering and half starved. Don't know if we can save him. But we can try."

He fashioned a sling out of a piece of Pearl's torn petticoat, then placed the pup inside, next to his heart.

"It'll remind him of his ma's heartbeat," he explained as he returned to his chores.

Pearl marveled at the tenderness in the boy. How could someone who had been so badly mistreated harbor such a nurturing, caring heart?

Soon the deer had been skinned and butchered. While Pearl and Gilbert set about cooking all the meat, Cal and Daniel began preparing the hide for tanning.

"This ought to make a fine jacket for you or your brother," Cal said as he worked on the supple skin.

"You're giving it to us?" the little boy asked.

Cal nodded. "It was Gilbert's kill."

"Then we'll make him buckskin leggings," Daniel said quickly, "to wear next winter when he's out hunting." His voice lowered to a wistful sigh. "I sure hope Gilbert lives to use them next winter."

Cal looked up from his work to spear a glance at the little boy. "What's that supposed to mean?"

"Pa." Daniel swallowed. "When he finds us here, he'll whip Gilbert good. And this time . . ." His voice trailed off.

In the silence that followed, Cal asked, "Has he ever whipped you?"

The boy shook his head. "No, sir." Cal saw the bleak look of despair that came into Daniel's eyes as he added softly, "Only Gilbert."

Across the cave, Pearl heard. And offered a silent prayer for these two sweet, gentle boys who had known so much hardship in their young lives.

* * *

Dinner was, as promised, a feast. There was tender roasted venison, as well as tubers dug from the banks of the stream and an assortment of plants. Once again, Pearl found herself enjoying the taste of the spices Gilbert had added to the meal.

As the others mopped up every drop of gravy with their biscuits, Pearl caught Daniel slipping tiny bites to the coyote pup, who sat between the boy and his brother.

"Have you given him a name?" she asked.

"I think we should name him Blizzard," Daniel said. "'Cause he was born in a blizzard." He turned to his older brother. "What do you think, Gilbert?"

"I don't think we ought to give him a name."

The little boy was crushed. "Why?"

"Because that will just make it harder to leave him behind when we go."

"Why do we have to leave him? Why can't he come home with us?"

"Because," Gilbert said patiently, "Pa would take one look at a coyote and shoot him, that's why."

"We'll hide him. We won't let Pa see him."

Gilbert drew an arm around his little brother. "Where are you going to hide a coyote pup on our place? You know you're only fooling yourself. He's a wild critter. You can't change what he is, any more than you can change Pa."

"But he likes me. Look." Daniel held out his hand, and the pup licked it. "If we leave him behind, he'll starve to death."

"Maybe." Gilbert shrugged. "Maybe not. At least out here he'll have a chance. But if we bring him home, he won't live a day with Pa around."

With a look of sadness, the little boy picked up the pup and cuddled it to his chest. "Come on, Blizzard. At least for now, you're safe. And tonight, you're going to sleep with me."

While the two boys sat in a corner of the cave, playing with the pup, Pearl washed their dishes and poured the last of the coffee for Cal. He stood by the mouth of the cave, smoking in silence. She found herself wondering where he went when he looked so sad and pensive.

As she approached, he looked up.

"You're awfully quiet tonight," she said softly.

"Got a lot on my mind."

"Anything you'd care to share?"

He shook his head. She was disappointed, but she didn't push. Maybe there were some things so dark and deep he would never share them with her. And though she longed to comfort him, the look in his eyes acted as a barrier.

A short time later, when the boys rolled themselves into their bed, Pearl knelt beside them. She tucked the furs around them, then bent to kiss each of them.

"Good night, Daniel. Gilbert."

"Good night, Miss Jewel," they muttered in unison.

She noticed that the little pup was nestled between them.

"My ma used to kiss us at night," Gilbert said softly. "Daniel is too young to remember. But I can still see her in my mind. I can even smell her."

"That's the wonderful thing about our minds." Pearl lingered beside him, smoothing the blankets. She noted that Daniel had already fallen asleep. "No one can take away our memories."

"Sometimes . . . sometimes I can't picture her face. And it scares me, that she's fading. But I can still remember the way I felt, warm and safe, when Ma was alive."

"Even though the picture fades, your heart will never forget," Pearl said gently. "And years from now, you'll still be able to recall the things she taught you."

"I promised her, when she was dying, that I would take care of Daniel." His voice wavered for a moment as he glanced at his little brother, the picture of innocence beside him. "But sometimes, it's so hard. Pa . . ." He stopped, then said, "There I go, babbling like Daniel."

Suddenly Pearl realized why this big, strapping boy stayed and endured his father's beatings. It wasn't because he was a coward, afraid to run away and make a life for himself. Or because of any loyalty to the cruel man who tortured him. He stayed because of a promise to a dying mother. The thought of his sacrifice nearly broke her heart.

Pearl took his hand in hers and squeezed. She felt tears sting her lids. "You're a very brave boy, Gilbert. And someday you'll grow to be a fine man."

"Like my pa?" His voice took on the hard edge of sarcasm.

"No." She brushed a strand of hair from his eyes. "You'll never be like your father. From everything I've seen, your mother's influence was too strong. You're like her, Gilbert. You're kind and decent and good."

"Nobody in town remembers that. All they know about the Ingrams is that our pa is a thief and a liar. And they expect us to be the same."

Pearl's voice throbbed with passion. "Not long ago, a very wise man told me that here in Texas, a person isn't judged by the cards he's dealt, but by the way he plays them."

For a long moment, she stared into Gilbert's eyes, and she could read the dawning of comprehension. She gave him a gentle smile. "Now why don't you get some sleep?" She bent and kissed him once more.

As she got to her feet, she glanced at Cal, who was still staring pensively into the night. At the fierce look on his face, she felt her heart turn over.

She went to him then, and slipped her arms around his waist. "Oh, Cal—" Her voice broke on a sob. "I can't bear thinking about that boy's pain."

Without a word, he drew her close and kissed her with a possessiveness that left her shaken.

They stayed like that, arms around each other, staring into the night, for over an hour. And when at last Pearl withdrew to her bed, she was content that some of their tension had eased. In each other's arms, she and Cal had found a measure of peace.

* * *

When they awoke in the morning, they could all feel the change in the air. The wind, which for days had howled out of the north, was now a warm, gentle southerly breeze. The sun, dazzling against the white landscape, was already beginning to melt the snowdrifts.

"If this keeps up," Cal announced, entering the cave with an armload of logs, "we'll be able to head home in a day or two."

Oddly, his words weren't greeted with smiles and cheers. Instead, Pearl and the two boys fell silent, each lost in private thoughts.

Pearl felt an ache around her heart. Would the love that she and Cal had discovered here in this cave be lost when they returned to the ranch? And what about the Ingram boys? How could she bear to allow these sweet children to return to a cruel father who so badly mistreated them? And if Rollie had died? What then? What would happen to two homeless boys? She had begun to care too much for them. But they weren't hers. She had no right to interfere in their lives. Did she?

Oh, Daddy, she thought. *If I've ever needed you, it's now. Please help me find my way through this maze.*

She forgot about her fears as she immersed herself in the task of preparing breakfast. The meal became a festive affair as everyone, their spirits lifted by Cal's lighthearted mood, began talking and laughing at once.

"After breakfast, Gilbert and I will test the trails, to see if a horse and wagon can manage them yet."

"You mean, you think we could leave today?" Pearl asked.

"We might. It all depends on the trails. If they're too slick, we'll wait until tomorrow."

"What can I do, Mr. McCabe?" Daniel asked.

"You can stay here and protect Miss Jewel," Cal said. "That's a mighty important job, son. Think you can handle it?"

"Yes, sir." The little boy beamed at being given such responsibility. "What about Blizzard, Gilbert?"

"You can keep him here," his brother said. "But you'll have to keep an eye on him. If the breeze carries the scent of his ma, he'll take off and try to find her."

"I'll take good care of him. And Miss Jewel," the little boy said solemnly.

A short time later, Gilbert and Cal took their leave, and Pearl set about cleaning up the cave.

As she worked, she called, "Would you like to do your sums, Daniel?"

"Yes'm." Leaving the coyote pup curled up in a ball beside the fire, the little boy picked up a stick and began to write the numbers Pearl gave him.

After about an hour, he glanced up with a worried frown. "Oh, no! Miss Jewel, where's Blizzard?"

He and Pearl searched the cave, but the little pup was nowhere to be found.

"Do you think he could have returned to the stream?"

Pearl nodded. "It's what Gilbert warned against." She picked up a blanket and tossed it over her shoulders. "Come on. We'll find him."

The two set out for the stream. Pearl was amazed at how much easier it was to traverse the terrain now that the frigid air had been replaced by gentle breezes. Though the mountain was still littered with mounds of snow, it seemed much less formidable as Pearl and the little boy made their way to the stream. There, on the banks, crouched the pup, nuzzling its dead mother.

"Oh, Blizzard." With great tenderness, Daniel lifted the whimpering pup in his arms.

"Come on, Daniel." Pearl started back to the cave. "We'll fix him some broth, and hope it will be enough to comfort him."

The boy stopped to nestle the pup inside his shirt, cooing words to him. When he looked up, Pearl was far ahead.

She swept aside the hide and took a tentative step inside. After the dazzling brightness of the sun reflecting off the snow, the gloom of the cave seemed even more pronounced. For a moment, Pearl couldn't see a thing. But as her eyes adjusted, she could make out a shape across the cave.

Her heart leaped to her throat as Rollie Ingram's high-pitched laugh greeted her. "Well, well. Now ain't this cozy? I was just beginnin' to think I'd missed you. But I was wrong. After a couple of days of setbacks, we're right back where we started, Miss High-and-Mighty Jewel. And it looks like old Rollie has the upper hand all over again."

Chapter Twenty-Two

Daniel pulled himself to the top of the snowbank. Cradling the coyote pup in his arms, he gave a laugh of pure delight as he slid down the bank, coming to rest against a half-buried boulder.

"Wasn't that fun, Blizzard?" he asked.

The pup licked his face.

"I don't care what Gilbert says," the little boy declared solemnly, "you're coming home with us. I'll never let Pa find you or hurt you. Never."

He tucked the pup back into his shirt and scrambled over several more snowbanks before he reached the cave.

"Miss Jewel is making you some broth. You're going to like it," Daniel said.

He shoved aside the hide and stepped inside. For several moments, he glanced around the cave, waiting for his eyes to adjust to the darkness. Then he spotted Pearl, standing at rigid attention on the far side of the cave.

"Miss Jewel, what's—?" He gave a gasp as his eyes made out the terrible scene. Just behind his teacher was his father. And in his hand was a knife, which he held firmly to her throat.

Rollie's face twisted into a mask of fury. "What the hell are you doing here, boy?"

"I..." Daniel swallowed and tried to speak, but the lump in his throat was choking him. Cal McCabe had trusted him to keep Miss Jewel safe. And he'd failed him. Failed her. Failed all of them. Miserably.

With tears stinging his eyes, he spun away and stumbled from the cave. Once outside, he took the pistol from his pocket and fired. The sound of the gunshot echoed across the hills. Then the little boy sat down in the snow and buried his face in the pup's fur. And cried as though his heart would break.

Cal's heart was in his throat as he ran. The signal could mean only one thing. Rollie was alive. Somehow he had survived the gunshots and the tumble down the ravine. And had come back for revenge.

He and Gilbert raced through the snow, their breath strained and shallow by the time they reached the cave.

They saw Daniel sitting dejectedly in a snowbank, tears still streaming down his cheeks.

"It's Pa," he managed between sobs. "He's inside with Miss Jewel. And he's holding a knife to her throat. I...left her alone while I went to chase Blizzard, and..."

"It's all right, son," Cal said gently. "At least you managed to sound an alarm."

The little boy shook his head. "Pa's going to kill her. I know he is. I saw his face..."

"Gilbert," Cal said sternly, "stay here with Daniel. Whatever you do, stay away from the cave." Before the older boy could argue, Cal pushed aside the hide and stepped into the gloom.

"You're right on time," Rollie called. "I figured that gunshot would bring you runnin'. And it's a good thing you didn't take too long. I couldn't wait much longer for all the fun to begin."

"Have you thought what you'll do after you kill us?" Cal asked.

"I'll have a drink to celebrate," Rollie said with a cackle.

"And then what?" Cal started forward, but Rollie signaled him to halt. He stopped, mentally calculating the distance between them. He had to find a way to keep Rollie distracted, until he could get close enough to jump him and wrestle that knife from his hand. The sight of it, pressed against Pearl's pale throat, had him seething with a wild, uncontrollable rage.

"You won't be able to return to your home, Ingram. You'll have to start over somewhere new. And what about your boys? Will you just expect them to keep quiet about what they know?"

"Them two piss-ants will do whatever I tell them," Rollie boasted.

"Really? Is that what you think?" Cal gave a short laugh.

"And what's that supposed to mean?"

"It means that you don't know your sons very well."

"And you do?" Rollie said with a sneer.

"Oh, I know them as well as I know myself. You see, Rollie, I've been them." Cal's voice had taken on a dangerous new edge.

Pearl heard the change in his tone, and was instantly alert. She studied Cal, and listened with a mixture of fascination and dread, suddenly aware that he was going to reveal the secrets of his heart, and wishing she could stop him.

"I had a father like you, Rollie. Actually, he was my stepfather. My real father died shortly after I was born. And my mother found herself widowed at the tender age of fifteen, with a new baby and a farm to run in a desolate section of Missouri." Cal's hands fisted at his sides as the memories, so long suppressed, washed over him. "For years I sensed that he was beating her, but I never witnessed it until the day he beat her so badly she couldn't stand. I was almost twelve years old. I got my father's old rifle and shot the bastard dead. And then I held my mother in my arms until she died. And after I buried her, in a grave beside my father, I started running, and I didn't stop until I found these Texas hills. I lived like an animal, never venturing out until after dark, afraid to light a fire, for fear it would lead someone to me. And when Onyx Jewel found me hiding out on his land, I looked like some kind of wild mountain creature, with hair down my back. My only clothes were animal skins. When he finally pried my story from me, he secretly contacted the marshal in Missouri and learned that the whole town had known about the beatings. No one was searching for me." Cal's hands tightened. "If anything, the whole town had cheered his death. Just as they'll cheer yours."

"Why, you..." Rollie's hand tightened on the blade at Pearl's throat.

Seeing it, Cal kept the words flowing, no longer caring how many secrets he revealed. "Onyx Jewel gave me back my life. And my self-respect."

During his narrative, Pearl had held her breath, feeling her heart break at his admission. How he must have suffered. And suffered still.

"Now isn't that a sad story..." Rollie's voice took on the whine of sarcasm, interrupting her thoughts. "So you figure Gilbert is going to turn on me someday and shoot his own father because of the beatings I've given him?"

Cal's eyes were bleak. "You haven't been listening, Rollie. It isn't Gilbert you should fear." In the silence of the cave, his voice thundered. "You damned fool! It's Daniel."

For several moments, there was no sound in the cave, as Cal and Rollie faced each other.

Pearl felt the scrape of the blade against her throat, and struggled not to swallow. But out of the corner of her eye she could see a sudden movement at the entrance to the cave, and she knew that both Daniel and Gilbert were standing just outside. It was impossible for them not to have heard every word Cal spoke.

The hide was pushed aside to reveal the two boys struggling over Cal's pistol.

"No, Daniel!" Gilbert cried.

But the little boy wrenched himself free and stood facing his father.

"Put that knife down, Pa," came the frightened little voice. "Or I'll blow your head off."

"Why, you little..." Rollie gave Pearl a shove and started across the cave toward his son.

In that instant, Cal darted forward and made a grab for his rifle. But before he could take aim, Rollie pounced on him, and the two men began wrestling for control of the weapon.

"You stop, Pa!" Daniel could hardly see for the tears streaming down his face. But, despite his tears, he took aim with the pistol.

In the blink of an eye, Rollie got to his feet and aimed the rifle at Cal's chest. "Oh, I'm going to enjoy this," he crooned as his finger closed over the trigger.

The sound of a gunshot resounded through the cave with all the force of thunder. For a moment, no one moved. Then Rollie clutched his stomach. Blood oozed between his fingers, spilling onto the floor of the cave. With a look of stunned surprise, he dropped to his knees.

"Daniel?" he managed to gasp. "You did this?"

"No." The gun slipped from Pearl's nerveless fingers and dropped to the floor. "I've never fired a gun before, and I know I'll never fire one again. But... couldn't let your son have that on his conscience for the rest of his life."

"You—" Rollie slumped to the floor of the cave. On his face was the same twisted mask of hatred he'd always worn in life.

His two sons clung together, averting their eyes as their father slowly gave up his life.

To spare them, Cal herded them from the cave and ordered Pearl to remain outside with them. They offered no objection. And as Cal returned to the cave, Pearl and Gilbert and Daniel huddled together, too stunned to speak, or even to cry. They merely clung to one another until, some time later, Cal led Rollie's horse and wagon outside. In the back of the wagon, beneath a blanket, lay Rollie's body.

Hours later, with Pearl and the boys on the wagon seat and Cal astride his horse, they began the long journey back to the ranch. No one spoke. And though it should have been a festive, triumphant return home, it had become instead a funeral procession.

For Pearl, there was no joy in the knowledge that, to gain her own freedom, she had been forced to take a man's life. But one thought kept her from sinking into despair. Her quick thinking had spared Daniel from repeating Cal's tragedy. The boy would not have to go through life knowing he had killed his own father.

Where had she found such unexpected courage?

A sudden thought came to her. Of course. Hadn't her father promised that he would always be at her side?

"Thank you, Daddy," she whispered.

"What did you say, Miss Pearl?" Daniel asked.

"I said . . . thank heavens for this fine day. How is Blizzard taking the trip?"

The little boy opened his shirt to reveal the round ball of fluff sleeping peacefully against his chest. "He's just fine."

Pearl gathered the two boys close and pressed a kiss to their temples. "And so are we. I think, given a little time, we're all going to be just fine."

In a tiny town like Hanging Tree, news travels with the speed of a prairie fire. Within hours of their return to the Jewel ranch, wranglers had carried the tale of Pearl's abduction by Rollie Ingram, and of her courageous handling of Cal McCabe's wounds. By far the most curious news was that Ingram's sons had braved a blizzard to find their beloved teacher, and that it was the prim and proper teacher herself who had shot Rollie Ingram to death.

"Lavinia Thurlong and Gladys Witherspoon are having such a fine time with this," Diamond said with a sigh.

She and her husband, Adam, had returned from Maryland just in time for all the excitement. They sat at the big scarred wooden table in the comfortable kitchen, surrounded by Jade and Ruby and Carmelita.

"It seems like every time we turn around, we set tongues to wagging," she added in exasperation.

Adam stopped behind her chair and laid a hand on her cheek in a gesture of tenderness. "You said it yourself. You're the closest thing this town has to royalty. Why not let them enjoy their bit of gossip?"

"Oh, Adam, why must you take every complicated thing and make it so simple?"

He merely laughed and turned to Carmelita. "I hope you're making those eggs for me."

"*Sí.* But not all of them." The housekeeper added red and green chilis, then set aside the egg mixture and removed a pan of corn bread from the oven.

At the sound of footsteps, they all turned toward the doorway. Pearl entered. As always, she wore a crisp gown, this one of palest pink, with mother-of-pearl buttons that ran from throat to hem. The flounced skirt was gathered here and there with deeper pink ribbons. Her hair was drawn back with pink combs.

Trailing behind her were Gilbert and Daniel, looking fit and rested. They were wearing new clothes, and their hair, freshly cut, was still slicked back from a morning bath.

"My, my!" Carmelita called. "You do look fine. Sit right down, and I will try to make up for the food you've been missing."

"What about Cal?" Pearl asked. "Aren't we going to wait for him to join us?"

"Oh, Señor Cal left hours ago." Carmelita moved to the stove, where she picked up the platter of eggs.

"Hours ago?" Pearl blanched. She'd wanted, needed, to see him. Ever since their return from the mountain, they'd been surrounded by people. If it wasn't her family wanting to hear every little detail of the ordeal, it was the marshal and his deputy demanding a statement.

"Did he say where he was going?"

"To the schoolhouse, to see if there was any damage. And from there to the north range. He thought he would be gone for several weeks."

"Several...weeks?"

"*Sí.*" The housekeeper gave her a gentle smile. "If you ask me, Señor Cal has a need to put all these bad things behind him and get on with his life. And you should do the same, Señorita Pearl. Perhaps you should pay a call to your school later on today and think about teaching class again soon."

"That's...that's a fine idea." Pearl stood and reached for her parasol. "If you'll excuse me, I think I'll have one of the wranglers fetch my rig."

"But you haven't eaten your breakfast yet."

Pearl took no notice of the spicy egg mixture as she rushed to the door. "I'm not hungry. But I'm sure Daniel and Gilbert will enjoy it."

The others watched in stunned silence as she moved gracefully across the kitchen and shoved open the back door. Once she was outside, her pace picked up a little as she crossed the porch. Then, as she headed toward the barn, she lifted her skirts in a most unladylike manner and began to run as fast as her legs could carry her.

Cal swept up the shards of broken glass and righted overturned desks, grateful for the chance to work. He didn't want any more time to think. It was all he'd been doing since his return from the mountain. And the only thing he'd thought about was Pearl.

He loved her. As he'd never loved anyone, anything, in his whole life. But he was convinced that love wasn't enough. No matter how hard he analyzed his feelings for Pearl, he always came to the same conclusion. They were definitely unsuited to one another.

Despite her heroic efforts during their emergency, she was a lady. A lady who would soon tire of the hardships of this life and return to a civilized place like Boston, a city with a dressmaker and a milliner, and a bakery shop on every corner. And, despite all the love he felt for her, he could never follow her there. He would wither and die if he ever had to leave this place.

At the sound of an approaching carriage, he set aside the broom and walked to the door. When he saw Pearl alight from the carriage, his frown deepened. He'd hoped to have several weeks on the range before having to face her.

He took a deep breath. It was just as well. He would make the break clean. And final. He'd have the rest of his life to nurse his broken heart.

"Carmelita said I might find you out here." Her voice had that breathless quality that always stirred his senses.

He avoided looking at her. "I thought I'd set things right before I head for the north range. That way, you can get back to teaching. That is, if you intend to stay around for the rest of the school year."

"And why wouldn't I?" She deposited an armload of wildflowers on her desk and began to set them in a bucket of water. "Unless, of course, you've decided that you were right all along, and you insist that the school be removed from Jewel land."

"Now why would I do a thing like that?"

"Because, if you recall, you exacted a promise from me. If the schoolhouse ever brought trouble to the Jewel ranch, I would close it."

"Pearl," he said, as gently as he could manage, "it wasn't your school that brought Rollie Ingram and his problems to our doorstep. He was trouble long before you came to Texas. And everyone knew that one day he'd meet his Maker at the end of a bullet. I'm just sorry that you ever had to be involved in that ugly scene."

Before she could open her mouth to protest, he added, "But I have no doubt that it was your influence that gave Rollie's sons the courage to redeem themselves. Without your lecture about honor, who knows what they might have done?"

He turned away, to avoid looking at her beauty. It was too painful. "I've been thinking, with all you've been forced to go through, you might be in a hurry to get back to civilization."

"But I am back to civilization. Oh!" She clapped a hand to her mouth as the realization dawned. "You mean, back to Boston?"

He righted another desk and replaced the fallen slate on top. "I figure by now it must be looking pretty good to you."

"When you nearly lose your life, a lot of things look good, Cal." Seeing that he had no intention of stopping his work or meeting her eyes, she crossed the room and placed a hand on his arm. "A lot of things that may have passed by, unnoticed, suddenly become very important." Her voice lowered. "For instance, a certain cowboy, who used to make me angry, now makes my heart beat faster."

"Now you listen to me, Pearl. What we had up on that mountain..." His voice nearly broke, but he forced himself to go on. "Well, that was just about the most special thing I've ever known. But I'm not fool enough to think I can have that forever."

"And why not?" she demanded.

"Because," he said, as simply as he could, "You're a lady, born and bred. And any way you cut it, I'm a raw cowboy who killed a man before I was a man myself. You deserve only the finest things in your life. And I—I can't give you anything except hard work that'll leave you old before your time. Any man who would ask a lady like you to share such a life is lower than a snake. So that's why—"

She silenced him by placing her hand over his mouth. At the first touch of that delicate palm against his lips, he felt the sexual jolt clear to his toes. He had all he could do to keep from dragging her against him and declaring his love like a damned fool.

"All right, Cal. You've had your say," she whispered. "Now it's my turn." She looked up at him with those big, trusting eyes, and he felt his heart turn over. "When I was a little girl, my father used to talk about his home in Texas. Oh, the things he described to me. They used to leave me wide-eyed with wonder. And I thought his adventurous life was like no other. And then I came here to experience, firsthand, his life. But unlike my father, who was so bold and brave, I found myself timid, frightened, helpless. Until you."

"I don't under—"

She smiled and pressed a finger gently to his lips. "Don't you see, Cal? In your arms, I became someone new. I was no longer that helpless, useless female I'd always been. In your arms, in your eyes, I was a woman who could do anything. Climb mountains. Overpower enemies. Survive in a wilderness by my wiles alone.''

He went still. It was true. She had become someone different during their ordeal. ''But none of that was because of me, Pearl. You found that strength within yourself.''

''Maybe. But don't you see, Cal? With you, I found a wonderful new sense of freedom. I can do anything I choose to do. And be anyone I choose to be. Oh, Cal, it was your love that unlocked that door and gave me my freedom. Why would I ever want to go back to that prison that once held me?''

His heart was beating so thunderously he thought it could probably be heard all the way to Hanging Tree. ''Then, if I ask you to stay here and be my wife, you won't think I'm lower than a snake?''

''I'll think you've finally come to your senses,'' she muttered against his lips.

He lifted his head a fraction, avoiding the temptation to kiss her. ''Will you? Marry me and put up with wolves and weather and cattle and all manner of vermin here in Texas?''

''Oh, Cal. I thought you'd never ask.'' She wrapped her arms around his waist and pressed her lips to his throat. ''Let's go tell the others. And go see Reverend Wade Weston. Oh, and the boys. I've been meaning to talk to you about them. I was hoping we could take Daniel and Gilbert in and make them ours. And that will mean Blizzard, of course, and . . .''

He decided the time was right for a kiss. And, for at least a few moments, it managed to silence her. But when she came up for air, she whispered, "And I was thinking we might want to make this cabin ours, since it was Daddy's first home, and it has a special place in my heart...."

"Woman," he muttered against her mouth, "I'm all in favor of making Daniel and Gilbert our sons, and living here in your pa's old cabin, as long as I can add a few more rooms, so we won't be walking into each other at every step. But first things first. I see a loft up there. And some straw. Now, if you have any pity in your heart, you'll at least give me a few hours alone with you."

Without waiting for a reply, he caught her in his arms and carried her up the ladder. As he laid her in the straw and stretched out beside her, he brushed her lips with his in the lightest of kisses. "Now that my wounds are completely healed," he muttered, "there are some things I've been meaning to teach you."

She brought her arms around his neck and drew his face close for a long, drugging kiss that left her head spinning. "I can't wait to learn," she whispered. "I've been told that, with the right teacher, I'm a very good pupil."

Epilogue

⁓⁓⁓⁓

"I don't think I've ever seen you looking so jumpy, Cal." Cookie shifted his pipe to the other side of his mouth before adding with a grin, "It'll only take a few minutes and it'll be over."

"I know. I know." Cal stood beside his old friend on the porch of the remodeled cabin and glanced at the wagonloads of people who continued to arrive and go inside.

As they passed him, everyone seemed to be talking about the fact that the newlyweds were leaving the elegant Jewel ranch to take up residence in this simple cabin, which had once been Onyx Jewel's home, and which would continue to serve as a schoolhouse, as well.

Cal and Pearl had insisted on holding the ceremony at their own place, rather than the big, fancy Jewel ranch. Much to the dismay of Lavinia Thurlong and Gladys Witherspoon, only the families of children attending the school had been invited to what the town was calling the biggest social event of the year.

Carmelita and Cookie had been cooking and baking for days, and the wonderful aroma of spices drifting from the kitchen had everyone's mouth watering.

Diamond, of course, was horrified, knowing how much the town gossips enjoyed such a spectacle. She had wanted it to be a private wedding, with only the family in attendance. But she had been outvoted. What was worse, she was being forced to wear a gown, a shimmering, silvery confection that was the perfect contrast to her thick red curls and sun-bronzed skin. As an act of revenge, she wore her sturdy, dung-caked work boots beneath the long skirt.

Seated beside her in the carriage were Jade, in an elegant green silk, with mandarin collar and frog closings, and Ruby in her trademark slinky red satin. On the opposite seat was the bride, who wore a gown the color of iridescent pearl, with a high neck and long sleeves buttoned from elbow to cuff. At her throat was her father's gift to her, a rope of gold with an onyx beside a perfect pearl. At her lobes were the earbobs Cal had bought for his bride—a delicate filigree of gold with matching pearls. He had presented them to her last night, a romantic night she would never forget. It had been their first in their newly renovated cabin.

Reverend Wade Weston rode up in a cloud of dust and strode forward, wearing his best Sunday blacks, to offer a handshake to the nervous groom.

"I've prepared a stirring sermon to assure that it's a memorable service," he said.

"Just see that it's brief." Cal had intended to say more, but just then he caught sight of Daniel and Gilbert, who had flanked the bride, stepping down from the carriage. They wore spanking new suits and radiant smiles. Spotting Cal, they raced to his side.

"Do we have to say anything?" Daniel asked nervously.

"Not a thing, son. All Gilbert has to do is hand me the ring." Cal turned to him. "You remembered the ring, didn't you?"

"Yes, sir." Gilbert withdrew a simple gold band from his pocket.

At the sight of his mother's ring, Cal felt his throat constrict. She would have loved his choice of bride. She would have been so proud. . . .

"I'm sure glad to hear we don't have to talk in front of all those people." Daniel peered through the doorway and saw a crowd nearly as big as the one at Sunday services. "Did all those folks come just to see you marry Miss Pearl?"

"I guess so." Cal could feel himself beginning to sweat, and he wished the damned thing was over. It was just the beginning, he fretted. Pretty soon, she'd have him hauling in wet laundry off the line, and putting dry britches on babies' behinds. But just then Diamond, Jade and Ruby stepped apart, and he caught sight of Pearl's sweet face. At once his fears dissolved. The truth was, he'd turn cartwheels in the middle of town, buck naked, if that little female asked him to.

She hurried over to join him and the boys. "Did you tell him yet?" she asked them.

"We were...waiting for you," Gilbert said, staring at the toe of his shiny new shoe.

"What's this about?" Cal wasn't sure he could stand many more surprises.

"Yesterday, when we drove into town for our suits, we had some...other business to take care of," the boy said.

"What other business?"

Gilbert reached into his pocket and withdrew an official document, which he handed to Cal. "Ma... that is, Miss Pearl...that is..." He stopped, swallowed, and gathered his courage. He wasn't much good at making speeches. "We met with the visiting judge. And we asked him to change our names, as a wedding gift to you. So now he's Daniel McCabe," he said, pointing to his little brother, "And I want to be called Gil McCabe. I thought Gil sounded more grown up than Gilbert. Like Cal. That is, if you don't object."

"Object?" Cal felt a lump in his throat the size of a boulder. He gathered the two boys into his arms and closed his eyes. It wouldn't do for his wranglers to see their boss crying. "I guess this will go down as the happiest day of my life. I acquired a bride and two of the finest sons any man could ever want."

Pearl's eyes misted. She truly felt as though her heart would burst with love.

Feeling a bulge under Daniel's jacket, Cal caught

him by the shoulder and peered down. "And what's this? Another surprise?"

"No, sir." Daniel pulled the wiggling coyote pup from its hiding place. "It's just Blizzard. I didn't want him to feel left out on such an important day. After all, he's part of the family, too."

At that moment, the music began to play, and the minister took his place. All heads swiveled to watch the bride and groom. But instead of a solemn procession, they saw a coyote puppy wriggle free and race through the crowd, with an embarrassed little boy chasing him, ducking between chairs, crawling through a forest of legs.

Cal and Pearl fell into each other's arms, laughing.

"Do you have any idea what you're getting yourself into, Mr. McCabe?" she asked.

"Not at all, Mrs. McCabe. But I know one thing." He shook his head in admiration. "You've begun to thrive on all this excitement."

She thought a moment, then nodded. "I think you're right."

"You are definitely your father's daughter," he murmured against her temple.

She pulled back and met his eyes. "I consider that the highest of compliments."

He bowed his head in acknowledgment. "And I know one thing more. That prim and proper life of yours will never be dull again, Mrs. McCabe."

"Promise?"

His smile remained. But his voice deepened with passion. "I do promise. With all my heart."

Oh, Daddy, she thought as she accepted Cal's arm and started toward the preacher. *You knew all along, didn't you? It was part of your plan to have me come here and find, not only this wonderful cowboy, but myself. Thank you, Daddy. I hope I've made you proud. Because you've made me the happiest woman in the world.*

* * * * *

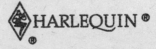

REBECCA

43 LIGHT STREET

YORK

FACE TO FACE

*Bestselling author Rebecca York returns to "43 Light Street"
for an original story of past secrets, deadly deceptions—and
the most intimate betrayal.*

She woke in a hospital—with amnesia...and with child.
According to her rescuer, whose striking face is the last
image she remembers, she's Justine Hollingsworth. But
nothing about her life seems to fit, except for the baby
inside her and Mike Lancer's arms around her. Consumed
by forbidden passion and racked by nameless fear, she
must discover if she is Justine...or the victim of some mind
game. Her life—and her unborn child's—depends on it....

Don't miss *Face To Face*—Available in October, wherever
Harlequin books are sold.

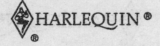 HARLEQUIN ®

43FTF

If you are looking for more titles by

RUTH LANGAN

Don't miss these fabulous stories by one of
Harlequin's great authors:

Harlequin® Historical

If you're a serious fan of historical romance,
then you're in luck!

Harlequin Historicals brings you
stories by bestselling authors, rising new stars
and talented first-timers.

Ruth Langan & Theresa Michaels
Mary McBride & Cheryl St. John
Margaret Moore & Merline Lovelace
Julie Tetel & Nina Beaumont
Susan Amarillas & Ana Seymour
Deborah Simmons & Linda Castle
Cassandra Austin & Emily French
Miranda Jarrett & Suzanne Barclay
DeLoras Scott & Laurie Grant…

You'll never run out of favorites.

Harlequin Historicals…they're too good to miss!

HH-GEN

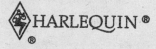

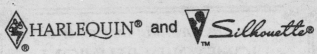

HARLEQUIN® and **Silhouette®**

are proud to present...

HERE COME THE GROOMS™

Four marriage-minded stories written by top Harlequin and Silhouette authors!

Next month, you'll find:

A Practical Marriage	by Dallas Schulze
Marry Sunshine	by Anne McAllister
The Cowboy and the Chauffeur	by Elizabeth August
McConnell's Bride	by Naomi Horton

ADDED BONUS! In every edition of *Here Come the Grooms* you'll find $5.00 worth of coupons good for Harlequin and Silhouette products.

On sale at your favorite Harlequin and Silhouette retail outlet.

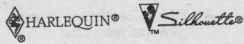

HARLEQUIN®   **Silhouette®**

HCTG896